# The
# Shadowing

Also by Rhiannon Ward

*The Quickening*

# The
# Shadowing

## Rhiannon Ward

ORION

An Orion paperback
First published in Great Britain in 2021 by Orion Books
an imprint of The Orion Publishing Group Ltd
Carmelite House, 50 Victoria Embankment
London EC4Y 0DZ

An Hachette UK Company

1 3 5 7 9 10 8 6 4 2

A CIP catalogue record for this book is
available from the British Library.

ISBN (Mass Market Paperback) 978 1 4091 9222 0
ISBN (eBook) 978 1 4091 9223 7
ISBN (Audio) 978 1 4091 9224 4

Typeset by Input Data Services Ltd, Somerset

Printed and bound in Great Britain by Clays Ltd, Elcograf S.p.A.

MIX
Paper from
responsible sources
FSC® C104740

www.orionbooks.co.uk

For Andy Lawrence

# Prologue

Those unfamiliar with the pocket-sized town of Southwell were often surprised at how sound carried once dusk fell. Even the smallest of noises bounced off the respectable brick houses and shuttered shopfronts, weaving along narrow alleys and cobbled streets, seeping through cracks in poorly fitted windows. It was a phenomenon that previous clerics of the decaying minster knew well. The order to speak in hushed voices when discussing Church business after dark was as much to ensure that gossip and idle chat wasn't overheard as any act of piety.

The first week of September had brought night after night of torrential downpours. They reminded Matthew Alban of the Bible stories his mother had read to him as a child. Unlike the relief Elijah felt at the rain on his back, however, Matthew had been assaulted every evening by shards of needles on his shoulders, causing his arm to tremble as he extinguished the flame of the large lantern hanging outside the coaching inn.

It was his favourite time of day: Annie, the servant girl in her bed, and the ostlers and pot-boy asleep above the stable. Once the midnight coach departed, it was just him in the night air and he liked to make sure all was secure against the encompassing dark.

He had long given up leaving a light on for strangers looking for an honest bed for the night. It didn't matter if they were on horse or foot – he wouldn't answer the door to them. It made a mockery of him calling his establishment a coaching inn, but he preferred strangers to pass by and seek shelter in other hostelries, leaving him and his regular guests, the ones he knew and trusted, to sleep in peace. He wouldn't forget the last time he'd opened the door to a stranger banging on the heavy wood as the moon hung swollen in the sky.

When he was satisfied that all the shutters were secured, Matthew climbed up to his room at the top of the inn and lay on the bed without undressing. He could feel dampness seeping from his underclothes through the rough cotton sheets into the mattress below. He tried to empty his mind to induce sleep, but the uneasy night air made for a suffocating rest. He'd just heard the distant chime of the grandfather clock striking the quarter-hour, when the night was punctured by a shriek of distress. Matthew, against his will, sat bolt upright, his stomach groaning at the effort after a late-night supper of pease porridge. The rain had stopped, he realised, and the silence was enough for the town to give up its secrets. Sure enough, another cry came – this time not of anguish, but of primeval pain.

This was no animal cry. The farmer at the edge of town had sent his pigs to market on the Saturday of last week and, in any case, Matthew knew it was the sound of a woman in pain. He lifted the damp blanket and, folding it in three, crossed the room to open the window and push it in the space where the shutter met rotten wood and pitted glass. Another cry came – softer this time – but he couldn't tell if it was the work of his makeshift wadding or that the wounded thing had run out of breath. It didn't matter either way. Some hurts refuse to heal.

As he returned to his bed, Matthew was sorry that his father had lost at cards the bullwhip that had been in the family for generations. He knew of a few people he'd like to use it on.

# PART ONE

## BRISTOL TO SOUTHWELL
## AND BACK

*Death is but crossing the world.*
William Penn

# Chapter One

It was the dream of the pit. Hester had two nightmares and each would wake her in a pool of sweat, crying out in terror. She'd got as far as the earth being shovelled onto her face – hard clods of soil which, had she been able to move, she'd have torn away with her hands. But she was dead, or near it, and she had to lie there until, as a blow crushed her cheek, she woke, gasping for breath. She sat up, aware of an ache in her belly, and groaned as she caught sight of the stained bed sheets. The night had brought her monthly bleed and with it spasms of pain radiating down her legs.

She rang the bell and Susanna appeared, looking surprised at the summons.

'Is anything the matter?'

Hester swung her legs onto the floor and nodded at the sheets.

'Will you help me, Susanna? I'd do it myself, but my insides are on fire.'

Susanna took charge, stripping linen away from the mattress and bundling it in the corner of the room. She disappeared to fetch clean sheets from the pine chest at the top of the staircase and returned, deftly making up the bed.

'You climb back in. Do you have your rags?'

Hester groaned. 'I'm all prepared.'

'I'll bring you a hot stone for your back. The pain will ease with heat.'

'Amos won't approve of me idling in bed.'

Hester felt the thud of apprehension in her chest. Her father wouldn't enter her chamber – climbing the steep staircase was beyond his ability since his stroke – but his words would be as sour as lemons when she next saw him. Susanna, however, was unimpressed.

'I'll tell him you're indisposed with women's problems. That usually shuts men up. What do they know of what we suffer?'

Nothing, thought Hester. But her father despised weakness in anyone. Pain was to be acknowledged and overcome with the right attitude.

'You won't tell him that you helped with my bed, will you? He'll be angry if he thinks I've relied on you.'

Servants, in Amos's opinion, were for attending to the house, not helping out family members encouraged to self-sufficiency at an early age.

'Leave him to me.'

Susanna hurried out at the sound of Amos's call. The pain continued to radiate from Hester's abdomen until, hearing her moans, Susanna reappeared with a stick of cinnamon bark for her to chew on. The old remedy worked. After an hour, the agony had subsided to a dull ache and Hester hauled herself up to face the long, dismal day.

It was an odd chance that she was thinking of her sister, Mercy, while she dressed. Hester had been given the only gown Mercy discarded during her leaving but, as it was a little tight, she'd left it hanging in the wardrobe. She was conscious of showing off her figure a little too improperly, especially in front of her father. However, a bout of vomiting sickness that summer had thinned her and, standing in front of her armoire, she was drawn to the blue wool dress. She pulled it over her, closing her eyes at the scent of her sister's skin. It was enough to push away the barriers that Hester had erected to anchor herself in the real world. When she opened her eyes again, Mercy was standing in front of her, smiling in the gentle way Hester loved.

'Go away,' she whispered, aghast, and her sister obliged.

Susanna came in while Hester was dressing, bearing another hot stone.

'Oh, you're up. I told the master that you'd be in bed all morning.'

'Then he'll be pleasantly surprised to see me.' Hester fumbled at the buttons on her bodice, refusing to acknowledge the thud of dread at the thought of seeing her father when she went downstairs. 'How is he?'

'As usual,' said Susanna in a lowered voice. 'What's the matter with you? Your hand is shaking.'

'I saw something, that's all.'

'What?'

Hester shook her head. She would not mention Mercy to Susanna. The maid knew of the spirits who appeared to Hester, but they were always shadows of the departed. Mercy, surely, couldn't be dead. The thought was too shocking. Her appearance to Hester just now must simply have been conjured by the act of putting on her sister's dress.

Susanna gave her a look. 'Keep your secrets, then.'

Susanna was sensitive when it came to Mercy, perhaps because it was she who'd uncovered her original vanishing. They'd breakfasted together as a family in those days, assembling around the table at eight o'clock prompt. There was no reason for the maid to be in Mercy's room. No one had a morning cup of tea in bed or required help with their dressing. They were all adept at readying themselves for the day.

Although she'd never admitted to it, Hester suspected that their clever maid must have had an inkling that something was afoot. Servants gossip with those from other families and

Susanna certainly liked intrigue. Perhaps she'd also picked up on a new heightened mood in the house. For, instead of sweeping the downstairs floors and brushing out the fires on that cool autumn morning, Susanna had pushed open the door of Mercy's bed chamber to find the bed unspoiled with a note lying on the pillow.

Mercy's last act as a daughter of the Goodwin household was to embrace the Quaker principle of thriftiness. Rather than put an envelope to waste, she'd simply written her message of farewell and folded the paper in half. Amos had never employed illiterate maids. He considered it an affront to the commitment to the education of women. Susanna was perfectly capable of reading a message, even in Mercy's hasty scrawl, so she was first in the house to discover the secret. Susanna carried the note to Hester's mother, Ruth, handing it to her and standing respectfully to one side as her mistress read the contents.

Afterwards, Hester had tried to discover the exact wording of the message, but Ruth wasn't telling and Susanna chose to deny that she knew. The details emerged soon enough, in any case. Mercy, aged twenty and betrothed to the son of family friends, had eloped with John Philips, tutor to the two young Goodwin sons.

Hester couldn't be sure what had shocked her more when her stunned mother told her the news. That Mercy had eloped, an act she'd only read of in thrilling tales smuggled to her by her school friends, or that the object of Mercy's affections had been Mr Philips, a man with a blemished face and thinning pale hair plastered to his scalp with a stinking lotion. How Mercy and he had managed to speak, let alone form an attachment, no one knew. Hester, alone at night and desperate not to submit to sleep, supposed that love found a way of overcoming obstacles.

Mercy's elopement had been the outrage of three years earlier.

A scandal, like most scandals, which ignited and died. Hester had loved her sister but mourned her in private. Amos decreed that Mercy's name was never again to be mentioned within those four walls and they'd obeyed him. Mercy had faded from family history as surely as ink on blotting paper. Hester's brothers, Asa and Peter, were despatched to school a few minutes' walk from their house, Amos forever repenting that he hadn't chosen this form of education at the outset.

Hester, shaking off thoughts of Mercy, descended the stairs while listening for her father's call. Sure enough, it came. His strength might have diminished, but his hearing was as sharp as ever. She heard his muffled words.

'Is it thee, Hester? Have my letters arrived? The mail is late this morning.'

'I'll check.'

Hester saw a single envelope sitting on the tin plate. Once, it would have been filled with correspondence addressed not only to the head of the family, but also their mother and occasionally Mercy, too. Now, with her father's business in decline along with his health, acquaintances had moved their attention to other more prosperous families.

Hester picked up the envelope and walked the short staircase into the back sitting room, which also doubled as her father's study since his illness. The house was still, only the ticking of the wall clock and the humming of Susanna upstairs in one of the bedrooms cutting through the silence. Amos was sitting, as usual, in the chair by the window, his broad back to her as she entered the room. He moved his head only slightly to acknowledge another presence. Rather than his habitual anger, this time Hester could sense his fury.

'Is it thee, Hester?'

'It's me, Amos.'

Her father still kept to the old ways, using only 'thee' to address his audience – a mannerism that encouraged ridicule from those outside their faith. There were also no distinctions made for familial ties, nor between master and servant. Hester called him Amos, as did Susanna. He'd have it no other way.

'Lying abed this morning, Susanna tells me.'

'The pain was so great I couldn't move, Amos.'

Her father didn't reply. Hester swallowed, aware that she was still frightened of this man.

'I've brought you a letter. Just the one arrived this morning.'

She moved forwards so that he could see her, placing the envelope in his hand. On the climb upstairs, she'd already examined the envelope, noting that the paper was of poor quality, almost translucent in texture, although the writing was confident enough, its bold strokes scoring the surface. Amos studied it for a moment, hesitated, then took a paperknife from his desk and deftly slit the top of the envelope.

Hester watched him scan the contents. His face, uneven after the stroke that nearly killed him, became waxen in front of her eyes. The lines grooved into the side of his face deepened. Hester, despite her fear, moved towards her father.

'Is everything well?'

'No,' he said. 'Everything is not well. What have I done to deserve such a wayward girl as thy sister Mercy?'

Hester reached out to grip the back of a wooden chair.

'Mercy?'

Her speaking infuriated him more. With a sweep of his hand, he knocked the inkstand flying, the liquid spraying across the carpet. She bent to retrieve the pot and felt a cuff on the side of her head.

'Amos, please.' She put a hand to her temple, trying to ignore the ringing in her ear.

He turned his attention away from her and back to the letter, reading through the contents another time. When he'd finished, he replaced the paper in the envelope and fixed his gaze away from her as she climbed to her feet.

'Thy sister is dead.'

The news took her breath away. It explained the morning's shadowing, as she'd come to call her visions. Mercy who, like her parents, had refused to believe in Hester's visions, had herself appeared briefly to her from the afterlife as a portent of the news she was about to receive. Feeling her father's eyes on her, Hester made an effort to compose herself. She must, for the moment, ignore the tingle in her spine at the thought of her shadowings, so long suppressed by Amos's beatings, beginning again.

'Dead? How?'

She gripped the chair tighter, feeling a splinter slide into her finger. She gasped at the pain but held on to steady herself at the news.

'That's no matter. Where's Ruth?'

Hester hadn't given her mother any thought all morning.

'Visiting, I suppose. I'm not sure where she's gone – she left before I dressed. Susanna might know.'

'Find her for me.'

It was an order from this man who still ruled the house with his iron will.

'Of course,' she replied, desperate to get away from him.

She climbed the narrow stairs to the first floor, following the sound of Susanna's humming. At the entrance to the boys' bedroom, she paused to watch the maid make up one of the small single beds. She stopped when she saw Hester, her lips forming a small circle of surprise.

'What's the matter? Is it Amos?'

'Mercy is dead.' Saying the name gave her courage and she stood firmer in the doorway. 'A letter came and it says that Mercy has died.'

'Never.' Susanna stared at Hester in shock. 'Is that who you saw this morning?'

Hester hesitated. 'For a moment, yes.'

'Oh, Hester. Don't tell Amos.'

Little chance of that, thought Hester. 'Do you know where Ruth is?'

'Visiting Mrs Perry. She took worse overnight and your mother was out before breakfast. What happened to Mercy?'

'I don't know. Amos won't tell me. He only said that Mercy was dead and asked what he'd done to deserve such a child.'

Susanna crossed the room. 'You stay here. I can run faster than you.' She peered closer. 'Did he strike you? I see a mark on your face.'

'Yes.' Hester's voice cracked at the unfairness of the blow that stung her scalp. 'Will you tell Ruth what's happened? She'll want to know. You tell her.'

The permission was, of course, unnecessary. Hester knew Susanna would spill the beans anyway. She was full of repressed excitement as she untied her apron.

'I'll go now.'

Hester heard the clack of her shoes down the stairs followed by the door shutting. She took a deep breath. She would need to go in to see her father, even though she'd rather have sat to digest the news in the bedroom she and Mercy had once shared. In that small, bare room they'd been confidantes, first of childish fancies but then, as they'd got older, allies in the face of Amos's brutality and Ruth's preoccupation with her charity work. Only in the last weeks before her elopement had Mercy withdrawn into herself, hugging her secret tightly. Now, Mercy was dead, the news foreshadowed by the dream of the pit and the vision of Mercy in her altered form. The shadowing had returned.

But no, she mustn't think of that. Amos thought he'd beaten out of her the nightmares that had haunted Hester from childhood and the tales of the spirits who disappeared when she tried to speak. According to him, there was only this life and where they went to beyond. No phantoms who flitted between the two. It was the Quaker belief and yet, from her first vision at the age of three, these shadows had appeared to her at times of crisis or when she was sick. Often they were faint outlines, other times recognisable forms like Mercy that morning. For a moment, Hester felt the presence of her sister – a tiny, faint breath against her cheek.

'Mercy,' she whispered. 'What happened?'

She listened for a reply but heard only a distant swishing sound followed by a thud. The atmosphere in the house took on a more menacing edge, causing Hester to hurry downstairs to her father's study. He was slumped over the table, his head turned to one side.

'Amos?'

Hester shook his shoulder, causing him to slide to the floor, his mouth working as he tried to speak. Amos was in the throes of a second stroke. As she knelt beside him, trying to loosen the neckerchief at his throat, she caught sight of the letter sitting on top of his desk. It had been removed once more from the envelope. Perhaps her father had wanted to reassure himself of the message. Whatever the reason, Hester could see the address written in the same confident scrawl at the top of the letter. It had come from a place called Southwell Union Workhouse. Mercy had died a pauper.

# Chapter Two

'It'll have to be you, Hester. There isn't anyone else who can go.'

Ruth twisted the fringe of her shawl as she sat at the oak table. The ledger where she recorded the family finances was open and Hester saw that a note had been made of the sum of coins handed over to the physician. Amos was confined to his bed after taking a draught of strong-smelling brew to induce sleep. It had done the trick. Her father was in a deep slumber and looked as if he'd already departed this world. Before leaving, the physician had warned that this second stroke might mark a significant deterioration in his faculties. Mercy, by her dying, had done something that her original disappearance had failed to do. It had mortally wounded their father.

'Hester, stop daydreaming. It's always the same. I talk to you and your mind is elsewhere.'

Hester saw that her mother had dropped the old-fashioned form of address. She'd been brought up in a more enlightened Quaker family but had adopted her husband's style of language in public. In private, she easily slipped into her old ways.

'I was saying, Hester, that it'll have to be you who sorts this matter out.'

'You want me to travel to Nottinghamshire?'

Hester was struggling to absorb the proposal. She was to be given the duty of representing the family on the long trek north – an unimaginable responsibility while Amos had been fit and well.

'You must.' Ruth picked up the ledger and closed it. 'I need to know what happened to Mercy. The letter tells us nothing more than that your sister has died.'

Hester watched her mother closely. She'd always been aware that Ruth had a small part of herself that she didn't allow anyone in her family to see. Even now, in the throes of her grief, she was holding herself back from Hester.

'You could write and ask for more information. The mail arrives quickly these days. We might have more news before the week is out.'

'I doubt that very much.' Ruth's voice was calm. 'The workhouses may be new but they're well governed. There will be a board of guardians, which the clerk will have to apply to for permission to reveal any details about Mercy.'

'There's no hurry, is there? Even if any reply goes through official channels, we can surely wait.'

A spasm of pain twisted Hester's insides, but she stood upright in front of her mother, years of training coming to the rescue.

'I don't want to be fobbed off with a few lines. They might condescend to tell me the cause of death, but they're under no obligation to tell me how she ended up in such a place. Our best chance to discover what's happened is to call on them in person and for that, I need you, Hester.'

Despite her misgivings, Hester's heart leaped in anticipation. The mission was a brief chance of escaping this house and seeing something of the world beyond the confines of Bristol.

'Will you tell Amos I'm going?'

Ruth turned her head. 'No, I don't think so. He might not notice your absence in his present state.'

'And what do I do when I get there? Arrange Mercy's funeral?'

'Of course not.' Ruth's voice was exasperated. 'Sometimes I forget how young you are, Hester. You'll find your sister already buried. The letter makes no mention of a funeral, but they don't wait around with their dead in the workhouses. Mercy will already be in the ground.'

Hester had no doubt Ruth was right. She was under no illusions how paupers were buried. There wasn't a poorhouse, school of correction or infirmary she hadn't entered as part of her visits with Ruth to the needy around the city. Once dead, the destitute were piled together in communal pits. For a moment, her dream flashed into her mind and her legs buckled.

'What is it, Hester?'

Hester hesitated, a lie ready on her lips. But Amos was in the twilight world and couldn't harm her.

'I had a dream again last night.'

'Which one?'

Hester was surprised. Her mother knew of her two nightmares but, under orders from Amos, refused to discuss them. She assumed Ruth had forgotten the details, but she'd remembered there were two.

'The pit,' she said. 'I was in the pit.'

Ruth sighed. 'You never talk of them now. It was too much to hope they'd disappeared. What about the sightings?'

Hester regarded her mother. Amos might be incapacitated, but the blow she'd received that morning showed she should still be wary of him. Ruth would be compelled to tell the truth if he asked.

'No. No shadowing.'

*Liar*, whispered Mercy.

Hester kept her eyes on her mother, who sighed.

'We can at least be thankful for that. Are you sure you're up to the journey?'

'Of course. I'll do it for Mercy's sake.' Hester coughed at her hypocrisy, the flutter of excitement still in her belly. 'What questions do you want me to put to the master?'

'First of all, you find out where Mercy is buried. This is for Amos's sake as well as mine. When he recovers, he'll want to know this, I'm sure.'

Recovers? thought Hester. This was surely optimistic given the physician's words. Her mother, as if reading her thoughts, made a knot in the fringe she was twisting.

'As you know, Friends aren't buried with the herd. We've fought hard for these exemptions. In Bristol, Quakers, poor or otherwise, are given single plots by Hermit's Cave. There must be similar arrangements in Southwell. Mercy wouldn't have hidden her upbringing. It's to be hoped she's had a Quaker burial.'

'But what if she's buried in the parish churchyard? None of us know what life Mercy was leading.'

Already, Hester could see she was on a fool's errand. Whatever news she brought back, it was unlikely to be good.

'Then you come back and tell me. Your father will ask when he recovers and I'll need to think of something to say.'

'All that way simply to find Mercy's grave.'

It was like an itch that she shouldn't scratch – the need to throw the worst at her mother. It was the dream's fault. The pit. It rocked her equilibrium and made her petty.

The look Ruth gave her daughter was full of hurt.

'One day, when you have a daughter of your own, you'll do well to remember those words. You're doing it for me as well. I want you to visit Mercy's grave and tell me what her resting place is like.'

'Once I've found the grave, then what?'

'Hester, I want to know how Mercy died. I won't be able to rest until I know. Workhouses have fevers that run through inmates. Typhoid, smallpox, cholera outbreaks, too. Ask the master. If necessary, find the physician who attended her, if there was one. Workhouses have doctors – not resident, but they usually call on the same one. Find out for me.'

The enormity of the task began to dawn on Hester.

'Are you sure they'll tell me? Perhaps they'll only deal with the head of the household.'

'Nonsense. You're of full age and from a respectable family. I shall send a response to the workhouse letter on the night mail coach telling them to expect you. You can leave the day after to-morrow. They'll be aware of your arrival.'

Ruth stood, finally relinquishing her shawl, and crossed to the window, where she gazed out onto the street.

'I'd rather have gone myself, but I can't be spared here. We've given you a decent education and you're sensible enough when you're not imagining things.' She paused, perhaps not convinced by Hester's denial of recent sightings. 'Stand firm when dealing with those in charge. My experience is that they treat you well once they've got your measure. You know this from our hospital visits.'

Hester nodded, although she hoped that the workhouse wouldn't be as dispiriting as Bristol Infirmary. Each time she visited, she recoiled from the smell of blood and gangrenous wounds. Workhouses were an unknown quantity, although she'd heard they were generally well run under the governance of a master and matron.

'Will you be all right, Ruth?' Hester asked, aware that while she was in another part of the country her mother would be confined to the sickroom, nursing an ill-tempered husband.

Ruth turned and made a face. 'Your father needs complete rest and will expect me by his side. Asa and Peter can stay with Cecily for the rest of the week, or possibly longer depending on Amos's recovery.'

That would please her brothers. Their aunt Cecily had a clutch of young sons, and the boys would be happier with their cousins than in this house of illness and silence.

'Then I'll go. And where will I stay?'

'I'll also send a letter by the mail coach to Dorothea Francombe. She's a school friend and lives near Southwell. You can stay with her overnight.'

She must be one of her mother's large network of Friends she corresponded with each week. This meant she'd be worthy, godly and deadly dull. Hester dreaded to think what she'd say when they discovered Mercy had ended her days in a workhouse near their home.

'Dorothea and I were close at school and we've kept in touch since.'

Hester hesitated. 'What shall I tell her about what's happened?'

Ruth returned to her vigil at the window.

'You can be honest with Dorothea. I'll tell her what I know in my message. She's a woman of the world. She'll receive my note by tomorrow and will meet you from your coach. You've a long journey ahead. There's plenty of time for them to get the household ready to welcome you.'

Hester thought of the mail coach speeding through the countryside with her mother's letters in the mail bag. How much quicker it would be than her own journey by stagecoach.

'Will I be riding outside?' she asked, her voice overeager.

Ruth, exasperated, shot her a look.

'This isn't a weekend jaunt to the country. Of course you won't be riding above the carriage. I can afford an inside place for you. I've sent Susanna to the booth at the coaching inn to find the quickest way to get you there. I'd rather you avoided changing at London, if possible.'

London. How she longed to visit the capital, even if it was to catch a glimpse of the city from a speeding coach.

Her mother's voice grew wistful. 'I wish I was going with you to see Dorothea. I have such fond memories of our childhood.

She's a widow now, although I can't quite see her in mourning. She also has a daughter a similar age to you.'

'That'll be nice,' Hester said without much hope. 'I'm sure I won't need to call on their generosity too much. I'll concentrate my efforts on the workhouse.'

'Hester.'

She stopped at the note in her mother's voice.

'I want you to find out why Mercy was in the Southwell Union, but be careful. People, including the poor, keep their secrets close. Be careful how you phrase your questions.'

'Mercy eloped with Mr Philips. Can't I ask what happened to him?'

'If you must, but it's unlikely to be good news. We must be down as next of kin for the Southwell Union to write to us.'

'Perhaps Mercy was a widow. It would at least account for her presence at the workhouse.'

'Or deserted,' said Ruth, her eyes meeting her daughter's. 'Let's not be fools. We owe Mercy at least that. If she was abandoned, however, leave it at that. I don't want to know what happened to Mr Philips.'

'The letter mentions nothing of him?'

Hester saw Ruth hesitate before she took the envelope from the table and passed it to her.

'You might as well be in full knowledge of the facts as we know them. You'll get a sense of who you'll be dealing with from the phrases Mr Kirkham uses.'

Hester took the note from Ruth's hand and skimmed through the letter signed by a Richard Kirkham, master of the Southwell Union Workhouse. His writing was a nauseating mixture of obsequiousness and pomposity. The writer was sorry to inform Mr Goodwin that his daughter was dead this very morning and it was his unfortunate task to tell next of kin. He was sure we would wish to know of Mercy's sad and untimely death.

Hester handed the letter back to her mother.

'Horrible.'

'Yes. It's rather a shock to be on the receiving end of such language. I hope I don't come across so pleased with myself during my visits around the city.'

'I'm sure you don't.' Hester paused, thinking of how she and her mother had blithely crossed the city with little regard to how they were being perceived. 'I hope I don't, either.'

Her mother grimaced. 'An attitude such as this takes years to perfect. You can count yourself safe in that regard.'

'Poor, tragic Mercy.'

Hester thought back to her sister as she'd last seen her – calm and composed as they'd walked together to see the construction of the bridge at Clifton beginning. They'd stood at the edge of the gorge watching the men shouting across at each other. Mercy must already have been plotting her escape with John Philips.

'I wonder how she ended up in the workhouse,' said Hester.

Her mother wiped a hand across her forehead.

'It's a place of last resort, like all workhouses. Mercy will have gone there because there was nowhere else to go.'

But there was the family . . . The thought hovered between Hester and her mother and she saw her mother turn so she didn't have to look her daughter in the eye.

'I'd like some answers, Hester. For my own peace of mind.'

Hester nodded. 'I shall discover what happened to Mercy and come straight home.'

# Chapter Three

It was an adventure, thought Hester. However appalled she was feeling at her sister's death, it would allow her to briefly experience freedom from her Bristol life. While she packed her trunk, her mind raced in anticipation of what was to come. Even the thought of the horses galloping full speed through the countryside, rather than the sedate trot of the cart they usually hired for days out, made the journey more thrilling. And, joy of joys, she was going via London.

Susanna had come back from the inn bursting with the news. If she was to reach the workhouse quickly, she'd need to take the coach from The Bush Tavern to The Swan with Two Necks in Lad Lane, London. From there, she could travel to Nottingham and pick up the Saturday market coach to Southwell.

The trip would take over a day and necessitate a change of horses every twelve miles or so to keep up the pace. Hester would leave Bristol at midnight and arrive at dawn the day after next. Night travel had once been viewed as dangerous and uncomfortable, but the roads had been rid of highwaymen. A network of innkeepers along the way would be keeping an eye out for any itinerant robbers looking to prey on a solo female traveller.

It was Susanna who accompanied Hester to the coach. Ruth wasn't willing to leave her husband and the boys had already been despatched to their aunt's. They were both in high spirits as they walked to the tavern, Hester's trunk already sent to the coach by cart. Together, they tried to think of what they knew about Nottinghamshire.

'Lace,' said Susanna, her eyes dropping to the plain costume of Hester. 'On a fine dandy, frothing at his throat and on his cuffs.'

'Robin Hood,' said Hester, her head full of the tales she'd read as a child, the books hidden from her father.

They paused, struggling to come up with any other references.

'I feel as if I'm going to the New World,' she said to Susanna, shivering from the wind at her back as the mild September's day began to cool. 'It feels so far away.'

'You'll be there and back before you know it. Have you had any other sightings?'

Hester shook her head. 'None at all.' She stopped. 'If Ruth asks, tell her nothing. I mentioned I had a nightmare the morning we heard of Mercy's death. She's suspicious that I'm holding something back.'

'She'll get nothing out of me.' Susanna reached down to squeeze her hand. 'Listen to that.'

They could hear the noise of the coaching inn two streets away. There was an air of excitement, the cries and calls of people on the move. Hester was astounded to see an assortment of carriages – gigs, chaise-carts, stagecoaches – lined up outside the tavern on Corn Street, all of them ready to depart.

'Where are all these people going?' she asked Susanna.

'Bath, Birmingham, Exeter. You name it, there's a coach that'll take you there. You won't see much of London, mind. It'll be a quick change for the Nottingham connection but, once you're on it, you can keep your seat until you take the market coach to Southwell.'

Hester was transfixed by the hubbub of activity, from ostlers taking charge of the horses, farriers inspecting hooves and boot-boys running between coaches as the landlord shouted orders.

Hawkers peddled their wares for the journey and the smell of stale beer permeated the air. She saw Susanna fascinated by two women of dubious repute standing to one side.

'Don't stare.'

Susanna's eyes widened as the pair were approached by two gentlemen who followed the women up an alleyway.

'They'll most probably be at it up against a wall.'

'Susanna!'

Hester laughed in shock, the act releasing the knot in her stomach that had appeared at the news of Mercy's death. Her maid went up to the window of the booth, inside from which a clerk pointed out one of the waiting carriages – a tall cab pulled by four horses that were snorting with impatience.

Hester boarded the coach, closely followed by two men, who rushed from the dining room at the inn, complaining that they hadn't been given enough time to eat their meal. The two gentlemen took seats opposite each other and promptly fell asleep. They might have been cheated out of the food, but judging by the ripe smell, they'd availed themselves of the alcohol on offer.

'Take care, Hester.' Susanna waved at her. 'And keep your mind in this world. Remember, no fancies. If you get a shadowing, tell them you're too busy to be scared.'

The day passed in a blur of busy inns, the coach stopping every hour or so to change or rest the horses. Sometimes she stretched her legs. Once, she bought a mug of brackish coffee, which she drank in a little side room, away from the raucous laughter coming from the main bar.

At eight in the morning, they stopped at a foul-looking place on the outskirts of London. The landlord and landlady were drunks. In their filthy dining room, she was served a greasy mutton chop and a hunk of bread. Conscious that there would be nothing else until she changed coach, Hester ate the revolting meal and, desperate to relieve herself, followed a sullen maid into the outside privy, which was as bad as she'd feared.

A heavy stomach, even if filled with bad ingredients, makes you sleepy. The two gentlemen had left at Reading to be replaced by a widow, a woman not much older than herself, who smiled at her while her hands worked knitting needles. As her heavy eyes drooped, Hester's last thought was to wonder if she would get to see London Bridge.

She awoke with a jolt as the woman reached forwards and tapped her skirts.

'This is journey's end. All change.'

Confused, Hester pulled her shawl around her and supervised the removal of her trunk from the carriage. The day was thick with fog, a London particular swirling around the coaches.

'I need to catch the coach north to Nottingham. How will I know which one is mine?' she asked a driver as she handed him a coin.

He pointed to a man striding up and down the yard. 'That's William Chaplain himself. He'll tell you.'

'He's the owner?'

'Of this and other coaching inns. There's nothing that goes on here without him knowing.'

Hester picked her way through the horses. There must have been over twenty in the yard, some attached to coaches, others being led away by ostlers.

'Can you help me?' she shouted at the man to get her voice heard above the din. 'I'm looking for the Nottingham coach. I'm told it leaves shortly.'

As she came out of the mist, she saw the man's expression change.

'It'll be leaving in ten minutes. I'll take you there myself.' He led her across the yard to one of the front carriages. 'Let me see your ticket.'

She handed him the paper.

She saw him whisper something to the driver and a coin change hands. He must have noticed the alarm in her face.

'You're not being sold into slavery, don't worry. I've asked the driver to take care of you. My aunt was a Friend. We run an honest business here.'

So that was it. Her plain clothes had given her away. She smiled, grateful for a kind gesture.

'Thank you.'

He tipped his hat and disappeared into the murk. Hester waited for the other occupants as her trunk was lifted onto the roof. Eventually, a heavy thud towards the front indicated that another traveller had paid for an outside seat and, grateful to be alone in the carriage, they set off.

The weather was foul and even the newly surfaced road could only just withstand the elements. Rocked and jolted as the drivers urged the horses onwards, Hester experienced her other dream on that long road north. Not the pit, but the inferno. First the crackling and then the burning of an unfamiliar building. Hester felt the heat on her face, the smell of singeing fabric assailing her nostrils, until, finally, the flames touched her skin, causing her to roar with anguish. She awoke with a jolt, grateful her cry was lost on the noisy road.

As she wiped the window with her gloved hand, she saw that night was falling, her second in the coach. At the next inn, she purchased more dirty coffee and resolved to keep awake until Nottingham. Release came sooner than she'd expected. At one of the horse-changing inns in the blackness of the countryside, the driver opened the door.

'The market coach will be along shortly to take you to Southwell.'

'You're sure it stops here? I thought I was to go into Nottingham.'

'As regular as clockwork. Don't you worry, miss.' The driver paused. 'You'll tell Mr Chaplain I looked after you, won't you?'

'I will if I see him on the return journey,' she promised.

Satisfied, the man pointed to a small veranda where a figure sat.

'You don't need to wait by yourself. There's another passenger for the market coach.'

Hester told the disgruntled innkeeper that she wouldn't be wanting refreshment and joined the woman on the bench. Now that the end was in sight, her stomach was somersaulting at the thought of reaching her destination.

'Heading to market, too?' The woman's accent was unlike any she had heard before, full of country fields and ripe apples.

'I'm going to Southwell, but not to the market.'

The woman turned to her. 'I thought you were one of the Nottingham Quakers. They sell their lace shawls there.'

'Lace?'

'Oh aye. You look surprised. You'll find a few of the plain Quakers like yourself, if that's what you're worried about. But it's the wets who sell at market.'

Wet Quakers – an unpleasant term used to describe those liberal in their dress. There were some in Bristol too, wearing ribbons, lace and gauze on their bonnets. Hester grimaced when she thought what her father's reactions would have been. The woman misinterpreted her gesture.

'We're all the same in God's eyes. Ribbons or not.'

'I'm sorry. It wasn't my intention to judge.' How I long to wear ribbons, she thought.

Her reply seemed to satisfy the woman.

'Family, then?'

Hester paused, wondering how much to reveal.

'I'm visiting the Southwell Union Workhouse. There's someone there I need to see.'

Hester turned to the woman, who frowned.

'The workhouse? It sits just outside the town. You can't miss it.'

'It's a decent place?'

The woman hesitated. 'You have business there?'

'I do.'

Hester found herself unable to confide Mercy's story to the stranger and realised that she was ashamed of her sister. Mortified that she'd ended up in such a place. She gazed into the inclement night, where the light of dawn was just seeping through on the horizon. No wonder she hadn't felt the presence of Mercy since she'd left Bristol. She was carrying shame and fear with her as heavy as her travelling trunk.

'Well, I suppose Mr and Mrs Kirkham are respectable, although they don't allow for any malingering. I hope your business is concluded satisfactorily,' said the woman as they both stood at the sound of horses' hooves. 'Because from what I've heard, you wouldn't want to get on the wrong side of either of them.'

# Chapter Four

The track to Southwell was worse than the road north and the horses' hooves clattered on the stone cobbles. Occasionally they badly judged the road, their misstep throwing Hester around in her seat. Dawn revealed dark, tin-coloured clouds hanging over the flat countryside, which let loose a torrent of needles. The carriage passed through a bitter squall, rain lashing against the doors, adding to the sense of claustrophobia.

There were four people crammed into the little coach and more unseen on the roof. A couple of elderly gentlemen, clearly friends, had squeezed themselves into opposite corners of the carriage and were discussing the finer points of the East India Trading Company. Hester's companion at the inn had wisely decided to try to sleep through the noise, her head bouncing a little as they jolted along the road.

Hester was chilled by the morning ahead. The excitement of the journey had worn off and she was bone-weary. She couldn't imagine what her reception at Southwell Union would be like. Hospitals and poorhouses were known quantities to her, workhouses a new beast. For years, paupers had relied on charity from the local parish and had been adequately fed and clothed. But the rumour was that the more children you had, the more money you received, so it was hardly worth your while going out to work. And the government had resolved to stop this abuse. Paupers were to be housed together and families split up.

Amos, of course, had been in favour of the plan. Like the legislators who introduced the Poor Law Amendment Act, he despised the weak and idle. Little was he to know that his own daughter would end up inside one.

*Mercy, where are you?* she silently asked her sister. *My journey is all about you.*

At a deep groove in the road, Hester's companion jerked awake. The elderly woman stared at her in wide-eyed wonder while she came to.

'You've had a good sleep.'

'It's the rocking – it reminds me of being a baby.'

Sleep wasn't a place of safety for Hester, but she smiled back at the woman.

'I think we must be nearly there.'

'Southwell is a beautiful town. It's small but perfectly formed. And it has a minster, fallen on lean times.'

Hester leaned to look out of the window. 'I hope this weather eases. I won't see much of the place at this rate.'

'Are you being met from the coach?'

Hester nodded. 'I'm staying overnight with family friends, and they've had a message to expect me. I'll have a chance to freshen up before I go about my business. I hope it's not too early a start for them.'

'They'll send a servant, most likely. If they're late, you can wait at The Black Griffin. It's respectable enough, although the land-lord has a rough-and-ready manner. You'll be fine if you don't linger for long. They'll look after your baggage until you need it, too.' She paused. 'This is when I know I'm home.'

Hester looked out of the window and saw a tall tree, its leaves beginning to turn brown, in the middle of a small green.

The woman looked at her. 'The oak. The strongest of all the trees. Not far now.'

Hester nodded. She wondered if Mercy had made this same journey when she'd eloped with Mr Philips. Perhaps the oak had been a symbol of strength for her, too. The hooves were more insistent now on the cobbles as if the horses sensed that their destination was close to hand.

'Whoa there.'

The coach slowed outside a building of grey stone, it's façade unwelcoming.

'Don't be deceived by appearances,' whispered Hester's companion. 'It's comfortable inside.'

They passed through an arch and the coach came to a standstill in the cobbled courtyard. Hester disembarked first, her legs stiff and cold. Stamping her feet, she felt the circulation return. She'd seen more coaching inns over the past day and night than in her previous twenty-two years. This one was quieter than the London hostelries, but there was nevertheless an air of activity. Above her was a gallery of rooms, the balcony laden with blankets and airing clothes.

She looked around for the Francombes, feeling disorientated after the long night. There was one woman who she thought for a moment might be Dorothea but, after only a brief glance in her direction, she hurried to embrace Hester's female travelling companion. There was no waiting gig that might be for her. She watched the two women go arm in arm across the wet cobbles. She'd need to take her companion's advice and have some breakfast and hope that the Francombes came for her while she ate.

She looked around the courtyard for a door where she could enter the inn.

'You go around the side, Quaker Jane.'

She heard a voice, harsh in the morning stillness, and she drew her coat tighter around her, looking for her accuser.

She found him standing in the recess of a door to the side of the building, a tall man and solidly built, his arms folded as he watched the driver retrieve Hester's trunk from the roof of the carriage.

'Were you addressing me?' she shouted across to him and watched in satisfaction as his face fell a little before he rearranged his features back into an expression of contempt. He hadn't expected her to answer back, that was clear, and she enjoyed a dart of satisfaction at his discomfort.

'Come to do your do-gooding among us poor folk. Where would you like me to direct you to? The hospital, prison or poor school?'

Furious, Hester picked up her bag and suppressed the desire to throw it at him. A fine Nottinghamshire welcome, she thought.

'I'd like some breakfast first. Do they serve it here?'

He inclined his head towards the darkness inside the doorway. Swallowing so he wouldn't see her dismay at the lack of anyone to meet her, she brushed past him, inhaling his scent of sweat and straw, not dissimilar to the horses she'd just spent the night near.

The room she entered was dominated by a hearth, where flames licked up a black kettle. Some of the rooms in the coaching inns she'd passed through were large enough to fit twenty people around, but this was a compact space with two comfortable chairs by the fire and a small wooden table nearby.

Whatever arrangement the owner of the coach had with the landlord, it clearly wasn't to present him with large groups of people early in the morning. She hesitated between the fireside and sitting at the table. Fearing she'd fall asleep near the heat, she pulled out a chair, taking off her bonnet and resting it on top of her bag.

The man had followed Hester inside and, ignoring her, disappeared to a room at the back. The coach had been scheduled to arrive at half past seven and, despite the weather, it had made good time. It couldn't be much later than eight o'clock – far too early to go direct to the workhouse. While the master wouldn't encourage residents to idle in bed, she must surely wait until ten to pay her visit.

She couldn't fathom what had happened to the Francombes. If they failed to make an appearance this morning, she'd have to work out where her coins would find her a bed for the night. She looked around the simple but clean room. Perhaps here would do. The woman in the coach had said it was respectable.

Footsteps signalled the man's return. He was carrying a coffee pot, which he filled with water from the kettle and placed in front of her. He still didn't look at her, keeping his eyes on a snoring dog lying prone in one corner of the room. She suspected he regretted his outburst once he realised he'd be forced to provide her with food and drink.

'Will eggs do you?'

She looked up. 'Please.'

He nodded and left to shout instructions to a kitchen servant. At a loss about what to do in the silent room, she took out a little calfskin book and opened it. The book was a luxury, a birthday present given to her by a friend, which she'd kept hidden under her mattress. Amos wouldn't have approved of either the extravagance of the binding or the subject matter of the novel. *Ivanhoe* was full of thrilling adventures, dastardly deeds and even a witch trial. To Hester's dismay, the words danced around the page as she tried to concentrate.

The eggs turned out to be delicious. They'd been fried in bacon fat and Hester finished them in minutes, along with three slices of bread. She caught a glimpse of surprise and humour in the man's eyes when he returned to clear away her plate.

'Why did you call me Quaker Jane?' she asked, her courage refreshed after the meal.

The man shrugged. 'It's just a phrase. We don't see many of

your ilk at this inn, although there's plenty in Nottingham. I only know of a few families in this town, one very respectable.'

'The Francombes?'

The man shrugged. 'That might be their name. They wouldn't come in here, would they?' His eyes swept over her. 'You're noticeable by your dress.'

And Quaker Jane is a well-known insult, she thought.

The man paused, his eyes sliding away from hers.

'I wouldn't have shouted across at you if I'd known you were on your own, ma'am. Solo travellers get a friendly welcome here. I thought there were others in the coach with you.'

Hester could see his apology had cost him his dignity.

'No offence taken.'

She watched as he added a log to the fire. His height and bulk reminded her a little of the man who delivered their weekly dairy supplies in Bristol. He looked like he should be on a farm, not serving coffee in this miniature room.

'You're welcome to stay until your friends arrive.'

'I'm not sure when that'll be. I was expecting them to meet me from the coach. It suggests a letter might have gone astray. I thought that if I went off on my business, it'll at least allow for today's mail to arrive.'

'The post's usually reliable,' said the man. 'Everything stops for the mail coach. Why don't you write a note to your friends? I can ensure it's handed at the correct door.'

'If they're not here when I've concluded my business, I'll take you up on the offer.'

The man shrugged. 'As you wish.'

Hester, more confident now a plan of action had been arranged, decided to take charge of matters.

'If it's possible, I'd like to leave my bag here and have a wash before I leave.'

'I can take you into the back room once you've finished. There's plenty of hot water. Joan will give you a hand if you need it. My other maid, Annie, is helping a guest dress.'

'I'm used to looking after myself.'

He ignored the comment, unimpressed.

'After, you can wait by the fire until the town wakes up. It'll be more comfortable there. Just shout if you want more coffee. I could even run to tea.'

'You don't by any chance know the way to Southwell Union?'

He frowned, his face darkening. 'The workhouse? What do you want with that place? If you've do-gooding on your mind, you'd be better off going to the asylum.'

What an odd man he was. His temper could change from polite to brusque in a flash.

'I need to inquire about a resident there.'

She could see he wanted her to continue, but she let him wait. Not from embarrassment this time. She was a lone woman far from home. She'd choose her confidants carefully.

He rested his hand on the table. 'You're determined to go?'

'I am.'

'Turn left out of the inn and you'll see a signpost at the cross-roads directing you to Upton. Follow that road and, after a mile or so, there will be large building in front of you. Would you like to hire a trap and driver?'

'I'll walk.'

'That's your decision. As I said, it's not far. You'll recognise the building as soon as you see it. Part prison, part hospital. All our taxes were poured into paying for it.'

'You don't approve of looking after the less fortunate?'

'Don't you go putting words into my mouth. The poor parishes did a fine job around here. I don't see how lumping everyone into a big building helps at all. Not a place like that, anyhow.'

'It has a bad reputation?'

He snorted and turned his back on her so she couldn't see his face.

'There's a porter's lodge on the west block. Give him a knock and ask for Mrs Kirkham.'

'Mrs Kirkham? What about her husband?'

'She's the matron though, isn't she? She can take you straight to the ladies' wing. You weren't intending to try to help the men, were you?'

He was barely being civil, she saw, and something she'd said had infuriated him.

'It's Mr Kirkham I need to see. I have to talk to him about a recent death. I'll stay by the fire until ten o'clock, if that's acceptable to you. Then I shall pay them a visit.'

He turned his head back towards her, but in the gloom of the room, she still couldn't see his expression.

'Someone died?'

'A relative.'

Hester watched as he busied himself with the plates, but she got the impression that he was listening very closely to her reply.

'I've come to discuss my sister, Mercy,' she said finally. 'And find out how she ended up in this distant town, so far from her kith and kin.'

# Chapter Five

Before leaving The Black Griffin, Hester managed a decent wash in the kitchen. The landlord took her through the main drinking room full of phials of spirits, the space made bright by pots of geraniums on the windowsills. Joan was a woman of Ruth's age in a percale dress with a stiffly starched cap that formed a coronet around her head. She gave Hester a keen glance and placed a washbowl and towel on the rough kitchen table. Hester saw the hot water was scented with dried heads of chamomile.

'That'll perk you up. You must be dead on your feet.' She handed Hester a clean square of muslin. 'Matthew says you're off to the workhouse. Best make yourself spruce. Mrs Kirkham has high standards.'

Hester sensed the woman's curiosity. She dipped her hands in the water's warmth and lowered her face over the bowl.

'Should I fear her?'

Joan sniffed. 'No reason for you to. Hold your head up high. She rules the roost there but has no jurisdiction over you. I hear you were expecting to be met.'

'I don't understand what's gone awry. Do you know the Francombes?'

'The name means nothing to me.'

'My mother's letter should have arrived here yesterday morning at the latest.'

'I'm sure they'll be along later. Do you have a return ticket?'

'All paid for.'

'Well, there we are. If the worst comes to the worst, you can stay the night here. We have accommodation to suit every person's means.' She winked. 'Even the tinkers get a night's sleep for a penny in the stables.'

As the minster bell rang out ten o'clock, Hester left for the workhouse. The market was in full swing, traders' cries ringing in her ears. She was glad to escape the crush as the town thinned out, following the landlord's instructions, which took her down a country lane towards the long red-brick building that dominated the flat landscape. She attracted a few curious glances on the road and one shouted across at her.

'Pauper's path is over there.'

She lowered her head, embarrassed at being mistaken for one of the needy.

'Thank you.'

It was a miserable trudge up past the kitchen garden to the porter's lodge. Hester felt the spirits of the poor souls who had made the long walk in misery and despair, although none showed themselves to her. In the distance, a clinking noise came across the air. Stone-breaking or bone-crushing was taking place behind the high wall, both tasks back-breaking.

She was aware of being observed and the shutter of the small booth slid open. She doubted if there was a less friendly face in Nottinghamshire. The man's eyes swept over her clothes and back to her face.

'You'll not be wanting assistance, then.'

'I have an appointment to see Mr Kirkham.'

The man frowned. 'Mr Kirkham never mentioned anything to me this morning.'

'He will have received a letter from my mother—'

'Never mind, never mind. I don't need the details. Go through the big door in the centre of the building. Little Pinch will be there to meet you.'

With a quick glance again at Hester, the man pulled the window shut.

Hester stepped through the porch into the entrance hall, bare except for a long table and two chairs placed against the wall. From behind a set of doors at the end of the room, she could hear children chanting their multiplication tables. In one corner, a bell hanging from a wooden frame had been placed on the table. Hester grasped the rope and gave it a shake, cringing as it chimed throughout the building. It had its desired effect, however, as she heard the sound of footsteps making their way towards her.

A maid appeared in the room, standing in her metal-soled clogs less than four and half feet tall. As she took in Hester's appearance, her eyes narrowed, casting an unfriendly glance behind her.

'We have the Primitive Methodists who do the visiting here. Mr Kirkham has told me to send any others on their way. We need no more bleeding hearts. Thanking you very much, of course.'

Her voice might have been more feminine than that of the pub landlord Hester had just encountered, but the tone of the words was as unfriendly.

'If you don't mind, I have a letter from your employer.' Hester held out the note and saw the girl hesitate. Unlike Susanna, this maid clearly didn't read. 'Perhaps if you take it to Mr Kirkham, he'll see me.'

The maid stared at the thin envelope. 'As you wish,' she said, snatching it out of Hester's hand.

With a swish of her skirts she was gone.

Hester considered sitting in one of the hard-backed chairs against the wall, but tension kept her on her feet. It also helped to combat the tiredness threatening to overwhelm her. She paced up and down the room, making her footsteps as silent as possible.

This had been Mercy's first view of the inside of the building, too. She'd walked the same pauper's path and had asked for help. *Where are you?* she asked again. *Don't tell me you've stayed behind in Bristol. I need you here beside me.*

The room remained silent until a door opened and a man, as tall as the maid had been short, entered. He had a florid complexion, which contrasted with his severe black coat made of decent cloth.

'My dear Miss . . .' He hesitated. 'Goodwin, is it?' he asked, checking the address on the envelope.

Hester moved forwards. 'Yes. I'm Hester Goodwin.'

'Indeed.' The man looked at her through narrowed eyes.

'The letter you hold was addressed to my father, who is unfortunately ill, and he's sent me in his place.'

'I see.'

His tone suggested he didn't see at all.

'I must admit, your presence here is rather a surprise.'

'As was your letter.' Hester struggled to keep the tartness from her voice. The meeting wasn't going as she'd anticipated, and the man looked like he wanted to grab her by the scruff of her neck. 'It was the first we'd heard of the Southwell Union.'

He didn't like that, she saw. He drew himself up and Little Pinch took a step backwards.

'I'm required by the board of guardians to write a letter to the family of those unfortunate souls who die within our walls. I try to be as prompt as possible with my duties.'

Duties? thought Hester. That's what Mercy had been reduced to. A duty.

'I understand. And we're very grateful for you doing so, as we were unaware that Mercy had fallen on hard times.'

'Is that so?' He flashed Hester a glance, no doubt assessing her dress, the third to do so since her arrival at the workhouse. 'I got the impression . . . well, never mind. You're here now. I have to say, I hadn't expected a reply, especially one so prompt and in person.'

He stared hard at her, emanating a hateful authority. How the residents must fear him. She mustn't show him how much he repelled her.

'My mother sent you a letter to tell you of my visit. Didn't you get it?'

'I've received nothing.'

It was as she'd feared – both letters had gone astray. Yet, the post was advertised as being reliable, with heavy fines if anyone attempted to steal or waylay correspondence carried by Her Majesty's mail.

'I'm sorry you've had a wasted trip from' – he checked the address on the envelope – 'Bristol. Perhaps I should make it clear in future correspondence that we really don't need a reply. In fact, I shall make a note of it. If that's all.' He turned to go.

'But, Mr Kirkham, I have no intention of returning home until I have more information.'

He'd gone very still. Little Pinch had retreated into the shadow of the room.

'Information? What information?'

Hester swallowed. 'To begin with, I want to find out where Mercy's buried.'

'Where she's buried?' His voice rose, which he immediately checked and dropped it to above a whisper. 'But, Miss Goodwin, your sister is in a grave in the churchyard.'

'In the parish church?' A sickness began to crawl through Hester.

Mr Kirkham, sensing himself at a disadvantage, began to fiddle with the button on his coat.

'You need to understand this isn't a private hospital. People who come between these four walls don't usually have family in the outside world with specific requests for their burial.'

'She didn't inform you that she was a Friend?'

'She did not. On admittance, she said she was from a respectable Bristol family. We assumed she was of the Established Church.'

He was trying to put a note of authority back in his voice, but a bead of sweat formed on his temple. And well he might be worried. Quaker rights for their own burial were enshrined in law.

'I'd like to see where she's buried. Is the grave marked?'

He clenched his teeth. 'Of course the grave isn't marked. She had a simple Christian burial. If I'd known she was a Quaker then, of course, I'd have made alternative arrangements. Although to be frank, Miss Goodwin, your sister would have been the first Friend here. They usually look after their own.'

Shame made Hester sharp. 'We had no idea she was here, or we'd have helped.' She remembered her mother's request. Ruth would want a description of Mercy's resting place. 'I'd still like to see the place where she was buried.'

'But I've told you, there's nothing to see.' He moved towards her as if to steer her away from the room and his presence. 'I can give you directions if you insist, but you'll simply find a country graveyard.'

'I will look anyway.'

He sighed. 'As you wish. Now, you'll have to excuse me.'

Hester stood her ground, ignoring her trembling legs.

'I'd like a little more information about Mercy's arrival at the workhouse. My mother demands it. I'd like to know if she came alone.' Hester glanced around as if by doing so she could conjure the figure of John Philips.

'Your sister came to the doors, just as you have done, and asked to be admitted. As she wasn't local to us, she had to wait a week for the board of guardians to meet and decide on the course of action. You appreciate that we have a duty of care to admit only those we're specifically responsible for, as set out in the Poor Law Act.'

'But you let her stay?'

'She was destitute and in dire straits. In the circumstances, we felt obliged to help.'

'What about her husband? Had she been abandoned?'

'Her husband? Miss Goodwin had no husband. If that had been the case, he'd be here alongside her. We don't provide relief for women with husbands to support them.'

'No husband?' Hester's voice sounded hoarse as she was aware of another wash of shame. 'None at all? You have no Mr Philips here?'

'I have no one by that name. Your sister was unmarried.'

Hester's ears pricked up at the malicious tinge to his words. Perhaps he was a man who thought all women were fools. Well, in Mercy's case, he was right. She'd eloped with Mr Philips and at some point they'd parted company. Hester couldn't understand why, at that point, she hadn't come back to the family. She pulled her coat tighter, suddenly aware of the cold.

'And how did she die?'

'We had an outbreak of cholera here. We disinfect new arrivals as much as we can, of course, when they enter. They use soap, are deloused and are given clean workhouse clothes. But once cholera is here, it spreads.'

Cholera. That, at least, was what Hester had been expecting and would be a piece of news she could safely take home to her mother. Cholera might largely be a poor person's disease, but no one was completely immune. At least they'd be able to tell other Friends without shame that Mercy had died of this deadly illness.

Of the rest, Mercy's abandonment and her resting place, Hester needed time to think about what she could tell her mother. She'd initially thought of sending a letter ahead of her return to Bristol, so her mother received the news in advance, but she saw now that would never do. Mercy had been abandoned and buried as a pauper and would have been tumbled into a communal grave. Hester doubted if there'd even be a hump in the ground to distinguish her last resting place.

At a noise behind her, she turned and saw that the little maid hadn't left the room as she'd expected but had been hovering nearby, listening to their conversation. As Hester caught her eye, she saw that the maid was trying to communicate to her.

'I am very sorry that your trip has been in vain.' Mr Kirkham came towards her, laying a proprietorial arm on her, which she longed to shake off. 'I can see you to the gate.' He steered her towards the front doorway.

Hester caught the eye of the maid again and saw she was inclining her head upwards towards the first floor of the building. Hester followed the maid's glance and stopped, forcing Mr Kirkham to come to a halt too.

'If I can't see where she's buried, then I'd at least like to see where she died.'

'But that's impossible.'

She turned towards him. 'Why?'

His chest swelled in outrage. 'We have certain regulations as to who is allowed to visit and where they're allowed in the workhouse.'

'Nevertheless, I would like to be shown the room.' Hester remembered her mother's words and drew herself up to her full height. 'You were kind enough to write to us and I've made a long overnight journey. I'd like to see where Mercy died.'

# Chapter Six

Matthew knew from the set of Joan's back that she wanted to discuss the girl. He'd sent the Quaker on her way, her shoulders squared, which had failed to hide the tremble of her hands as she'd handed him the coins to pay for her breakfast. She'd smelled of soap after her wash – a change from the over-scented hussies who would be coming in at eleven o'clock for their first glass of stout. He'd watched as she'd crossed the street and disappeared from sight, a traveller in an unfamiliar town. Perhaps he'd been wrong not to warn her. If she'd been a man, he wouldn't have hesitated to call out a word of caution. In the end, uncertainty had held his tongue.

Although he disliked do-gooders, from the Unitarians to the Primitives in the chapel at the edge of town, he'd been embarrassed by the way she'd looked him in the eye as she'd answered him back after his taunts. That was the trouble with giving women a bit of freedom – they thought themselves the equal of you and yet they were indeed the weaker sex. Would that woman with the conker-brown hair and fine grey eyes be able to roll the barrel along the uneven floor as he was about to do? Of course not. And her self-assurance would do no better with Kirkham up at the workhouse. Thinking of the man brought another stab of conscience. He should have warned the girl with more forthright words.

Joan came out into the courtyard, undoing her pinny and balling it up to place it under her arm.

'That's me for the morning. I've some errands to run. I'll be back in time for the mail coach. Annie's in the kitchen attending to her tasks.'

'God help us, then.'

'Oh, leave the girl alone. She'll get the hang of things soon enough.' Joan looked around the courtyard. 'Still no one come to claim the Quaker girl? She hadn't expected that. To come all that way and find she wasn't even expected.'

'How did she act in the kitchen?'

'Fearful but trying not to show it. She asked about a family called the Francombes. The name meant nothing to me. Do you know them?'

Matthew shrugged. 'They don't frequent my hostelry.'

Joan laughed at this and slapped him on the arm.

'Look at you. I didn't think for a minute . . . Never mind. I'm sure she'll be all right.'

He tried to join in with her mirth, although his smile felt as fake as his words.

'Perhaps she'll ask for a bed at the workhouse.'

Joan's mood turned sober and she shot him a look.

'We don't make jokes about ending up there.'

He nodded and turned his back to her so he wouldn't have to discuss the woman again. No. He shouldn't have made that joke, although Joan's reticence had a very different origin from his own.

# Chapter Seven

Mr Kirkham was furious, Hester saw. His red face turned purple, flecks of spittle gathering at the corner of his mouth.

'It's impossible. I'm a busy man. I don't have time to conduct a tour of the building. You'll need to leave.'

Behind the man's anger and resolve, Hester detected bluster. Little Pinch kept her gaze on her, willing her to stand firm, and Hester briefly closed her eyes, remembering her mother's words. *They treat you well once they've got your measure.* At that moment, she felt Mercy appear alongside her. *At last,* she told her sister. *I supposed I was on a fool's errand.* When she opened her eyes, she realised Mr Kirkham saw the act as an indication of weakness.

'Don't distress yourself, my dear. The workhouse really isn't a place for gentlewomen.'

Hester regarded him coldly. 'I've been sent here for a purpose, which I intend to honour. You cannot show me her grave, and yet it's the law that Quakers are allowed their own funeral arrangements.'

She saw him swallow.

'My next step would be to inform the board of guardians. Surely they believe in the freedom to practise our own religion. However, if you show me where Mercy died, I'll consider the matter closed.'

He was infuriated, she could see. He opened his mouth to

speak, but they were distracted by a cat creeping in, enticed by the smell of cooking food in the kitchen.

'Get that bloody thing away from here.' He lashed out with his boot but missed the animal, instead kicking Little Pinch, who was trying to shoo it away.

She stood, smarting from the attack, then scurried away towards the kitchens as if her skirts were on fire. With a pang, Hester thought of Susanna who, she was sure, would have stood up to this man. She caught his eye and, perhaps ashamed by his attack, he nodded his head.

'Very well. I'll take you to the dormitory.'

Mr Kirkham adopted a schoolmaster's tone as he escorted her through the building, trying, Hester thought, to restore his damaged pride. He was obviously proud of the building and his place within it.

'This is the kitchen. Dinner is cooked by the inmates with overall direction from Mrs Kirkham.'

Hester glanced around as they passed through the room. A couple of women, clothed in coarse dresses and day caps, were clearing up after breakfast while Little Pinch was leaning over a chicken plucking feathers as fast as she could, her little body shaking.

'Will I meet Mrs Kirkham?'

'You will. She's in the dormitory for undeserving women as we speak. You'll meet her when we get there.'

Undeserving women? thought Hester. Surely Mercy's poverty hadn't made her into an improvident resident. She'd arrived as a single woman in need. What was so undeserving in that? Mr Kirkham had moved on.

'The undeserving women's day room. Your sister spent much time in here nearing the end.'

It was a mean whitewashed room with five hard-backed chairs

forming a circle. Hester frowned. Surely a woman with cholera shouldn't have been allowed to mix with others.

'She died quickly after contracting the illness?'

Mr Kirkham coughed as they crossed to a set of stairs. 'My wife can answer any questions you have. Up we go.'

He allowed her to lead the way and Hester was conscious of his eyes on her back as she climbed the narrow steps.

'To the left are the beds for the deserving poor. We recognise, of course, that some people are unable to provide for themselves and this is what the workhouse was built for.'

'May I see?'

Before he could answer, Hester poked her head through the door and looked at the row of beds, all neatly made. A dormitory for women whether they were married or single. There was likely to be an identical room elsewhere in the building housing the deserving males. Children would be similarly distanced, huddled into beds with other small souls. The antithesis of a family unit. They might as well be orphans. She kept her expression polite as she considered the room.

Mercy had arrived and been given a bed not in this dormitory, but one reserved for the wilfully poor. It could only mean that when she'd presented herself at the workhouse, she'd told them of her elopement with Mr Philips and her subsequent abandonment. That must be it. Lumped in with the immoral and idle. This, Hester decided, was where the truth and what Hester told her mother would diverge. She wouldn't lessen Mercy in her parents' eyes. The room she saw before her would be the one she described to Ruth and to Amos, if he recovered.

At the sound of coughing, Hester realised that a bed was occupied. From underneath the thin blanket, she could hear a woman muttering, her words unintelligible. Hester hesitated, wondering whether to go to the woman's aid.

'Never mind her. Through here,' said Mr Kirkham, growing impatient at Hester's dawdling.

He stopped in front of a closed door, behind which there was a murmuring of voices. Hester went cold, suddenly seized by a force pulling her away from the room. She spun round, but Mercy was nowhere to be seen. The grip on her was icy, sending waves of shock through her body. She reached out a hand and steadied herself against the wall. Mr Kirkham was oblivious to her distress.

'My wife has plenty to keep her occupied. I think I can leave you here with her. She can answer any questions you have, but please don't detain her longer than necessary.'

Hester, still stunned, became aware of a smell. Not the foul rotting flesh odours she'd to endure when she visited Bristol Infirmary but a vague nauseating scent that made her want to retch. She thought about taking out the handkerchief from the pocket of her skirt, but she was determined not to show any weakness in front of this man.

'Has the outbreak of cholera passed?' she asked.

He turned to her, amusement fighting with anger.

'My dear lady, do you really think I'd be showing you this room if there were any infectious patients here?'

Mr Kirkham knocked at the door, which opened at once. Mrs Kirkham was a buxom woman stuffed into a burgundy plaid dress, her shoulders covered with a shawl. From underneath a lace cap, a shrewd pair of coal-black eyes in a face of high colour like her husband's assessed Hester.

'Ah, Mrs Kirkham. I have here a Miss Goodwin.'

At the mention of her last name, the woman frowned. 'Goodwin?'

'Indeed. The same name as Mercy, who so unfortunately passed last week.'

'I'm hardly likely to forget, am I?' She swept her eyes over Hester, her hand still holding the door.

Mr Kirkham's voice remained expressionless. 'This lady has expressed a wish to see where her sister died. I've said that it's perfectly acceptable in the absence of a grave to visit.'

A look passed between the pair and the woman nodded, stepping back to let her enter.

'Miss Goodwin hasn't been *fully* acquainted with the facts of her sister's death. She knows there was an outbreak of cholera, but that is all.'

'Of course.' Mrs Kirkham gave her a chilly glance and opened the door. 'Then you'd better come in.'

Hester turned to thank the master, but he'd already started to go.

'Stop blabbering,' he shouted at the woman huddled under the bedclothes in the adjoining room.

She hoped Little Pinch had made herself scarce.

'Well, don't stand there,' said Mrs Kirkham.

Hester felt the ice creep through her veins once again, but she took a breath and stepped over the threshold. The room was identical to the one she'd left, filled with twelve beds, six on each side. On one of them, two girls sat side by side, their hands clasped together.

'We were just saying our prayers,' Mrs Kirkham said, glancing at Hester. 'However, given that we're in the presence of a Quaker who doesn't share our ways, I think we might just say amen and finish them early.'

Hester frowned at the voice filled with mockery.

'Are these the only women in this wing?'

Mrs Kirkham laughed, showing a fine set of teeth.

'We're nearly full. Mr Kirkham will be in trouble with the board. They don't like the undeserving rooms to be filled. These are women who have willingly chosen to be poor.'

'Willingly chosen?' Hester set her face at her. 'Who would willingly choose poverty?'

'We all have a choice at one time or another. The other dormitory is for the afflicted, the old and infirm. We must look after our sick.'

'And here?' Hester looked around.

'This is where women who think they can live off the charity of others are housed.'

'If this dormitory is full, why are these two women—'

'Separate? I've been asked by the parson, Reverend Flint, to ensure these girls receive extra religious instruction.'

Hester, now in the grip of a coldness so icy that it reached her bones, had to brace herself against the temptation to flee. One of the girls, a flaxen-haired beauty of about sixteen, glanced up and the look she gave Hester was full of understanding. The girl put her finger to her lips.

'And Mercy, was she given extra instruction too?'

The other girl sniggered. She was little more than a child, thirteen at most. Mrs Kirkham looked at Hester with what appeared to be pity.

'Your sister did indeed require additional instruction.'

Hester looked closer at the figures on the bed and saw that they were dressed in the same attire she'd seen the women wearing in the kitchen, a brown cloth of rough quality. The younger girl was tall and thin, like a beanpole, and the sacking hung loosely at her shoulders until it met the unmistakable swell of her stomach. The flaxen-haired girl looked to be at a more advanced stage. Mrs Kirkham stared at Hester, taking in her scrutiny.

'I see the penny has dropped.'

# Chapter Eight

'Mercy was expecting a baby when she died,' said Hester, feeling the air relax and a warmth spread through her.

*I understand*, she told Mercy. *Your secret is out.*

Mrs Kirkham watched her with an expression of grim satisfaction. No wonder Mr Kirkham had been in a rush to depart. He was leaving it to this gleeful woman to break the news to Hester.

'She came here seven months gone. Some workhouses leave the women out in the hedgerows to give birth, but we pride ourselves on a more public spirit.'

'Did she say how she'd managed to find herself alone?'

'She gave an account to the board of guardians after admittance. She'd been abandoned, as is usually the case.'

'Was she confined to bed?'

'Of course not. Expectant mothers are required to work.' She glanced across at the girls. 'Once they've said their prayers, they'll be joining the others.'

'And Mercy?'

'She helped in the laundry. She was a decent worker.'

'So where did she contract cholera?'

The fair-haired girl looked across at Hester, frowning. It was the same everywhere. Inmates, patients, the sick. All afraid of the disease sometimes called the blue death on account of the tinge of sufferers' skin.

'We think she brought it with her. Her last abode was a common lodging in Nottingham. She probably picked it up there.'

A common lodging – the cheapest place to stay where, for four pence a night, you could buy the use of a bed.

'And her husb . . . the man we thought was her husband. A Mr Philips?'

'Disappeared.' Mrs Kirkham smacked her lips. 'She told Ellen the story, didn't she?'

The girl looked over to Mrs Kirkham to check she could speak.

'Go on. Tell Miss Goodwin the story.'

Ellen swallowed. Hester saw her lips were dry and cracked, causing a trail of blood to wind its way down her chin.

'He disappeared in Nottingham. He left her in a coffee house in the city. Told her he had an interview for a teaching position. She waited for six hours before she realised he wasn't returning.'

Hester felt bile rising in her throat and thought she was going to retch.

'Abandoned?'

*Abandoned*, echoed her sister.

'And what happened to the child?'

'The baby didn't survive,' said Mrs Kirkham. 'I called the midwife when the birth was near, but cholera attacks every bone in your body. We buried Mercy with her child in her arms. I hope that gives you comfort.'

*Liar.*

The voice was loud in Hester's ear and she jumped, to the amusement of Ellen, the tiny child soon to be a mother. Was it Mercy who had spoken this time or a different spectre, for Hester sensed another presence in the room? One without the calmness of Mercy; a restless spirit. She studied Mrs Kirkham. Her words rang hollow, everything about this woman radiating false bonhomie.

'Which bed was she in?' she asked.

Mrs Kirkham rolled her eyes but pointed to a small cot near a mean window, the grey skies seen through smeared glass – that would have been Mercy's last view of this life . . . She walked across to the bed, but all sense of her sister was gone. Another woman's nightdress hung on the peg above the headboard.

The sad truth of Mercy's end was clear. She'd been deserted by Mr Philips, and he'd reneged on any promise he might have made about a wedding. Hester was at a loss to understand why Mercy hadn't written to her family to say she was with child. Amos might be strict, but even he was worldly enough to know about women becoming pregnant by lovers who couldn't or wouldn't marry them.

'I think I've seen all I need—'

Before she could finish her sentence, a cry came from behind the door. Ellen looked across at her and raised her eyebrows as Mrs Kirkham hurried out of the room, closing the door with a snap behind her. Left alone with the girls, Hester became awkward, but, out of Mrs Kirkham's presence, the inmates relaxed.

'It's old Meg. She gets confused and lashes out. They keep her chained to the bed. Mrs Kirkham has gone to help as there's a danger she'll hurt herself.'

The speaker was the flaxen-haired girl. Her voice held the trace of an accent, one she associated with the sailors in the Bristol docks.

'You mean the woman under the bedclothes? She's chained?'

'She needs to be in the asylum.' Ellen glanced at her hands, raw from hard work.

'Then why don't they send her there?' Hester asked.

The girl shrugged, appraising her. 'We've not been told. Perhaps they're full. Plenty of people with the madness in Nottinghamshire.' She paused. 'Funny you turning up. You could tell

Mercy was respectable. A cut above us all. Not that she was stuck-up. Mucked in like the rest of us. Must have been a to-do when she eloped.'

Hester pushed away the memory of Amos's rage.

'I feel we failed Mercy. If she'd written, we could have done something to help.'

'Never got her letters, then,' the girl replied, her tone tart.

Hester felt the need to defend her father. 'She sent no letters to us.'

'She did, didn't she, Elisabet?' Ellen glanced across to her fellow inmate. 'She told us she'd written to inform her family of the baby.'

'I don't think that's the case,' said Hester, listening for the whisper of Mercy, but all the spirits had departed for the moment.

She remembered her father's consternation at receiving the letter from Mr Kirkham. He couldn't have faked such a reaction. The news that Mercy had died had induced his stroke.

Two pairs of eyes regarded her, neither accusing her. They knew enough of the world to appreciate families were complicated, especially when it came to illegitimate children. She guessed that Mercy had told a white lie to explain her presence in the workhouse when she was clearly from a respectable family.

'Was Mr Philips informed of the death of the child?' Hester asked.

Ellen cackled at that, showing a row of teeth belonging to a woman thirty years older.

'I think "mister" is a little strong for that old sod, don't you?'

Hester was determined not to look shocked while there was still information to be squeezed out.

'Was it a boy or a girl, the child?'

'A girl,' whispered Elisabet. 'Now gone.'

'I know.' Hester's throat constricted.

The girl shook her head. 'All gone,' she whispered at her. 'They've all gone.'

'Elisabet,' said Ellen, her voice full of warning. 'Be careful what you say.'

Hester frowned as Mrs Kirkham reappeared at the door, a little ruffled and in high colour. In the distance, a bell rang, the chime identical to the one Hester had made on arrival.

'I'm afraid I'm needed downstairs, Miss Goodwin. You'll need to see yourself out. Can you remember the way?'

'Certainly.' Hester wasn't at all as confident as she sounded. 'Perhaps one of the girls . . .'

'The girls stay here.'

Hester shrugged and turned to leave. 'I'm sure I'll find my way.'

Nodding, Mrs Kirkham hurried away.

'Goodbye, then,' said Hester.

'Bye,' said Ellen, standing up and stretching her arms. 'I'm in the kitchen today. They'll have "holified" soup after the prayers I've said today.'

'Don't joke,' whispered Elisabet, following Hester to the door.

'Where are you from?' Hester asked. 'I can hear your foreign accent. I've heard a similar tone in the sailors at the hospital I visit.'

The girl rubbed her eyes. 'Sweden.'

'Then you're a long way from home.'

'I came over on one of my uncle's ships. I met my Joe on board and he brought me to Nottinghamshire.'

'Will you return? To Sweden, I mean. This is no place for you here.'

'It depends. Joe always said that if I was in trouble, the workhouse would help. When he died, I asked to be admitted until the baby's born, then I'll try to get a passage back. Only . . .'

'Only what?'

'Elisabet, be careful.' Ellen had been listening intently to their conversation, despite their whispers.

'I am careful.' She leaned forwards to push open the door, her face brushing close to Hester's.

'I thought it a good idea. Now I'm not so sure. No one told me about the angelmaker. She appears when there's a birth. I don't want her around me when the time comes.'

'The angelmaker?' What a strange term, thought Hester. Our faith has no place for angels and yet the word speaks to me. 'What do you mean by angelmaker?'

Hester's question panicked the girl. She grasped Hester's sleeve, holding on tight.

'Don't let the angelmaker take my baby. She wants it for her own end. If I see her, it's already too late. Do you understand?'

Hester stared at her, aware of the spirit of Mercy next to her.

'Is it a spectre you see?'

The girl stared at her, her eyes wide.

'I'm sure of it. A pale lady. She arrives by night. She shan't take my baby.'

'Elisabet, what are you saying to our guest?'

Mrs Kirkham had swept back into the room.

'Nothing, Mrs Kirkham.'

'Then let Miss Goodwin leave.'

Astonished, Hester stepped through the doorway and turned to say her goodbyes, but the door had already been shut in her face.

# Chapter Nine

Outside the gates of Southwell Union, Hester had a moment of brain fever. The workhouse stood behind her and she was desperate to escape its shadow. But the town turned its cold face on her, calling across the fields that she wasn't to take a step nearer. Well, she couldn't turn back. The two girls in the workhouse were beyond her help and would no doubt be sent to their allotted tasks the minute she left. The only thing for her to do was to return to The Black Griffin and see if any inquiries had been made for her there. Otherwise, she'd take a room and wait for the return coach the following morning.

As she walked away, she was conscious of a pair of eyes watching her retreat. Not a supernatural presence, but a living observer making sure she left the grounds. She turned and saw a figure in the central upper window. It afforded the watcher a view of all the courtyards. No one breaking stones or washing at the pump would escape scrutiny. Well, they'd got what they wanted. She was leaving with plenty of questions and few answers.

After retracing her steps along the pauper path, she hesitated. To the east she could see a square church tower, away from the direction she should take to the town. Mercy had been buried in the parish church according to Mr Kirkham. If there wasn't a grave, she could at least describe Mercy's resting place to her mother.

In the churchyard, the graves were marked by simple tablets and crosses free from sentimental words. Amos would approve.

Only one stood out among the neat rows – a stone-carved angel sheathed in a gown similar to a Greek goddess with her wings spread as if for flight. She stopped to inspect it. Angelmaker, Elisabet had said. Perhaps it was a reference to this grave marker, chilling in its piety. She stepped nearer and read the inscription: Eliza Evans – Aged 82. Hester grimaced. Not the angelmaker, surely.

Hester stared around the quiet churchyard, taking in the scene. She'd tell Ruth that Mercy was buried in a place of peace, although it felt like a lie. The atmosphere wasn't one of serenity but of desolation. The canopies of the trees met, casting a shadow over much of the church, but she could hear no birds nor other animals. In one corner, near an ancient yew, a square of earth was visible, the soil recently turned. Was this the communal grave, opened whenever a pauper needed burial? The gravedigger would know, or the parson. She owed it to Mercy and her lost child to at least try to find their resting place.

Church buildings were an unknown quantity to her. She was used to worshipping in bare white rooms furnished only with a table and long benches. The plain, unadorned design was meant to bring you closer to God and the Quaker faith rejected anything that might be there simply for show. 'If you want the trimmings, you can go next door,' Amos frequently pronounced. However, this church was a house of God and couldn't be so terrible.

She followed the path to the church door and pushed it open, peering into the murk. A rush of stagnant air greeted her, smelling of the grave. No candles were being wasted to guide any passing pilgrims. She held out a hand and scrabbled against the wall to guide herself into the body of the church. At first, she thought she'd interrupted a service. The pews were full and the cleric was at the front with his arm raised as he delivered a sermon. This must be Reverend Flint, the parson keen that Elisabet and Ellen received extra instruction. It must also be he who had buried Mercy. He looked at least eighty, a thin, decrepit-looking man with an air of the zealot about him.

Hester moved into the shadow, not wanting to interrupt his address. It was a fire-and-brimstone speech, so far removed from the loving God she felt at Friends' meetings. The congregation remained still, seemingly engrossed in the words. As her eyes became accustomed to the dark, she realised the people were odd shapes, some slumped to one side, others appearing without arms or heads.

She crept into the back of a pew and gave one of them a push. With a whoosh, it slid to the ground. A straw man like a scarecrow, its face of painted sackcloth, stared up at her from the floor. Hester took a step back, appalled at the garish face and disjointed limbs.

'What—?'

'Leave my congregation alone.'

She jumped as the parson moved towards her.

'How dare you interfere with the faithful. What are you doing here?'

Hester suppressed the urge to flee at his tone. 'Reverend Flint?'

'What of it?'

'I'm looking for the grave of my sister, Mercy. She died at the Southwell Union last week.'

'If she's from the workhouse, she'll be buried in the pit.'

'The pit?' The nightmare rushed towards Hester, knocking her off-kilter.

He leered at her. 'It's a communal grave. Do you want me to take you there? You want to lie next to your sister, do you?'

Terror made her furious. 'You hateful man.' She pushed herself along the pew. 'What's wrong with everyone here?'

God help Mercy in this foul place. She reached the light of the day and caught sight of the stone angel. She turned to ask him a final question, but the words died on her lips. He was staring beyond her.

'Who is it that follows you?'

Hester spun round, but there was only the chilly graveyard and leaves blowing around her feet.

'There's no one there.' She took a deep breath. 'Does the name angelmaker mean anything to you? A pale lady?'

'Heathen,' he screamed after her. 'I see you in your Quaker garb now. Come to spy on me, have you? Harlot.'

She stumbled forwards, tripping over her skirts until she moved out into the sunlight, the man's voice ringing in her ears.

# Chapter Ten

Hester hurried towards the town, sick at heart. Any sense of the spirit of Mercy being close by had vanished and she couldn't stay in this place a minute longer. There might be a coach south this evening and if so, with her return already paid for, she'd be on it. She'd make the booking at The Black Griffin and wait it out there. The inn was cordial, even if not friendly.

Absorbed in her thoughts, she hardly noticed the barefoot girl pacing the wood pavement outside a milliner's. It was the child she was nursing who broke into Hester's thoughts, its bawls making an uncanny echo on the road.

'Is your baby well?' Hester took a step forwards and the woman shrank back, clutching the child to her chest. She was dressed in a grey shift, too long for her, which gave her a train like a filthy bride.

'Don't touch him,' she whispered, her voice as thin as a coil of smoke.

Hester froze and took a step back. 'I don't wish you any harm.'

'Have you seen my child?'

Confused, Hester looked at the swaddled baby. 'Your child? But it's in your arms.'

The woman looked down at the little bundle and nodded. 'My baby.'

She's lost her wits, thought Hester. There's nothing I can do to help. She took a few steps, then had a change of heart and dug around in her reticule for a coin. She turned to give it to the girl, but the street was empty.

Oh no, thought Hester. No more shadowings, please.

It was a relief to see The Black Griffin. She'd discuss her predicament with the landlord. Despite his truculence, he had a competent manner and would surely advise her of the quickest way home. When she turned under the arch at the entrance to the inn, she saw a woman standing under an umbrella to shade herself from the October sun. As she lifted the parasol, Hester saw a handsome dark-haired woman whose face broke into a smile.

'Hester, my dear. I'd have recognised you anywhere. You're the living image of your mother.'

Hester realised how much tension the day had brought when she had to fight back the tears at the kind words. The woman came forwards to embrace her.

'You must call me Dorothea, my dear. This is my daughter, Caroline. She's been so excited to meet you.'

From out of the shadows came a girl, taller than her mother with the same near-black hair. She wasn't in Quaker clothing; a cerise ribbon was woven through her bonnet and fine gold thread edged her cape. It made her look very dashing, Hester thought with a pang, aware of her drab outfit, a feeling only heightened as the girl fixed her eyes on Hester's plain grey bonnet.

'I'm mortified that we weren't here to meet you from the coach earlier today,' said Dorothea. 'The letter only arrived this morning and we made haste as soon as we received it.'

'I was worried that news of my arrival wouldn't reach you at all.'

'We guessed once we'd read the letter that you'd be arriving today and we hoped we'd catch you in time. When we got here, the landlord said you'd arrived by market coach but that he had your trunk and you'd be back for it soon enough. So we decided to wait.'

Hester looked around for the landlord, but the courtyard was empty, awaiting the next carriage.

'Ruth and I never considered there would be an issue with the mail. She wrote three days ago and we've been told the post is fast on the new roads.'

Dorothea shrugged, glancing at her daughter. 'Accidents do happen – coaches overturn, mail is lost.'

'Mr Kirkham at the Union hadn't received Ruth's letter either. I suppose it's likely it'll arrive today, as yours did.'

Caroline looked down, clearly embarrassed by talk of the workhouse but unsurprised. Ruth had obviously mentioned Mercy's circumstances in her letter to the Francombes. Dorothea, however, was unperturbed.

'Let's not talk of that place now. We must take you straight back to our house. You'll need a rest after such a tiring and upsetting morning. You can tell us more there.'

'We've had dealings with both Mr and Mrs Kirkham in the past,' said Caroline, linking her arm through Hester's. 'You don't need to explain anything on that score.'

The landlord came out of the inn carrying Hester's trunk on his shoulder. He placed it in a trap and returned inside without a backwards glance. Neither of the Francombes paid any attention to him or to the ostler who helped them up into the carriage. Dorothea took the reins and with a flick at the grey mare, they trotted away from The Black Griffin.

They passed the spot where the spectral girl had appeared. The street was still empty, only a small boy sweeping the road no doubt in exchange for a few pence. The trap made a circle of the town, passing the minster, impressive in its architecture, even though it had an air of decline.

'Have you been inside?' Hester asked.

Dorothea looked surprised. 'Of course. It's not our faith, mind, but we attended a recent marriage there.' She looked at Hester. 'You'll find us a little more relaxed here than you're used to, I think. Don't worry. I won't spill anything to Ruth.'

'I'm not concerned. It isn't Ruth who would have a problem with it,' said Hester.

Quakers had once had a closer relationship with the Established Church. Her own grandparents on her mother's side were buried in a churchyard in the Anglican parish of Chew Magna near Bath. The vicar had allowed those of all faiths to rest within the boundary walls, but Amos had strictly forbidden his family to visit any place of worship other than the meeting house. As she regarded the minster, she saw a flash of grey disappear up a lane.

'What is it, my dear?' asked Dorothea.

Hester shook away the image. 'It's nothing.'

It's happening again, she thought. If Amos finds out, sick or not, I shall be in trouble. The visions had first appeared to her as a young child. Sick in bed with a fever, she'd been aware of a comforting figure sitting on the chair next to her cot – her maternal grandmother who had died six months earlier. When she'd mentioned it first to Ruth, who had then spoken of it to Amos, both of her parents had been convinced that the visions were part of her illness.

However, the hazy figures, as insubstantial as shadows, had continued to materialise throughout her childhood. Whether it was the neighbours' daughter who had died of scarlatina or the butcher's boy who had fallen off the cart, the shadowings brought comfort. Despite Amos's ragings and Ruth's disbelief, Hester knew they were nothing to do with her imagination. How else could she conjure a previous maid's sister who had died in childbirth – a young woman with a birthmark on her cheek? The maid had only mentioned the disfigurement long after the woman had appeared as a shadowing.

Her visions came in times of crisis and when she was feeling low in mood. Hester had never been frightened of them. Until now. She didn't fear Mercy, but there was another presence, she was sure of it, and one that wasn't showing their true form.

A jolt shook Hester from her reverie and she saw Dorothea's eyes on her.

'It's always disorientating being so far from your home. You'll feel better once you're at Guy House.'

The trap drew up outside a handsome narrow building of similar proportions to the Goodwins' residence in Bristol but with a far grander air, from the gleaming polished brass door knocker to the well-clipped privet hedge that enclosed the front garden. A maid opened the door, taking Hester's travelling coat.

'Bring us some tea, please. Hester has had quite a morning, I think,' said Dorothea. 'And ask Jack to take the trunk off the trap.'

She ushered Hester into a small room decorated in fern-patterned wallpaper. Hester felt herself begin to relax.

'So,' said Dorothea once they'd settled. 'Mercy died in the workhouse. I know condolences don't always help, but I want you to know I truly am sorry. I never met Mercy, but your mother's letters were always full of stories of you two girls. I feel like I know you already.'

Hester hid her start of surprise. Although Ruth wrote innumerable letters to her network of acquaintances, one travelling as far as Scotland each month, Hester had always assumed the notes would be full of Quaker news, not family chatter.

'You were at school with my mother?'

'I was. We've kept in touch since. It's always a good thing to keep a reminder of your childhood. It reminds you that each of us has taken a different path.'

'Never mind about that. Let Hester tell us about the workhouse.'

Caroline sounded bored as she played with her teaspoon, giving it short raps on the wooden chair arm, an act that would have earned Hester a clout from Amos. Dorothea, probably used to her daughter's capriciousness, ignored her.

'Sorry, Hester. Do tell us your story.'

I don't know where to start, she thought. Her mind was full of Mercy on Earth and in spirit, and the two expectant mothers she'd met, along with the girl on the street cradling her baby. Mothers and their children. Trying to gather her thoughts, she stalled.

'You said you knew of Mr Kirkham. Do you make visits to the workhouse?'

Mrs Francombe pulled a face. 'I'm afraid not. I've never been inside the building. It's new to the town, you see. Well, it was erected a decade or so ago, but that constitutes new for Southwell. When it first opened, we did try to visit, but we were turned away. Mr Kirkham apparently doesn't like Friends.'

And there I was, turning up in my grey clothes demanding information, she thought.

'Any particular reason why not?'

Dorothea shrugged.

'I don't know, but we're not welcome there. Perhaps the master wants to go about his work unhindered, or maybe he had a bad experience with someone from our faith.'

Hester remembered Little Pinch's words.

'The maid I met in reception mentioned something about the Primitive Methodists being allowed access.'

'Well, they do good works in the town and I'm sure they're keeping an eye on things inside the workhouse.' She paused. 'Were you treated cordially?'

Hester thought of the befrocked gentleman who had grudgingly escorted her to the dormitory.

'Well enough. . . . I got the impression that they'd rather I'd not been anywhere near the place, but they were cordial. You had no idea Mercy was in the workhouse?'

Mrs Francombe raised her hands. 'My dear, none at all. If I'd had even an inkling, I'd have marched down there myself. Poverty is nothing to be ashamed of, and we could have done something to help her, I'm sure.'

'Any sign of her husband?'

Caroline's voice was cool and Hester was reminded that although she lived in the bigger city, this girl was the more worldly. Hester would never have asked the blunt question, with all the hidden implications, in this lovely drawing room.

'It appears that no marriage took place,' Hester said, watching for their reaction.

Dorothea sighed. 'It's a common enough story. Your poor parents.'

Hester felt the familiar wash of shame.

'I don't understand why she didn't write to us,' she burst out, letting the frustration of the day spill into the room. 'You've said yourself it's a common story. Why didn't she send us a message? She told the girls in the workhouse that she did, but I'm sure no letters arrived.'

Dorothea glanced at her daughter. There was a pause, with only the ticking clock on the mantelpiece.

Finally, she said, 'I remember your father from the wedding. It was only a brief time, but he did appear a little . . .' She paused, searching for a word. 'Rigid.'

Hester tried to hide her anguish. Rigid was an understatement. She wondered how many times Mercy had paused, on the cusp of writing to the family, but had her hand stayed by the thought of their father's outrage and displeasure.

'It's a fair assessment of Amos.'

'Ruth says he's much diminished after his stroke.'

Hester swallowed. 'He is.'

'And did you find out what your mother wanted to know? Have you discovered how Mercy died?'

'Of cholera.'

'Cholera? I never heard of an outbreak there. I'm surprised it took away such a healthy girl. It usually preys on the sick and elderly.'

'She was weakened,' said Hester, lifting her head. She could feel the heat from her burning cheeks and couldn't stop her eyes from filling with tears. 'Mercy was with child when she died.'

'Oh, my dear.' Dorothea rose and came to join her on the sofa, putting Hester's arm around her shoulders. 'What a day you've had of it. And what became of the little soul?'

'Buried in the parish churchyard,' Hester said, the tears finally falling. 'But no grave to mark either of them. What on earth am I going to tell my father?'

'Never mind him.'

Hester raised her head at Caroline's brisk tone. Her mother gave her a look and turned back to Hester.

'You tell Amos that there's no Quaker plot in Southwell. If he doesn't like it, he can start searching his conscience for his role in this tragedy.'

'You don't know what he's like when he's angry,' whispered Hester.

'No, I don't, but I can imagine. Listen, my dear. If you look beyond our clothes and way of living, we are of the faith, too. We've all had to make sacrifices over the years as dissenters. Mercy and her baby are buried in a simple grave and put to rest. It's as much as we'd have done. Of course, Amos would want to know where she was buried, but it's known to God and that's enough.'

I wish this woman was my mother, thought Hester with a stab

of disloyalty. Ruth, for all her competence and kindness, bowed in every way to Amos's will. Hester had never got to know her mother as an individual even on their visits to the needy. Her mother's talk was of family matters and practical affairs. Hester couldn't begin to think what Ruth must have been like as a school friend of Dorothea, who, she guessed, would never allow herself to be dictated to by a man such as Amos.

'It's a quiet place where Mercy is laid to rest, I suppose.'

'You went to visit?' asked Caroline. 'I hope you managed to avoid the parson. He's as mad as a fruit bat.'

Hester shook her head. What act of loyalty was it that stopped her from sharing what had greeted her inside the church?

'What was the workhouse like inside?' asked Dorothea. 'It has a reputation for being well run although very strict.'

'It was clean and neat but devoid of any form of comfort for the people who pass through there.'

'I heard it was bleak. Shallow tin baths and boiled onion for dinner. Yet, Mr Kirkham lives like a king.'

Hester, suddenly weary, suppressed a yawn. 'He didn't seem the extravagant type.'

'Appearances are deceptive. What a time you've had of it, Hester. Come, let me take you up to your room. Have a rest, and we shall spend the evening coming up with a plan to let your father know what happened to Mercy. Don't worry too much about your mother. Ruth was always eminently sensible.'

Hester was both touched and relieved by the solicitude of these two worldly women. It had been a day of sorrow and discovery – only now could she allow herself to reflect on the strange message Elisabet had whispered to her in the dormitory: Don't let the angelmaker take my baby.

# Chapter Eleven

Hester was woken by a rap on the door. A maid, bringing in her tea, was followed by Dorothea Francombe, all bustle and solicitude. It reminded Hester of how different things were in this family. She was used to Susanna, their only maid, doing the hard labour helped by various members of the Goodwin family, including herself. It was the Quaker model – everyone responsible for clearing and tidying their own mess, which blurred the distinction between master and servant. Dorothea was a robust woman and could easily have carried the tray in herself, but that was maid's work and this, Hester guessed, was a house with defined roles.

'Now, we have a guest for dinner tonight,' said Dorothea as she was leaving the room. 'A Mr Edward Holland, who I'm sure you'll find to be great company. He's an eminent doctor in the town and a special confidant of Caroline's.'

Hester wondered if she was being given a warning. It was the sort of thing her own mother had done when Mercy had been courted by Mr Cook, the man selected by Amos as a respectable suitor. Once an agreement had been reached, Ruth had made sure all of her acquaintances knew that both Mercy and Mr Cook were off the market. Little good that had done. Well, she'd soon see if there was an attachment between the doctor and Caroline. It would make for a good story to tell Susanna, if nothing else.

Hester dressed in her spare gown. It was as drab as her travelling dress but lighter and more suitable for an evening engagement.

Before she went down, Dorothea came back into the bedroom.

'I have something for you. I don't want you to refuse it. It's a gift in regard of my dear friendship with your mother.'

She held out a cream evening shawl made of lace so intricately worked Hester could only gaze at it in wonder.

'For me?' she asked.

'And to keep. You've had a terrible day, and a thing of beauty always helps to raise the spirits.'

Hester draped the shawl over her shoulders. It hung on her as if she were sheathed in a chrysalis.

'It's the most beautiful thing I've ever worn.'

Satisfied, Dorothea nodded and they descended the stairs together. As they entered the drawing room, Caroline was at the piano alongside a man who was turning the pages for her. He saw Hester and smiled.

'Your guest is here,' said Edward.

Caroline stopped playing and looked up at her companion rather than at Hester. Edward Holland was a lean man with light brown hair cropped short in the style of Prince Albert. His features were serious. Hester had expected a foppish young man – perhaps it was that type she thought would attract Caroline – but his expression was one of calm intelligence. He must be much beloved by his patients, she thought. It was the face you'd want to see in sickness.

Hester took his outstretched hand and saw that he was older than he appeared at first glance. Perhaps nearing thirty-five. His gaze was thoughtful as he looked her over and she was glad of the shawl hiding her dowdy dress.

'Can you play, Miss Goodwin?' asked Edward.

Hester shook her head. 'Not at all.'

She didn't add that music, art, reading and dancing were all on Amos's list of forbidden activities.

Dorothea glanced across at her with a sympathetic expression. 'Never mind, Hester. There's more to life than being able to pick out a tune on the piano.'

'What *are* your accomplishments, Miss Goodwin?' asked Edward.

Despite his light tone, Hester thought she heard a flicker of interest in his words as he turned to the music.

Hester hunted for something to say.

'I like to read,' she said.

'Oh.'

Caroline made it sound as if it were the dullest thing ever.

'And what are you reading at the moment?' asked Edward.

'Mr Scott's *Ivanhoe*. The witchcraft passages are fascinating.'

They looked at her in astonishment and Hester could feel herself growing hot at their scrutiny. Goodness knows what had induced her to come out with such a statement. She could only think that she was tired by the day.

Caroline broke the silence by laughing. 'Hester, that's very funny.'

Glad to be of service, Hester thought crossly, but she was aware again of Edward's scrutiny.

There were just the four of them at dinner that evening. Edward focused his attention between the three women, asking Hester questions about life in Bristol. She answered readily enough but was conscious that talk of hospital visits bored Caroline.

'You're not a Friend?' she asked him.

'Goodness, no, although my mother was. She became an Anglican when she married my father, but it's through her that I know the Francombes.'

He paused and his expression closed as if an unhappy memory had surfaced. Dorothea laid a comforting hand on his arm.

'Do you associate with those outside the religion, Hester?' asked

Caroline, taking a grape from a plate. 'I can't imagine socialising only with Friends. How deadly dull that would be.'

How rude she was, Hester thought. Caroline had clearly been indulged, but that was no excuse for her forthright questions. It was almost as if she wished to antagonise Hester, or perhaps she wanted to appear clever in front of Edward. Well, she wouldn't allow herself to be cowed.

She shook her head. 'Unfortunately not. I shall have to pretend to Amos that there were just us three women tonight.'

Her reply delighted Caroline, who clapped her hands.

'Your father does sound stern. Don't worry. We shan't tell.'

With a pang of guilt, Hester thought of Amos lying stricken in a darkened room in Bristol. Edward poured himself a glass of wine.

'You arrived at The Black Griffin, I believe? What did you think of the landlord, Matthew Alban?'

So that was the man's name, thought Hester. Matthew Alban.

'I got a decent enough welcome, although he did call me Quaker Jane.'

Caroline snorted while Edward frowned into his glass, regarding the amber liquid.

'He needs to keep a civil tongue in his head if he's to continue trading. This town isn't short of coaching inns. I hope he didn't give you any bother.'

Hester caught a hint of anger. It sounded as if Matthew Alban had already made an enemy of Edward.

'He gave me accurate directions to the workhouse. He was polite enough.'

'You should never have gone to the workhouse alone. The landlord should have sent word to the Francombes that you were here. Even if the original letter hadn't arrived, your mother and Dorothea are in touch regularly. She wouldn't have turned you away and could have accompanied you there. Southwell Union is no place for a young gentlewoman.'

'I'm used to visiting the poor. It was no worse than the houses I visit.' Hester saw that she'd embarrassed the three of them.

This wasn't strictly true. The workhouse had been true to type, but the sense of something skewed once she'd made it to the undeserving women's dormitory had thrown her. The sensation couldn't be accounted for simply by the unfriendliness of the Kirkhams.

'Do you visit the patients there?' she asked the doctor.

He looked surprised. 'Who, me?' Hester saw Caroline smile down at her plate. 'They call their own man in from town. Not that I think much of him. He's a reputation for liking the drink. And stronger, I've heard.'

'So it'll be he who attended to Mercy when she contracted cholera? I've been informed this is what killed her.'

'Almost certainly – if they called a doctor. But the disease can strike quickly. There might not have been time.' He made a face.

This was a physician who would be wonderful assisting in childbirth or prescribing you with potions for a fever. But cholera suggested pestilence and poverty, and Hester couldn't imagine Edward inside the workhouse. Although soberly and respectably attired, he projected affluence and propriety.

'What's it like there?' he enquired.

He asked the question idly. Perhaps he was making conversation, but she wanted to give an accurate answer for Mercy's sake. She deserved more than to have the place where she spent her final hours dismissed over a fruit bowl.

'It has an odd atmosphere.' She frowned, trying to replicate the sensation she'd felt earlier, but just caught the tail of its shadow.

'So I've heard. It's likely a miserable job physicking to those people.'

'Why?' Hester asked. 'Are they not as in need of a decent medical service as any other?'

'Of course.'

Hester saw she'd made him angry.

'How little you think of me. I was going to say that it allows you no opportunity to develop a relationship with the patients.'

'I'm sorry.' Contrite, Hester picked up the wine that had made her heady. 'Does the term angelmaker mean anything to you?' she asked, remembering the words of Elisabet.

'Angelmaker?' Caroline was the first to react, although Hester saw she'd hardly caught her attention. 'It sounds a little churchy. They didn't try to convert you while you were there, did they?'

'No. One of the girls who was with child mentioned an angelmaker who appears in the dormitory. I wondered if you knew what she meant. She was worried that the woman would take away her baby, but she didn't give me any more details.'

'What nonsense,' said Edward. 'I know for a fact that babies are born and remain at the workhouse until the family are in a position to leave. Of course, because of the separation of families, none are actually conceived there.'

Hester felt her face going hot at the frank talk.

'The girl who spoke of it was overwrought. She suggested it might be a ghost.'

Dorothea reached across to refill Hester's wine glass.

'There are often spectral stories attached to places where groups congregate. I heard something similar at one of the almshouses in the parish. Tales of a shadowy woman who appeared to the poor when they were about to die. I wouldn't be surprised if the story has been taken to the workhouse. These tales travel, unfortunately.'

'A woman who appears to the poor?' asked Edward. 'What did she look like?'

'A grey lady, I was told.' Dorothea made a face.

'The girl I met mentioned a pale lady. Perhaps it's the same spectre,' said Hester.

'Well, there you are, then. I told you tales travel.'

'A grey lady?' Caroline cast a glance at Hester's dress. 'Perhaps she was a Friend.'

Dorothea smiled at the comment, which made Hester smart.

'Pay no attention to the story,' said Caroline. 'These ghosts are always women. I remember something similar from my childhood. An old crone who would offer to guide you through the streets with a lamp but was leading you away from your parents into the otherworld.'

Hester shook off the images of the graveyard where the marble statue had chilled her.

'So, let's talk about something else,' said Edward. 'Tell me, Hester, what do you think of our prime minister? Is your father a Whig?'

Dorothea smiled at him. 'Shall we move into the drawing room to continue this discussion? And, Hester, please don't worry about the tales from the workhouse. There's really nothing to concern yourself with.'

Hester looked at the kind but uninterested faces illuminated by the firelight and nodded at them.

'Of course, nothing to worry about at all.'

## Chapter Twelve

The day dawned bright as Matthew entered the courtyard to await the arrival of the London coach. His elderly dog had identified the sound of the hooves over the street chatter and, at the sound of the hound's bark, he swung open the large gate. He'd hoped for a quiet morning after his disturbed sleep the previous night, but the sight of the gaggle of three women waiting on the pavement assured him this wouldn't be the case.

The youngest of the three he recognised as the girl from the previous day. The red bloom of her cheeks had paled, but her eyes were as alert as ever when she lifted them up to acknowledge his presence.

The other two – the Francombes, the girl had said – were smartly dressed with an air of affluence. They were a different type of Quaker to the girl, he could see. The older girl looked a pert miss, the ribbons from her bonnet hanging down in pretty curls, which she tossed over her shoulders. She ignored him but was aware of his scrutiny.

Matthew would dearly have loved to know how the girl had got on at the workhouse. He had no insider to update him and he'd been minded to ask her when she arrived for the return coach. He'd have made his voice deliberately casual, of course, but he'd have listened carefully to the information. Flanked by her two companions, however, he wouldn't be able to approach her. He wondered again at her pale cheeks. Had the visit to the workhouse revealed something distasteful?

As the horses rattled into the courtyard, the three women took a step back to avoid the shower of dust. Matthew moved forwards with the steps but needn't have bothered. The carriage was empty. The morning after market day was always the quietest and besides, not everyone liked to travel on a Sunday. Was it the Sabbath for Quakers, too? He wasn't sure but, whatever, the girl had no qualms about travelling on that day.

He took her bag and swung it up onto the roof of the coach, leaving the driver to fasten the straps. As she climbed aboard, he caught her eye.

'Did you find what you were looking for?' he asked in a low voice.

She glanced at him, her gaze assessing. 'Yes and no.'

'But you're on your way now. You won't be returning?'

She turned to check on her two friends, who were admiring one of the horses.

'What is it about this place?' she asked. 'What haunts it?'

Matthew, assuming she was talking about the inn, stepped back as if slapped.

'This place not fit for your do-gooding, Quaker Jane?'

'I didn't mean . . . never mind.'

She turned her face away from him and her gaze remained straight ahead as the horses left the courtyard. The woman's two companions left soon after and Matthew turned into the room where the girl had wolfed down a hearty breakfast the previous day. The maid, Annie, and the dog fled at the look on his face, but Joan remained standing in the doorway.

'I wonder if she found what she was looking for,' she said.

'I bloody hope not. The workhouse is a place where you're better off not asking any questions,' Matthew replied, closing the door behind him with a bang.

## Chapter Thirteen

Hester had never been so happy to see the streets of Bristol. At The Bush Tavern, she jumped out of the coach into Susanna's arms, the pair of them swinging each other round in giddy delight.

'How did you know I'd arrive at this time?'

'I didn't, but there's only two London coaches, and I'd have returned this evening otherwise.'

'I am glad to see you. How's Amos?' Hester asked, conscious of the news she'd soon have to share.

It would be easier to deliver it to Ruth rather than her father, but Susanna's answer was a relief of sorts.

'He's still bad. He can barely speak, and what comes out is gibberish. Do you have news?'

'Yes – none of it good.' Hester looked into the shrewd eyes of Susanna. 'It's only fair that I tell Ruth first.'

'Then talk to me afterwards.'

She directed the trunk to be delivered by cart to the Goodwin house and linked her arm through Hester's.

Ruth was making up a milk pudding for Amos when they arrived home. She looked older than when Hester had left her earlier in the week, her dress hanging like sackcloth on her thin frame. Susanna made herself scarce, disappearing into the scullery to scour the soaking pans.

'Hester.' Ruth embraced her, a rare show of affection.

Hester hugged her back tightly, surprising both of them. Ruth smelled of warm milk overlaid with iodine.

'I'm so pleased you're back. Tell me.'

Hester kept it brief, leaving nothing out except for the sightings. Her mother regarded her calmly when she'd finished.

'You did well. It was no easy task to hear of those things. We tell Amos nothing.'

'Nothing whatsoever?'

'Hester, he doesn't even realise that you've been away. If he recovers, I'll decide what to tell him then.'

When Ruth had swept back upstairs, Susanna emerged, looking up at the clock.

'I can't spare time to have tea with you, but you can talk to me while I make pastry.'

'How much did you overhear?'

Susanna gave her a look of reproach. 'Everything, of course.'

'And you're not shocked?'

'That's what happens, isn't it?' Susanna had her arms deep in flour as she rubbed in the butter. 'They have their wicked way with you and then leave you high and dry. Poor Mercy.' She paused, glancing up at Hester. 'She never mentioned anything to you?'

Hester shook her head. 'Nothing at all.' She couldn't stop the hurt from spilling out. 'And I thought we were close. We used to confide almost everything to each other. Yet, I suspected nothing.'

'Don't take it to heart. Everyone has their secrets. I should have warned her what might happen, though. Take it as a lesson from me. Don't give away what you can't afford to lose.'

Hester coloured at the thought of Edward's eyes on her.

'And how do you know?' she asked. 'What experience do you have of men?'

'None. Which is the way it's going to stay until I'm married. Despite the best efforts of any lad I've ever stepped out with. I keep a hatpin for the purpose. Any funny business and they get a spear in the thigh. Or elsewhere.'

Hester caught Susanna's eye and laughed.

'I've missed you, Susanna. What did you think of John Philips? Mercy's beau.'

'Mercy's cad, you mean.' Susanna considered the question. 'Devious. He looked at you out of the side of his eyes. Never trust a man who does that.'

'Did you know about him and Mercy? Be honest, Susanna. I'm not a child now.'

Susanna paused for a moment, wiping her forehead with a floured hand.

'Yes,' she said finally. 'I caught them talking in the kitchen and Mercy asked me not to tell so I didn't.'

'Just talking?'

'That's all. But that was enough with Amos in his prime, wasn't it? I never imagined the fools would elope.' She sounded furious. 'As I said, he was a cad.'

Hester sighed. 'Mercy was no one's fool. I wonder how you tell? At the beginning, I mean, when there's just the sweet words.'

Susanna pushed Hester out of the way.

'You can't tell. That's the problem.'

As she undressed that night, Hester felt the knot inside her stomach begin to tighten once more. She'd done what she'd set out for and yet she felt no peace. She was glad of her comfortable bed – less luxurious than the one in the Francombes' guest chamber, but one where she knew all the hollowed-out ridges and warped springs. Her door opened and Susanna stood on the threshold holding a candle.

'Is all shut up for the night?' asked Hester.

'As secure as the prison. Ruth has gone to her room, but she won't be there long. Amos is unsettled. Did you see him?'

'Briefly.'

Hester had found she could barely look at her father. Even in mortal illness, he gave off a frightful power.

'Do you want me to sleep with you tonight? It's a night for terrors.'

Hester nodded and moved to make room for Susanna. How she'd missed these confidences. She'd always trusted Susanna. With just a couple of years between them, Hester and Susanna had always had a bond that felt more like sisters than maid and mistress.

'How did you know?'

Susanna placed the candle on the little table. 'I could see it in your eyes. I knew you wouldn't say anything about it while Ruth was up and about. Are you having your nightmares again?'

'Yes, but dreams I can cope with. My shadowings have started again in earnest and that frightens me more.'

'Tell me what you've seen.'

Hester, glad of Susanna's warmth next to her, lay back on her pillow.

'You remember Mercy appeared to me the morning we learned of her death? I thought that would be it. On the journey north, I felt nothing, although I had the nightmare of the fire. Once I arrived at the workhouse, though, she came once more. I could feel her standing next to me as if alive.'

'That's all? You have nothing to fear from Mercy.'

'There was someone else. Not Mercy. Another spirit. A little desperate, I think.'

'Evil?'

'No, not evil. Not benign, either.'

'And you saw it?'

'No. I saw Mercy but not the other. And there's another thing. As I was leaving, a woman mentioned an angelmaker. Such a strange turn of phrase. She was scared that this angelmaker – a pale lady, she said – would come and take her unborn baby.'

'Angelmaker?' Susanna made a face. 'Does it mean anything to you?'

'No, nothing at all. I asked the girl, Elisabet, if she were a spectre and she said she was sure of it.'

'And you saw nothing?' asked Susanna.

'No. Afterwards, I went to the churchyard to look for Mercy's grave. It's a strange, disquieting place. The parson was quite mad.'

Susanna snorted.

'On my return to the town, I saw a woman carrying a child looking for her baby.'

'A real one or a shadowing?'

'I fear the latter.'

'Why?' Susanna turned over onto her stomach.

'When I spoke to her, she asked me if I'd seen her child, even though she was carrying the baby. The shadowings, if they speak, often make no sense. Also, when I looked back, the woman had gone.'

'Down an unseen passage, perhaps.'

'I don't think so, Susanna.'

'Thank God Amos isn't up to much,' said Susanna, blowing out the candle. 'You'd be black and blue if you told him you were seeing your spectres again.'

# Chapter Fourteen

As life began to settle into a routine of sorts, Hester became aware of a presence behind her in the street as she made her way to Bristol Infirmary to resume her visits to the sick. It was an unpleasant task. The building with its harsh, institutionalised rooms brought back too many memories of Southwell Workhouse. The hospital, however, gave her respite from her pursuer, who never entered the building.

It stayed in the street – a figure she felt following her from ten yards behind. Hester never looked round, not once, but used the glass of the shopfront windows to remind herself that her shadow wasn't real. No one else was aware of anything untoward, but she noticed dogs barked as she passed and horses shied in the street to the fury of their masters.

Amos had begun to deteriorate, sinking into that twilight place between the living and the dead. Ruth sat with her husband every hour of the day, feeding him morsels of bread and spooning him soup, leaving Susanna to run the rest of the household. Hester was astonished at Ruth's calm acceptance of what had happened to her daughter. It was another example of how little she knew of her mother's true feelings.

Ruth knew how Mercy had died and where she was buried, and that was enough. A simple communal grave didn't worry her, and she accepted that Mercy had been abandoned by Mr Philips with a calm resignation. Hester, however, wasn't at peace. The brooding atmosphere of the workhouse played on her mind. It was a place of secrets, and how Mercy had ended up there was the biggest mystery of all.

'Are you sure she didn't write to us?' she'd demanded of her mother one afternoon, cornering her as she'd emerged from Amos's chamber.

'Hester, I ask you to let it be. I never saw any letter from Mercy. I'd have known her hand immediately. She didn't get in touch with us.'

Hester saw that her question had agitated Ruth.

'What would you have done if she had written?'

Her mother hesitated. 'You're nearly twenty-three, Hester, so there's no reason why you shouldn't hear of these things. There are places, lying-in hospitals, where women can go when they're in the position that Mercy found herself in. We could have paid for her to be placed in one of these.'

'You think Amos would have allowed this?'

'I know he's a strict man, Hester, but family is family. I'm sure he'd have helped out.'

'And what would have happened to the child?'

Ruth sighed. 'There are foundling hospitals. That would have been a last resort. We might have been able to place the child with parents unable to have their own. Not everyone is so blessed.'

'But—'

'Please, Hester, I don't want to discuss this any more. Mercy didn't write, and therefore we're talking about conjecture. Let the past be.'

It was the only conversation she was to have with her mother about Mercy while her father was alive. Amos's condition worsened and Ruth's pinched face was a reminder to Hester not to bother her with other painful issues. The nightmares stayed away and Mercy appeared only once, dressed in the uniform of the workhouse. She held her hand out to Hester, who reached to take it but couldn't quite touch the fingers grasping for her touch.

Gradually, Hester began to notice a shift in the house. Amos stopped eating and the physician pronounced that, unless he began to take food, it would only be a matter of days. Susanna took the news badly, to Hester's surprise. She was aware that Susanna and Amos had held each other in high esteem, but perhaps her affection ran deeper than Hester had realised. Susanna moped around the kitchen, withdrawing into the scullery when Hester wanted to talk.

Finally, a week to the day after Hester's return to Bristol, the morning dragging as she waited to set out for a service at the meeting house, she went looking for Susanna. The maid was perched on a window-seat, darning a scorched tablecloth. She moved to make room for Hester – a clear signal that she'd be happy to talk. Hester rifled though the pile of sewing Susanna had laid at her feet, picking up a pair of her own stockings to mend. Her father would have approved. They sewed in silence for a few minutes.

'What's on your mind, Susanna? You've been preoccupied the last few days,' asked Hester.

Susanna kept her head bent over her work, her hands busy with the needle.

'I've been thinking about your visit to Nottinghamshire and your tales of spectres. We seem to be surrounded by death at present.'

'Because of Amos, you mean?' asked Hester.

'Amos, Mercy, her baby. It's as if the shadows are waiting to reclaim us.'

'Susanna!' Hester placed her stocking in her lap. 'It's not like you to be so morbid.'

'It's your fault, Hester. I can almost see that workhouse dormitory based on your description.'

'Then I'm sorry I painted such a vivid picture. Why does it upset you so?'

Susanna bent her head over her work once more.

'Who is to say the workhouse doesn't become my own home in the future? One accident, and I'm at the mercy of strangers' charity.'

'But you don't need to worry about anything. You've a place with us as long as you want.'

'But will you be able to afford to keep me when Amos dies?'

'I assume . . .' Hester stopped, aware that she knew little of the family finances. 'I can talk to Ruth. I'll do everything to keep you, and we'll find you alternative employment if we find ourselves compromised. You won't end up in the workhouse, I promise.'

Satisfied, Susanna held up the linen cloth, which she'd made a passable attempt at mending.

'I'll never find work as a seamstress,' she said mournfully. 'Shall we set out for the service?'

Hester slid onto the bench of the meeting house feeling some of the eyes of other families on her. Ruth was missing a Sunday meeting, which was almost unheard of, but an agitated Amos had knocked over a glass of hot milk that had been left cooling on the side that morning, scalding her arm. The meeting was an escape, although Susanna was dismayed when she saw how packed the room was.

'Gawd. I hope the spirit doesn't move too many people.'

Hester lifted her eyes and met the gaze of Mrs Cook, whose son had originally been promised to Mercy. The family friend was of a kindly nature, and whereas some might have gloated at Mercy's fate after her elopement, the woman's gaze remained sympathetic. Hester, embarrassed, slid her eyes away to rest on two women dressed in sober blue topped by the most exquisite lace. The women kept their eyes forwards, but Hester feasted on the dress and dearly wished she could wear something similar.

After the service, most of it blessedly in silence, she and Susanna escaped into the drizzly morning, where they watched the two smart girls lift their parasols and hurry down the street.

'I haven't seen them before,' said Hester. 'Do you know who they are?'

'They've been here for months. Goes to show how much attention you pay to other Friends. They're lacemakers from Nottingham.'

'Nottingham?' Hester gazed after them. 'That accounts for their beautiful clothes.'

'And you never even made it to the city,' said Susanna. 'Although you did come back with a beautiful shawl. What's the matter?'

'Do you think there are many people from Nottinghamshire in Bristol?'

'How should I know?' Susanna sighed. 'All right, probably. People gravitate from all over for the trade. What do you want to know for?'

'I'm wondering if any might know of Southwell Union.'

'Well, no point asking those two. They're respectable. They've opened a shop in the city and it's doing well. You'd be wasting your time.'

'But we could ask if they know of someone. When I took the carriage to Southwell, the woman travelling with me said it was famous in the county. What do you think?'

'I think you need to put that whole business behind you. Is Mercy appearing again? Tell her she needs to rest in peace and stop mithering you.'

'It's not Mercy. She just seems to have gone . . .' A look at Susanna's face and Hester decided not to mention her pursuer.

The two girls were at the Wednesday meeting, this time sitting on the raised platform. One of them spoke during the service, her Nottinghamshire accent barely noticeable. As the meeting came to an end, Hester gave Susanna a push.

'Get moving. I need to catch the girls before they leave.'

The day was dry but windy and the girls emerged from the building holding onto their bonnets.

'May I speak to you for a moment?' asked Hester.

The two stopped, neither showing much curiosity.

'I hear you're from Nottingham. I was in the county recently. In Southwell, if you know it?'

'I know of it,' said one of the girls, a tall fair woman.

'You're far from home,' said Susanna. 'I hear you've opened a shop in the city.'

'Best lace you'll find in the South West,' said the other girl.

'Do you know of many women from Nottingham in Bristol? There's a community, perhaps.'

'We hear of people in passing,' said the light-haired girl. 'Are you looking for someone?'

'No one specific. We're looking for someone who might know of the Union workhouse in Southwell,' said Hester.

The two girls exchanged glances. They know our story, thought Hester.

'We've heard of it,' proffered the dark-haired girl, 'but that's it. You want us to find someone who has visited, perhaps?'

'I'd dearly love to speak to someone. I stayed with a family in Southwell but they knew very little.'

'Leave it with us,' the girls said in unison and laughed.

Hester and Susanna stared after them, watching the girls' erect backs as they walked down the street.

'They knew about Mercy,' said Susanna.

'I know. Bad news travels fast. But they were glad enough to help.'

'Glad they'll never have to make use of the workhouse, more like.'

Susanna pulled her shawl over her head. From across the city, they heard a bell toll. She caught sight of Hester's face.

'What is it?' she asked Hester.

'Not long for Amos. I can feel the chill of the grave.'

Hester saw Susanna shudder.

'What's the matter?'

'I don't like it when you talk like this,' said Susanna. 'Especially within earshot of the meeting house. What would our Quaker friends say?'

'It's not my fault the shadowings appear to me.' Hester felt herself redden at the rebuke.

'Many would see your visions as the work of the Devil. Witchcraft even.'

'Then it's just as well they don't know.'

A heaviness washed over Hester. It had always been the same. Her sightings were something to be hidden, with the threat of a beating from Amos hanging over her if she even dared mention them. But she'd grown used to the company of her insubstantial companions, who were never frightening or malicious.

'Never mind.' Hester took Susanna's arm. 'Let's talk of something else.'

# Chapter Fifteen

Amos died at 4 a.m. the following morning – that strange hour when no one but the nightwatchman or those tending to the sick are awake. Ruth roused Hester from her slumber, shaking her shoulder.

'The end is near, my dear. Do you want to come?'

Hester wanted to say no, to stay in the warm fug of her bed. But ever the dutiful daughter, she slipped her feet into slippers and sat with her mother, listening to Amos's death rattle until they were both aware of a terrible silence. Ruth stood and lifted a sheet over her husband's face then left the room. Hester, refusing to be left alone with Amos, found her mother staring out of the drawing room window, her eyes on the empty street.

'Did he say anything before he died?'

Ruth didn't turn.

'Not a thing.'

'Not even about Mercy?'

'I think, Hester, that might have been too much to hope for.'

Over the following days, Ruth took over all arrangements for the funeral and would allow Hester no role, leaving her to absorb the reality of a world without her father. Ruth's distance was no surprise to Hester, although perhaps she'd hoped her mother might drop her guard during her mourning. Hester's brothers remained at their aunt's house, taking comfort from their noisy cousins, their absence giving Ruth the space to focus on the preparations.

'Will you manage?' Hester asked Susanna on the morning of the funeral.

A small tea was organised for after the burial and Susanna had been baking throughout the week to feed everyone. She saw that the maid had been crying, her eyes rimmed red and her face flushed. Susanna pushed past Hester.

'We'll be fine.'

'I hadn't realised Amos meant so much to you,' Hester called after the maid, feeling the need to comment on Susanna's distress.

She received no reply.

As Amos was lowered into the ground, she felt the reassuring presence of Mercy next to her. Not in physical form but recognisable by the rustling of her skirt and, in the damp October air, the smell of the lavender powder she'd used. Twice she turned to check if she could see Mercy and twice she caught the eye of Susanna, standing at the back of the small group of mourners, who frowned and shook her head. Not a day for a shadowing.

Back at the house, Ruth, despite her grief, had arranged matters for the wake in a manner that Amos would have heartily approved. Their mourning was subdued and restrained in the Quaker way. Hester and Susanna ran up and down the stairs with pots of tea and plates of seed cake, Abernethy biscuits and sponge fingers. As Hester served the guests, snippets of conversation came to her.

'You can't keep an eye on them all the time. She's not the first Friend to elope.'

'Boys are so much easier than girls . . .'

The conversation, as she'd feared, was about Mercy and not Amos, who had all but been forgotten at his own wake. Ruth, however, appeared not to notice and looked more animated than Hester had seen her in a long time. When the last guest had left, Hester found Susanna sitting alone at the kitchen table, enjoying a cup of tea. When she saw Hester, she poured another cup and kicked a chair.

'Take a seat and join me.'

Hester sat down, enjoying the dark drink Susanna brewed below stairs.

'That went well enough, didn't it?' asked Hester.

'Ruth is exhausted, though. Is—'

They both jumped at the sound of a knock.

'Who on earth can that be?' Susanna opened the kitchen door, letting in the cold afternoon air, and peered into the dark. 'Oh, it's you. Come in.'

Hester turned in her chair to see one of the Nottinghamshire lacemakers enter. It was the fair-haired one, her face just peeping out of the hood of a cloak.

'I can't stay long. We've just closed up the shop and we have work to do tonight. We have a commission to finish.'

'You have some news?' asked Hester.

Susanna scowled at her. 'Let the girl get settled at least.' She threw the old tea leaves into the sink and added a heap of new to the pot. 'Busy or not, you'll manage a cup on this cold night, Miss . . .'

'Call me Mary. Tea would be most welcome.' The girl pulled down her hood and took a seat. 'Autumn is coming in fast. I'll be brief, as I know you must both be tired. I heard that there was the funeral today. I did wonder whether to delay my visit until tomorrow, but we shall be even busier then.'

'I don't mind,' said Hester. 'I'm grateful you've made the trip. You've found someone who knows of the workhouse?'

'I have. It didn't take long at all. Lacemaking involves not only the weaving of the threads, but also bobbin and material suppliers, needlewomen to attach our work, washers skilled in keeping it clean. All play a role. Our last commission was for

Mrs Johnson. Do you know of the family?'

Hester shook her head. 'They mean nothing to me.'

'It's a decent enough household to work in, although the master made his name from slaving.'

Hester grimaced into her tea. There were plenty of such families in Bristol – even some respectable Quakers had their foundation in the abominable practice. The outlawing of the trade at the beginning of the decade had, Hester hoped, signalled a new dawn for Bristol, a city that had long been associated with slave ships. The problem was that while Quakers had been at the forefront of the abolition movement, some continued to share the spoils of the practice. The lacemaker's employer had grown rich on the back of the misery of millions of people.

'When we were starting our business in this city, we were advised to call on Mrs Johnson. She has a particular fancy for delicate lace. It's not uncommon. Some women, especially the gentry, fall in love with the work we do. Mrs Johnson is one such woman.'

'Then you should have a steady stream of work,' said Hester.

'I hope so. There's a girl in the Johnsons' employ. A laundry maid. The mistress recruits all of her washing staff from Nottinghamshire, as they know how to wash lace properly. I thought of them when you asked me if I could find someone who knew of the workhouse. And would you believe it, she especially likes the girls from Southwell Union, because they're the best washers of all. Properly trained by the matron, apparently.'

Hester thought of Mrs Kirkham and the sharp orders she'd given the girls. They would be well trained all right.

'And is there such a girl in her employ now?'

'They don't stay long. The wages are poor, I understand. But one of the washers has spent time in the workhouse. Her name is Kitty. She's a diffident young thing but, as Mrs Johnson rightly assumed, excellent at washing lace.'

'When did she arrive at the Johnsons'?'

'About two months ago. Straight from the Union.'

'Two months?' Hester stared at Mary. 'Then she might remember Mercy. Can we ask?'

'I could arrange for the two of you to meet. The girl has a strange reputation, though. One of the other laundry maids told me that the girl likes to tell stories to the maids at night.' Mary lowered her voice. 'There's four of them in a room together. Typical. The grander the place, the more cramped the servants' quarters.'

'What kind of stories?' Hester asked.

'I'm not so sure. The workhouse seems to have cast a long spell over the girl. She cries at night at the thought of being sent back there.'

'I can imagine.' Hester went cold as she often did when a shadowing was about to appear. Not now, she silently pleaded. 'Do you think she'd meet me? If she's a servant, her time off will be limited.'

'The junior maids are given leave to go to church on a Sunday,' said Mary.

'Then we'll tempt her with a hot meal,' said Susanna. 'I know just the place.'

'You think she'll do it?' asked Hester.

'She's gone hungry. In my experience, those who have wanted for sustenance always take you up on the offer of a feed.'

'Susanna. Where *did* you get such a cynical view of people from?'

Susanna snorted, surveying the remains of the baked meats from the funeral.

'Your father.'

# Chapter Sixteen

Susanna was wrong about one thing. The girl didn't just want a meal, she wanted money. Hard currency was difficult for Hester to obtain. Finances were tight. Even the simple funeral needed paying for and she'd returned all the unspent money her mother had given her for the journey to Southwell. In the end, she took one of her plain shawls – not the thing of beauty that Dorothea Francombe had given her – to Thomas Drew Pawnbrokers. He frowned when he saw her dress but willingly exchanged the shawl for four shillings. She burned the ticket when she got home, as she'd never have the funds to redeem the garment.

They arranged to meet in a coffee shop near the docks. While Hester had passed through the district on the way to visit pauper families, she'd never stopped to enter any of the food establishments. Susanna, aware of Hester's inexperience, steered her to a table and ordered them coffee while they waited.

Hester looked around her, captivated by the clientele. This was a different world to her ordinary one – a life where in your spare time you didn't visit the sick and do good works but you relaxed with strangers, refreshing yourself with the dark pungent brew that could make your hair stand on end. The place had a queer mix of patrons. In the corner were three sailors, their occupation given away by their tanned faces and naval rig uniforms. Near the window was a gentleman with a woman of more dubious respectability, and on the adjoining table two ladies, similar to

Susanna and herself, who were conversing, their heads bent together as they gossiped.

The place made Hester think of the last hostelry she'd been in, The Black Griffin in Southwell. She'd enjoyed the silence of that solitary breakfast. Here, the bustle set her teeth on edge, noise layered upon noise, although she could see Susanna was in her element. Hester waited for the door to open, anticipation making her edgy. When it did, a wan girl in her Sunday best appeared along with the lacemaker, who steered her towards their table.

'I can't stay – I've too much work to do. Now, this is Kitty. She's been promised a meal and some coins.'

Kitty, who had driven a hard bargain, looked modestly at the floor.

'I have the money.' Emboldened, Hester looked at the girl. 'I'll pass them to you after I've heard your story. I also have some questions for you. It doesn't matter if you can't answer them all. The money is yours.'

With a nod, Mary left them and the girl sat. They ordered three meals of mutton chops – honest cuts of meat – accompanied by more coffee. They ate in silence, none of them starving but with the appetites of healthy young women. As the plates were scraped clean, the girl became nervous, cupping the mug for warmth, darting looks to Hester as if unsure that what she was about to tell them was worth the money. It was Susanna who took charge.

'So, Kitty, you now need to sing for your supper – you know how it goes. Tell her your story and she'll give you the money. A fair exchange. And there's no need to hold anything back. Don't worry about the clothes she wears. She's been to Southwell. She knows what the place is like. You'll find no airs and graces from her. Her sister ended up there like you. She's not proud.'

Hester wasn't sure whether to be offended or flattered by the speech and decided on an encouraging smile. Kitty didn't look reassured but blew on her coffee, which must have been stone cold, a final time.

'I went there about a year ago with my family. There was no-where else left for us to try. When we first got there, it weren't too bad. The place isn't always full. Sometimes there are a lot of poor to look after and other times not so many. When we arrived – me and my mam and two brothers – the place were quiet.'

'You were split up?'

'Of course.' The girl looked surprised that Hester should be asking. 'The boys slept in the children's dormitory along with the other young ones. They were given lessons in the morning and then had work in the afternoon. But they were good lads. No holding of the rations from them for bad behaviour.'

'And your mother?'

The girl looked at the table. 'My mother was sick, so it was bad. We were split up almost immediately. Me in the room for the able-bodied undeserving women, on account of my ability to work, Ma with the old and infirm next door.'

'Is your father dead?' asked Hester.

'I wish. A wastrel,' said the girl with some satisfaction. 'Used to come round drunk, and that's how us three were born.'

Hester kept her face straight but saw Susanna glance at her. Hester was unshocked. On her visits to the poor, it had been clear many a child had been conceived after a night of drinking.

'So we never had any money. The vicar were a kind man. He wrote "poor" next to each of us when we were baptised, which my mother weren't happy with. She said it would be forever there for all to see, but that's what we were, poor. On the charity of the parish.

'Then the workhouse had more room and we were told that was it. We'd all four have to move there. There were this board of guardians. All four of us made to stand in front of this table while Ma explained our circumstances.'

Hester leaned forwards. 'Was Mr Kirkham there?'

'Mr and Mrs Kirkham were both present. We were accepted and that was that.'

'Tell me about Mr Kirkham.'

Kitty looked at her empty cup.

'I don't know what to say. I don't think he ever noticed my presence. I was in the laundry all day. They were training me for service work, so Mr Kirkham wasn't around much.'

'You know Little Pinch?'

The girl's eyes lit up. 'Little Pinch? Of course. Was she doing all right?'

Hester said slowly, 'I think she's well. I only spoke to her briefly. She seemed scared of Mr Kirkham.'

'Oh, we were all scared of him. He has a vicious temper and he likes to drink at night. It leaves him with a bad head in the morning.'

'And Mrs Kirkham?'

'Well, she was matron, in charge of the women. I don't know how she spread herself about, but she managed it well enough. It didn't matter if you were in the kitchen, laundry or the cowshed. She knew what you were up to and what you were supposed to be doing. Eyes in the back of her head, she had.'

'And were you scared of Mrs Kirkham?'

'I've felt the sting of her hand too. I dare say I deserved it.'

Hester contemplated the girl. Harsh but fair seemed to be as far as Kitty was prepared to go when it came to the master and matron. It couldn't account for her feeling of unease when she'd entered the undeserving women's dormitory.

'Kitty, tell me. Did you meet my sister, Mercy?'

'I knew Mercy a little. I didn't get to talk to her much, of course. We were in different dormitories on accounting of . . .' Kitty coughed. 'On accounting of her condition and suchlike. Then I left just after her baby was born.'

'But Mercy was with the undeserving poor, too.'

'Not on the top floor, she weren't. That's where most of us slept. The first floor was for special cases.'

'What do you mean, special?' asked Susanna.

Kitty shrugged. 'You went there, didn't you?' she asked Hester.

'I was given a tour of the downstairs and first floor.'

'Well, there's the same type of dormitories at the top. The first floor was reserved for the sickest of the deserving poor and the undeserving girls who had got themselves in the family way and suchlike.'

'The expectant girls were bedded together?'

'Probably easiest for them. And your Mercy was there. Disowned by her family, she told me.'

Kitty frowned at Hester, but she saw there was no rancour in the girl's eyes. It was just the way of the world.

'She wasn't disowned, Kitty, I promise you. She was ashamed to ask for help.'

Kitty shook her head. 'Begging your pardon, miss, but that's not right. She wrote at least twice. The clerk had to arrange postage. Perhaps they thought it would ease the burden on the workhouse if she returned home.'

'I think you're mistaken, Kitty.'

'I'm not, miss. One day, I watched her go up to the mail rider and ask if he had a letter for her. Mrs Kirkham were ever so angry that a resident would speak directly to the driver. She was punished for that, I think.'

'How was she punished?' asked Hester, her mouth dry.

'How they disciplined everyone. Deprived them of food, of course.'

'You're sure she wrote to us in Bristol?' Hester looked at Susanna, who uncharacteristically refused to meet her gaze.

'Twice at least, I heard, and I'm sure she received a reply. When

I spoke to her, begging your pardon, she was despondent that she'd been disowned by your father.'

Hester looked across at Susanna, who shook her head. Not a gesture of denial but telling her not to interrupt. Hester felt a bubble of fury begin to form inside her chest.

'Tell me about the undeserving poor wing.'

Was it Hester's imagination or did the girl shrink?

'I was there because I had no choice. Deserving or not deserving doesn't come into it. If I left, the whole family would have to leave. That's the rules. So I stayed and was lumped in . . . excuse me, miss . . . with the idle and profligate when I were just trying to do right by my family.'

'You didn't like it there? The place looked clean enough if a little drab.'

'Oh, miss, it wasn't just that.' Kitty leaned forwards. 'That wasn't the half of it. Bare spaces I don't mind, but this was much, much more. It has unhappy spirits.'

Here it was again. A tale of a spectres. But was it the old wives' tale that Dorothea and Caroline Francombe had traded half-smiles about, or the presence she herself had felt in that chilled room?

'I'm sorry, I can imagine what the place must be like at night.'

Kitty nodded. 'It's fearful. No one wants to see the pale lady. If you're with child, she'll take your baby, too.'

'The pale lady?' Elisabet had used the same description. Here was her chance for more detail. 'Tell me about her. Why do you say she takes the children?'

But Kitty's mind was elsewhere.

'Begging your pardon, miss, but what became of your sister's bairn?'

Hester felt the food she'd just eaten settle as a lump in her stomach.

'The baby died along with Mercy.'

'I'm sorry, miss, but she didn't.'

The girl's diffidence had gone. She grasped Hester's hand, her fingers as cold as ice.

'What do you mean?'

'The baby was born alive. A little girl it was, and Mercy was as proud as punch. But then she died of the childbed fever and there was nothing they could do.'

'I was told she died of cholera. Her and her unborn child.'

'Cholera?' The girl stared at her in surprise. 'There was no cholera in the workhouse. Never has been. They say it's because of the fresh water supply.'

'I thought cholera travelled by air. The miasma is responsible for it,' said Susanna, confused.

Hester turned to the maid. 'Thinking is changing. There's evidence that the sickness is carried by water. In any case, I was told Mercy arrived with cholera from her common lodgings.'

'Oh, no. That's not the case. She was perfectly well when she arrived.'

Hester could see Kitty was adamant on this point.

'Why tell me she died of cholera, then?' Hester asked Susanna, who shrugged.

'Mercy died of childbed fever,' said Kitty. 'Caught an infection. But the baby was alive and well when I left.'

'Then what happened to the child?'

The girl's eyes were as round as saucers. 'I don't know. Perhaps it were the pale lady who got her.'

The pale lady. Hester held onto the girl's fingers, squeezing them tighter.

'You'll have your money soon, Kitty, I promise. But tell me about the spectre.'

Kitty dropped her voice to a whisper. 'I don't know much. They say she's a mother who lost her own child and goes through the corridors lamenting the loss of her baby. Then, when she finds a newborn, she takes it as her own.'

Hester frowned, remembering the girl she'd met on the street corner in Southwell.

'I saw a woman dressed in grey rags while I was there. Perhaps I, too, have seen the pale lady.'

'Be careful, Hester.'

Susanna was warning her that she shouldn't speak of her shadowings, but Hester saw that Kitty, wide-eyed, was nodding.

'It's a place of spirits, I'm sure.'

'But this girl was despairing. There's nothing to be afraid of, Kitty.'

'That's not what I heard. She stalks the corridors with her candle, waiting to snatch away your soul. If you're unlucky, she takes your baby, too. She likes women with child, they say, and if you're really, really bad, she leaves you to the living and just takes your child.' Kitty raised her voice, causing the sailors to look across at them.

Hester took a deep breath. 'I spoke to a girl there named Elisabet. Do you know her?'

Kitty nodded.

'She called the pale lady the angelmaker. She asked me to make sure that the angelmaker stayed away from her and her baby.'

Kitty frowned and shook her head. 'I never heard her called that, only the pale lady.'

'And did you meet women whose babies had been taken? Are the stories based on fact?'

'There was one baby who was born while I was there. It ended up in the nursery along with the older children.'

'And that's all?'

Kitty shrugged and Hester got the impression she'd offended the girl. It was a nonsense story full of fancy and easily disproved by the rational Hester, yet what had happened to Mercy's baby? As she remembered that icy dormitory and the tired souls she'd seen, with Mercy standing alongside her and the desperate spirit who had whispered in her ear, Hester felt the slow creep of dread up her spine.

# Chapter Seventeen

Hester and Susanna made their way back to the Goodwin house in silence, each absorbed in their own thoughts. Mercy's child might live and, to Hester, the idea was both intoxicating and appalling. Mrs Kirkham had clearly told her the baby was dead and buried alongside its mother. This was the reason the sightings had begun again since her visit to the workhouse, she was sure: Mercy was desperate to communicate to Hester that her child hadn't simply died with her.

The baby's welfare had also been uppermost in Mercy's mind while she was alive. Mercy knew Amos's temperament but had nevertheless sent a letter, Hester suspected, to plead for the future of her child. She'd written to Amos asking for charity and forgiveness. Kitty's words had rung true and had echoed those of Elisabet and Ellen in the workhouse.

As they neared the house, Hester turned to her maid.

'Was it you who intercepted the letters?'

Susanna stopped. 'I swear to you, Hester, that I'm not involved in any conspiracy. If Amos had told me to intercept letters from Mercy and carry them direct to him, then I'd have done it, but with a heavy heart. I promise you, I'd confess it now if that were the case.'

'But he didn't?'

'I swear to you, Hester, he did not. But—'

'But what?'

'It's got me thinking.'

'You noticed something?'

Susanna hesitated, aware that she was going to incriminate another.

'Sometimes the tin plate was empty when I'd go to collect the letters. The mail rider had already been and the post taken direct to Amos. I could tell by the fresh pile of correspondence on his desk.'

Hester frowned. 'Nothing strange in that. Ruth may have simply got there first.'

'Of course, but your mother liked to leave it for me,' said Susanna. 'You know how demanding Amos is. She used to creep out of the house for her visits to other Friends after Amos's stroke. If the post had arrived, it simply stayed on the tray until I attended to it.'

'When did you notice the change in routine? The fact that post was bypassing you. Recently?'

Susanna nodded.

'And yet Amos called for me to bring up the post the day we learned of Mercy's death,' said Hester. 'He didn't act like a person with something to hide.'

She caught sight of Susanna's expression.

'Is there something else?'

'I took a package to the post office about six weeks ago. It had a Nottingham address.'

'The workhouse?' asked Hester.

'I honestly don't remember. Your father often wrote to institutions. I noticed Nottingham, but not if it was the workhouse.'

'You say package rather than letter.'

'A small parcel. About the size of my palm.' Susanna held out her hand.

'What could he have sent Mercy?'

'I don't know,' said Susanna. 'Whatever it was, the post began to be left for me again. Please don't say anything, Hester. My position is precarious as it is.'

'I shan't incriminate you, but I will have it out with Ruth anyway.'

Hester found her mother in the dining room, scrutinising the books. At the sight of Ruth's dejection, some of the fire in Hester abated. Ruth, however, immediately saw something was wrong.

'Hester, what's the matter? Is everything all right?'

'Why did you lie to me about Mercy writing to Amos?'

Ruth pulled her shawl tighter around her body and Hester saw the marks of exhaustion under her eyes.

'I don't know what you mean.' Ruth turned from Hester, her tone defensive.

'The letter plate was often empty when Susanna went to check it. You saw a letter from Mercy and took it yourself to Amos. From then on you took charge of the post. I'm right, aren't I?'

'As I told you before, Mercy never wrote to us here.'

Hester very nearly changed the subject. Her mother, as far as she could tell, had never openly lied to her. Ruth lived a life of truthfulness but not openness. It was her mother's private nature that gave Hester the courage to dig deeper.

'I'm sorry, Ruth, but I don't believe you.'

'I said—'

'I know what you said, but I think you're lying to me.'

It was the accusation that shocked Ruth into a confession, Hester saw.

Ruth put her face in her hands. 'Of course, you're right. I'll never forgive myself.'

'Did you see its contents?'

'Amos wouldn't tell me what was in the note. He flatly refused to discuss it. I told myself Mercy had written to ask for forgiveness, that was all.'

'So why did you lie to me about it when I asked you before my visit to Nottinghamshire? Amos was too sick by then to have stopped you from telling me.'

Ruth took a deep breath and clutched at her throat.

'Mother, are you all right?' Hester poured a glass of water from the carafe and put it to Ruth's lips.

She choked and recovered. 'Forgive me, Hester. I was a little faint for a moment then.' She attempted a smile. 'You called me "mother".'

'I did?'

Ruth smiled. 'Perhaps, with your father gone, we might slip into more modern forms. As for Mercy, I assumed she was asking your father for his forgiveness. A form of reconciliation. And also, I supposed, for some money. I never once thought she was in such dire straits. It's all my fault. I can see the accusation in your eyes and you've every reason to be angry. Now your father's gone, I see that I should have stood my ground much, much more.'

'She received a reply, it seems.'

'He answered?' Ruth stared at Hester, aghast. 'How do you know?'

Hester thought of Susanna's plea.

'One of the women I met in the workhouse told me. We both know he wouldn't have written telling Mercy to return home. A package was sent. The girls at the workhouse knew it and didn't judge us. But I do. I'm ashamed not only of my family, but also of my dress and my very faith. Aren't we supposed to practise what we preach?'

'Of course we are. Hester, I shall never forgive myself. Some days I feel as if I have nothing left to live for.'

But there was, thought Hester. There was a living baby. Or at least a child who might have lived. Hester regarded her mother, wondering what to say next. Now would be the time to reveal about the baby. Hester's eyes dropped to the bill book.

'Are our finances bad?'

Ruth sighed. 'We're very constrained, Hester, I won't deny it. The boys can continue their education. The school has grants for widows and they've been promised an education until they're eighteen.'

'I could try to find some work.'

'I don't think it's come to that yet, but it might. Your father's illness has taken its toll on the family finances. I have until the autumn to make plans to see what's possible so that we can continue to thrive. I'm nearly at the end of my tether.'

Hester tucked away any thought of mentioning the child. Her mother's skin was almost translucent with worry and she wouldn't add to it, she decided. She turned to go.

'I'm not a child any longer. Don't keep things hidden from me, please. I can't help if I'm in the dark.'

'Hester.' Her mother pulled out a letter from underneath the cloth-bound book. 'There's something I want to discuss with you. I've received an invitation to go with your aunt Cecily to Bath. She's taking a house for the month of October. You know she hates high summer in the town, but Bath is so pretty in the autumn. She's invited us all to go with her.'

'What will you do with the house?'

'I'll shut it up. It'll be more economical. Susanna would come with us – we'll need a maid. What do you think?'

Hester thought of the two families cramped together in rooms in Bath and made a face.

'I suppose it would be fine.'

Hester's dream that night gave lie to her words. She'd feared falling asleep in case a nightmare returned after the revelations of the day but, instead, it was a childhood memory she dreamed of.

Mercy and herself as children walking to the Quaker school they attended. They'd stopped to let a fine coach speed past and had caught a glimpse of a society lady, her hair impossibly high and powdered a luminous white. They'd held hands in awe as they'd watched the departing coach, and Hester had said she'd love for them to be the women inside, replete with jewels and fine clothes.

'Not for us.' Mercy gripped Hester's hand tightly. 'We shall grow old as respectable Quaker women.'

In her dream, Mercy grew fainter and fainter until she resembled the shadowing Hester occasionally glimpsed. Waking with a start, Hester fumbled for the candle and made up her mind. She could not, would not join that fickle and vain society in Bath while the mystery of her niece remained unsolved. She'd find a way of returning to Southwell.

# Chapter Eighteen

The solution to Hester's dilemma came from an unexpected source. The family had begun to shut up the house in readiness for the temporary move to Bath. Susanna was in a filthy mood as she didn't want to leave the city and spent most of her days banging around the rooms to show her displeasure. Hester, dreading the trip to Bath, spent sleepless nights thinking of a way to return to Southwell. The nightmares stayed away, but Mercy and that other spirit remained alongside her. The message was clear. Our journeys aren't over and nor is yours.

Hester, awake in the dark nights, concocted devious plots in her mind. The most promising involved her writing to the master of Southwell Union and demanding, as sister of a deceased inmate, the right to visit infirm visitors to check on their welfare. But it was hopeless, she knew. They'd simply say no and she'd be no further forwards.

Ruth entered her chamber while she was dressing a few days before their departure to Bath.

'I've received a letter. You'll never guess from whom.'

Hester's heart lurched. 'Not more bad news.'

'On the contrary. It's from the Francombes. You appear to have made a favourable impression, and Dorothea has invited you back to stay.'

Hester bent her head over her buttons so that her mother wouldn't see her face.

'Could you spare me?'

'My dear, you know I'd hate you to go. I've been looking forward to having the family back together in Bath, but Dorothea is being quite insistent. She can be very persuasive when she tries. What do you think?'

'I was looking forward to Bath, too,' lied Hester.

'Then I shall write and decline.'

'No! Ruth, no.' Hester lowered her voice. 'It's just, I've been thinking about those poor women I met in the workhouse.'

'The residents?'

'If I accepted Mrs Francombe's invitation, I could visit the workhouse as well as spend time with the family.'

Ruth looked surprised. As well she might, thought Hester. She knew her daughter had never exactly embraced with fervour the acts of charity she'd undertaken in Bristol.

'I don't see why not. Didn't you say that Dorothea hadn't been welcome there? What makes you think you'll get a more favourable response?'

'I won't. If you think it a good idea, I wonder if you might write to them and ask. They did seem embarrassed about Mercy. Perhaps they'll relent if you put pressure on them to have me.'

Hester was aware of her mother's scrutiny.

'Is there something you want to tell me? You did inform me of everything from your visit?'

At least Hester could answer this honestly.

'I promise, Ruth, I gave you a full account of my visit to the workhouse.' She shook away thoughts of Kitty.

Ruth sighed. 'Come November, we'll have our hands full picking up the threads of our lives once more. We have to go on without your father and that's exactly what we'll do, although there will be some difficult decisions to be made about this house. Perhaps a spell away on your own would do you the world of good.

Bath would be so dull for you. Could you stand being so near the place where your sister died?'

'Mercy is gone. I wouldn't mind at all.'

The rustling came again and Hester felt her sister lean against her. She didn't dare turn.

'Is anything the matter, Hester?'

Hester kept her expression neutral. 'All is well. Did Mrs Francombe give a reason for inviting me?'

'It seems that Caroline, her daughter, has asked for you.'

'Are you sure?'

Hester couldn't hide her surprise. Caroline, although polite, had given the impression she found Hester a provincial bore. Perhaps she just needed someone to lord it over, thought Hester uncharitably.

'That's what she says here in this letter. Well, what do you think? It really is up to you, Hester.'

Hester thought of the shadow that had followed her the last few weeks. Not Mercy, still pressing against her hip, but that other figure she'd first encountered in the workhouse. Could she rely on shaking it off in Bath, or would that desperate spectre follow her until she freed it from its agony?

'Ruth, I'd like to go. I know money and space are tight in Bath. In any case, it will only be for a few weeks.'

'Are you sure? I'm so pleased that Dorothea liked you, too. What's she like now, Hester? I remember her being such a charming girl. Brimming full of life.'

Hester considered. 'She's still charming but so different from us. She gives off an air of affluence and contentment.'

'That doesn't sound like the Dorothea I knew, but we all change. I forget we're respectable matrons now. Let me write and tell her that you're going to come. They're going to send money for your fare, which will be very welcome. Given the invitation has come from them, I think we can accept it without any scruples.'

'And the workhouse?'

'Do you really think it would help the women there if you visited?'

Hester thought back to the dormitory housing, to desperate Elisabet and resigned Ellen – both to be used in her pursuit to find out what happened to her sister.

'I think it would be good for both me and for them,' Hester lied. 'The maid I met at the entrance said the master didn't like Friends. He prefers the Methodists.'

Ruth threw her head back and laughed at this – the first sound of merriment Hester had heard in the house for weeks.

'Does he now? Well, as you say, Mr Kirkham owes us a favour. A fine stink I'll raise if he declines your visits. Burying Mercy in a communal grave . . . You leave it with me.'

Hester heard no more about it for a week or so. The weather turned muggy for September. Bristol, near the sea, was accustomed to the iron weight the early-autumn season brought. Ruth had written to the Francombes, and it was agreed that whether or not she had Mr Kirkham's prior permission to visit the workhouse, she'd be travelling to Southwell.

Hester had little to pack and would have happily taken on the chore herself, but Susanna was keen to help. Together, they filled the portmanteau with the well-made but oh-so-drab dresses, capes and undergarments that made up her wardrobe. Hester knew she'd look like the poor relation next to Caroline, but there was nothing to be done about it. Even if there had been money to buy new gowns, the thought of replacing an old grey wardrobe with new ones in the same colour was too dispiriting.

Hester could see Susanna wanted to talk to her.

'What are you going back for?'

'I've been invited by the Francombes.'

'That's not the reason you're going though, is it? It's Kitty's words that have done this.'

'Perhaps.' Hester folded the precious shawl and laid it on top of the clothes. 'I know now that Mercy's story was more than dying of cholera in the workhouse. I should have realised it at the time. She appeared to me for a reason. I need to go back and discover what's happened to the child.'

'Perhaps we should tell Ruth first.'

'No!' Hester gripped Susanna's shoulder, surprising them both. 'Don't mention it to Ruth. She's had enough, hasn't she? She doesn't need to know about the baby. At least until I know if the child is alive or dead.'

'But . . .' Susanna's voice dropped to a whisper. 'Suppose it's dangerous? What's happened to the child if it's alive? There might be people who don't want you meddling in their affairs.'

Hester thought back to the grim building with its patina of respectability.

'There's no danger. I simply haven't been given all the facts. I intend to rectify that.'

Susanna sighed. Always a fusspot, she seemed to have got worse since Amos's death, but Hester's mind was made up. She helped the maid to pull shut the portmanteau and secure it with cord, impatient to get going.

'I promise, Susanna, that I'll return unscathed and free of the sightings. I have nothing to fear from Southwell.'

# PART TWO

## SOUTHWELL

*Though we be looked upon as the weaker vessels . . .*
*we can stand our ground.*
Women Friends of Lancashire

# Chapter Nineteen

William Chaplain remembered Hester from the previous trip when she changed coaches at The Swan with Two Necks. He lifted his hat to her, but there would be no coins given to the driver this time, now that she was a seasoned traveller. She'd been careful to avoid the greasy chops served in the foul inn outside London and remembered to use the fields as a toilet rather than the stinking holes in the floor.

At each stage, the coach was packed to the gills with passengers both inside and on the roof. Rather than resulting in an unpleasant journey, Hester enjoyed the sense of being surrounded by people. Not one of the journeyers suspected that there was another passenger alongside them.

In her Quaker grey, Mercy sat next to Hester in the coach. Her form was only just visible, like a painting completed in the palest of washes. Whether she was happy Hester was returning to Southwell was hard to say, but her expression remained placid, her eyes fixed on her sister. At one point on the journey, as they were alighting at an inn, a bull mastiff barked at the spectre, baring its teeth. Its master gave it a kick and extended an apology to Hester, which she accepted with embarrassment.

By the time the fly coach turned into the arch of The Black Griffin, she was as weary as she remembered the first time round. The only bonus was that she was spared an early-morning arrival, reaching Southwell at the respectable time of three o'clock in the afternoon. Unconsciously, as she alighted, she looked to the place where she'd first seen the landlord, Matthew Alban, but the doorway was empty. In the opposite corner of the courtyard, Dorothea Francombe stepped down from her gig and hurried to meet her.

'At least I've made your arrival this time! I can't even begin to tell you how happy I am that you're staying with us. Caroline is naturally thrilled, too.'

Hester looked behind Dorothea to see if her daughter had accompanied her but saw only the door to The Black Griffin open and Joan appear. Her eyes widened in surprise, but she acknowledged Hester with a nod. Dorothea turned to follow her gaze and frowned when she saw the kitchen woman standing against the door frame.

'My gig is waiting. Let's get you away from here,' said Dorothea. 'Boy, bring the portmanteau to my horse.'

As the stable hand struggled with Hester's trunk, Dorothea steered Hester towards her gig. With an expert flick of the reins, they were off, trotting sedately through the cobbled streets. Hester, always sensitive to a change in atmosphere, saw at once that Southwell had changed since her first sight of it in the early September sunshine. October had cooled the town, bringing a chill wind and giving the place an air of a town bracing itself for winter. Leaves rained on their heads as they passed under a canopy of branches, irritating the mare, who shook its head, causing the cart to rock.

'Steady.' Dorothea flicked the whip, an act unlikely to reassure any animal. 'Now, Hester, first of all, I have some news. Your mother wrote to me to say you wanted to visit the workhouse on a weekly basis. I take it you haven't received a reply.'

'Not in Bristol. Ruth has now gone to Bath, and so they've been asked to respond to me in Southwell.'

'Well, they've written to me to say they've agreed to your proposal.'

'They wrote to you?' said Hester, turning to look at Dorothea. 'Why not direct to me?'

'My dear, Ruth must have told them where you were staying. Perhaps she told them to direct their reply to me. I am known in the town.'

'I see. I'm surprised they acquiesced so easily.'

Dorothea glanced at her as she steered the horse round a corner.

'So am I, to be honest. I'm not sure what Ruth put in the letter, but you're to be allowed to visit the women's wing for two mornings a week. They've suggested Mondays and Thursdays. I advise you fall in with their suggestion, given they don't usually like to have visitors at all.'

'That's excellent.' Hester felt the triumph of success lift her spirits.

'So that's settled, then.' Dorothea flicked at the horse to speed it up as it showed signs of slowing in front of a cart of apples. 'I hope you won't find us too unworthy. I'm afraid Caroline and I spend our days in more frivolous pursuits than visiting the poor.' She spoke with a light tone, a woman happy at her place in the world.

Hester shifted uncomfortably in the seat. Pale grey was most definitely not the colour to wear after days of travelling. She was grubby and damp. Dorothea was elegantly dressed in a dark burgundy woollen cloth. Stuffed into her corset and best travelling frock, Hester had been sweating profusely since leaving Bristol.

'You're uncomfortable?' Dorothea shot her a look of sympathy. 'You know, my dear, you can maintain your air of dignity without resorting to cloth dyed the hue of dishwater. Do you have dresses of any other colour?'

Miserably, Hester shook her head.

'Well, never mind. Let me see what I can do. You're about the same height as Caroline, although perhaps a little plumper.'

'Oh no, please don't go to any trouble.'

'No trouble at all,' said Dorothea comfortably. 'You can wear your grey things to the workhouse.'

As the horse trotted sedately through the town, Hester felt a clutch at her arm. Dorothea had both hands on the reins, so the touch wasn't hers. Mercy, although thinned to transparency, had used her energy to make herself felt and Hester sensed her exhaustion at the effort. What was it that her sister wanted?

She looked down at the street and saw, on the dirty pavement near a boy sweeping the crossing, the woman and child she spoke to after her first visit to the workhouse. The baby was slumbering this time, its little mouth open as it rested its head on its mother's shoulders. The woman was a substantial figure, not a shadowing, surely. She caught Hester's eye and took a step towards the gig.

'Where have you taken my child?'

Hester turned her face away. 'I don't have it.'

'What was that, my dear?' asked Dorothea. 'I'm afraid your words were lost in the wind.'

'It doesn't matter. Who is that girl we just passed?' she asked. 'The one holding the baby.'

'Which girl?' Dorothea looked round. 'I didn't see anyone.'

Hester was too tired to reply and closed her eyes for the rest of the journey.

At Guy House, she was shown to the room she'd occupied on her earlier visit as her trunk was hauled up the stairs. A maid, timid and deferential, began to unpack while Hester sat in the chair, trying to stay awake. They were both startled by the arrival of Caroline, who appeared in a whirlwind, bounding over to kiss Hester on the cheek.

'You're here! I'm so pleased you agreed to join us for the month.'

Hester made an effort to look alert.

'I have to say, the invitation was a very welcome surprise.'

'I could just see you were desperate not to return to Bristol. Now, I have lots of activities planned to raise your spirits.'

Hester, flattered at how pleased the girl was to see her, allowed herself to be led to the sitting room when what she really would have loved was to lie down in those cool sheets for an hour or two and revive her energy. Caroline, however, wanted to recite the schedule for the whole of Hester's stay.

'Sunday is a bore because we visit other Friends. They change each week, but there's no fun to be had. Monday to Saturday, however, the time is ours. Market is Saturday, of course, and that's worth a visit, not least because such pretty silk is sent down from Macclesfield.' She stopped. 'What's the matter? You're not going all prim on me, are you?'

'Not at all. I'd love to wear some ribbons while I'm here.'

It was true. Frivolous, of course, but who was to stop her?

'Well, that's all right, then. On Thursdays there are recitals at the assembly rooms. Why, Hester, you're making a face. You're going to tell me you don't like music.'

'The problem is that two mornings a week I'm to visit the Union workhouse. Thursday is one of the agreed days.'

'You're not actually planning to go, are you?' Caroline frowned. 'Mama and I thought it was just a ruse to make sure your mother would let you visit us.'

Hester hesitated. She'd decided on the coach north to proceed with caution. Ruth had warned her once that people kept their secrets close and she wouldn't gain anything by showing her hand too early.

'Ruth is bound to check. I'll need to undertake my visits. It's the reason she allowed me to come in the first place.' Hester looked down at her hands while telling the white lie.

'Oh well,' Caroline said. 'It's not too bad, especially if it's morning. I don't usually get up before eleven.'

Caroline's frankness made her laugh.

'You shall just be putting ribbons in your hair when I return from the workhouse.'

Caroline grimaced. 'Don't mention that horrible place. Now, let me tell you who was also delighted when I told him that you'd be returning to Southwell.'

'I can't possibly think.'

Hester found herself bristling at Caroline's arch tone, although she could guess what was coming next.

'Don't tease, Hester. How many admirers did you have time to attract during your previous visit? I'll warrant the only man you met was Edward Holland.'

'Doctor Holland?' asked Hester, furious to feel a flush staining her cheeks. 'But I thought he was promised to you.'

'Me?' Caroline was dismissive. 'We've grown up together. He's most definitely not got any romantic interest in me. Well, what do you think of him?'

Hester hesitated. 'He seemed very respectable.'

'He's a catch. Lots of mothers in Southwell have their eyes on him for their own daughters. Anyway, we're having dinner at his house tonight. We're honoured. He doesn't often issue invitations to his rooms. You'll see for yourself how pleased he is to see you.'

Hester groaned.

'What's the matter?'

'I'm so weary, I'm sure I'll be yawning into my soup the whole evening.'

Caroline, delighted, laughed. 'It's going to be so much fun. We'll be great friends, I know.'

# Chapter Twenty

'She's back.' Joan stood in front of Matthew, her hands on her hips.

'Who?'

For a moment, Matthew was consumed by images of the wench he'd had the previous night. She'd made him pay, which he hadn't realised would be part of the bargain when he'd invited her up to his room. He was usually adept at spotting the professionals, but he'd been caught out and it had cost him a shilling, and it wasn't even money well spent. If the trollop wanted more of him, she'd soon be sorry.

'The Quaker. Hester her name was. She went up to the work-house last month.'

Matthew remembered all right, and could feel a spurt of shame as he thought about her tart response to his rudeness. She'd gone to the workhouse and had been upset about what she'd found there. Well, that was no surprise. What was surprising was that she'd decided to return. This, he reasoned, was not good news.

'What are you telling me for?' Worry made him abrupt with Joan, but he saw she took no offence.

'Thought you'd like to know. I liked the girl.'

'Let's hope she stays away from the Union.'

She stared at him. 'You don't think that's the reason she's come back, do you? She was met by that Quaker family. She looked like a visitor, not a woman with a purpose like the last time.'

Matthew shrugged and, giving up, Joan disappeared back into the kitchen. He found he couldn't settle at any task after Joan's news. A new stable lad answered him back and he clipped the youngster around the ear, ignoring the injured look on the boy's face. When he saw he'd have no peace that afternoon, he changed his shirt and made his way towards the churchyard. The sexton was thankfully absent, so he wouldn't need to explain his presence as he picked his way through the graves, his eyes peeled to the ground. When he'd done a sweep of the graveyard, he let out a sigh of relief. There was no newly tilled soil. There had been no deaths at the workhouse recently.

# Chapter Twenty-One

Edward answered the door to their knock and ushered them through the cramped hall towards his living quarters on the first floor. It was all Hester would have expected from a doctor's rooms, from the respectable striped wallpaper to the solid oak furniture, but the house had a sterile air, the sense of rooms only barely lived in. As she was climbing the stairs, Hester thought she heard a sob from behind one of the doors on the ground floor, but Edward showed no sign he'd heard the cry. After they'd been settled in a long drawing room, he gave his apologies and Hester listened to his footsteps echo as he descended the stairs.

'Poor Edward. I wonder what's wrong. He looked a little pained.'

Caroline dropped onto a sofa and began to fan herself, although the evening was cool and she was in a dress that showed off her elegant shoulders.

'A problem with a patient, perhaps.'

Dorothea lifted the lid of a small pianoforte and began to play a tune from memory. Although Hester had heard Caroline perform on her first evening at Guy House, she was surprised that Dorothea could also play so well. Dorothea caught Hester's eye and smiled.

'Your mother and I used to play duets.'

'Ruth can play the piano?'

'Of course. Please don't tell me your father didn't allow her to practise.'

'We don't even own an instrument.'

She saw Dorothea look down at the keys and frown.

An elderly housekeeper announced that dinner was ready and Edward joined them in the sitting room, full of apologies.

'Is everything all right?' asked Caroline. 'You look most put out.'

'Everything's well. I have a patient who isn't expected to last the night and I'd promised him a draught to relieve his discomfort. His servant was waiting for me to dispense the phial. He's gone now, so we won't be disturbed.'

But it was a woman's sob I heard, thought Hester. Perhaps he's being discreet.

'Do you use rooms here for your consultations?' she asked.

'I rather think,' said Caroline, 'that Edward's patients are used to him going to them.'

Edward smiled. 'Well, you're both right. Of course I see patients in their homes, but I do also have consulting rooms here on the ground floor. Working people often prefer to come to me. I have a small room for meeting my patients and a large one for surgery when necessary.'

'You're a surgeon?' asked Hester.

'I trained under the best barber.'

Hester winced, looking down at her plate, where slivers of venison bled into green leaves.

'Sorry, forgive my sense of humour. I have a medical degree, but even us educated men need help when presented with broken bones. I was taught how to splint a leg and repair a torn shoulder by the best barber in town.'

Dorothea looked at Hester to see her reaction.

'You visit the hospitals, I believe. You know there are good or indifferent doctors. Edward here is one of the best,' she said.

'Of course.'

Edward was smiling, but his words were confusing. He'd surely meant to shock her when he mentioned the barber, and he had done. Not because she was naïve in such matters but because she hadn't expected him to be so forthright about the baser aspects of his work. A medical man's no-nonsense approach to his job, perhaps, but she was overcome by the painful dislocation of someone who doesn't belong.

She looked across at her companions. The three of them in the candlelight made an attractive triptych. Both Dorothea and Caroline were wearing pale yellow gowns and had pearl earrings that shimmered in the light. Edward was more distracted than he'd been during dinner at the Francombes, and she saw him glance at the large clock in the corner of the room.

'So, what are your plans while Hester's in town? I hope to join you for at least one excursion if I can get away from my patients.'

'We shall have to work around Hester's plans. She's to visit the workhouse twice a week while she's here.'

'The workhouse?' asked Edward, making an effort to hide his surprise.

Dorothea gave her daughter a look of reproach.

'Don't tease, Caroline. Hester's resolved to make herself useful while she's our guest. She'll be visiting the Union two mornings a week, Edward.'

'It's not much of a holiday for you, is it?' Edward smiled across at her. 'Can we persuade you to change your mind?'

Hester shook her head. 'It's all arranged. I was wondering about the physician to the workhouse. Am I likely to encounter him?'

'Old Bant? He's called in occasionally, I suppose, but even doctors of Bant's reputation still want paying and I've heard the Union are tight-fisted. If you're lucky, you won't see him at all.' He studied her, choosing his words carefully. 'I'd advise you not to consult with him if you're unwell yourself.'

'He's incompetent?'

'I dare say he's better than receiving no medical care whatsoever. At least I think so.'

'He lives in Southwell? How many physicians does the town have?'

'Goodness, Hester, these questions,' said Dorothea. 'In the unlikely event of you being unwell, we'd call for Edward here.'

Edward gave a small bow. 'Thank you, Dorothea. In answer to your question, Hester, there are two of us. I'm the youngest and therefore the most popular.'

'If you're going to be sick, you might as well enjoy being ministered to,' said Caroline, laughing.

'Then Doctor Bant doesn't live inside the workhouse?' asked Hester.

'Good heavens, no. He's in some dingy lodging by the river.'

'Who appointed him? The master?'

Edward snorted. 'Old Kirkham? He doesn't have the power. Bant was appointed by the board of guardians. They're always looking at saving costs, including who physicks. You get what you pay for.'

'You're not still thinking about Mercy, are you?' asked Dorothea. 'I'm sure they did everything they could for her and her child.'

Was it her imagination or were the three of them listening closely to her reply? No, Hester assured herself, their expressions were just those of polite interest. So, what accounted for the sense of the air thinning in the room? Mercy wasn't present, she was sure of it, and yet Hester sensed her pursuer from Bristol. The spectre had followed her to Southwell and it was in this room that she was trying to communicate to Hester.

*I don't know what you want from me,* Hester told the spirit. *You have to be more forceful.*

Even as she spoke, she realised the danger of her words. Her sightings had always been just that. Spirits who materialised for a short while and disappeared. Now, she was feeling Mercy's touch, but she could at least trust her sister. The other more desperate spirit was an unknown quantity. With a jolt, she realised her companions were still waiting for an answer.

'I was just wondering about medical provision, that was all.'

'Never mind old Doctor Bant,' said Caroline, changing the subject. 'You'll have your work cut out trying to think of conversation topics to discuss with the women. I'm sure the matron will insist on only improving subjects.'

'No more nonsense about the pale lady,' said Dorothea, smiling.

'Of course.' Caroline stared at Hester for a moment. 'You must tell us if you hear any more about the pale lady. Remember? The spectre who appeared to the woman you spoke to. It's the spirits who interest us.'

Hester kept her expression neutral. 'I hadn't intended to make any further inquiries,' she lied, looking at Caroline's mocking expression.

'Quite right.' Edward smiled across the table at her. 'Keep your feet on the ground and your wits about you when you get to the workhouse. You're going to need that strength.'

## Chapter Twenty-Two

The next morning, while her hosts slept, Hester slipped out of the front door in search of the workhouse physician. No explanation was needed to the maid. It was Monday morning and she'd already been given notice that Hester would be leaving the house early to visit the Union. She'd refused breakfast – the knot of dread had returned and hunger made her senses sharper. She'd need all of her wits about her when dealing with the Kirkhams. Stepping out onto the pavement, she took a deep breath of icy air and set off, avoiding the eyes of curious street hawkers who, sensing a lack of custom, gave her a wide berth.

The area close to the River Greet was one of the worst parts of town, the streets reeking of rotted animals and excrement. Edward's vague statement that the physician lived 'by the river' got her as far as a dingy maze of streets, but she couldn't identify which passage or building belonged to a Doctor Bant. Dithering over which way to turn, she saw a young boy sweeping the road and called across to him. He turned a startled face to her, his nervy manner one of a child used to being treated badly.

'Can you tell me the way to Doctor Bant's house? The doctor who physicks to the workhouse.'

'Bant? You'll find him down that passage, next to the street lamp. His room's on the first floor – you climb the stairs from outside.'

She slipped the grateful child a penny, which he took in his grubby hands.

'Thank you. You take care, miss. Taste whatever he gives you like this . . .' He stuck out a pink tongue and put his finger on its tip. 'Some tonics can do you more harm than good.'

'I'll be careful,' she promised.

The passage was ill-lit with only the pale dawn visible through the rooftops to guide her way. She looked around to see if any thieves were following her progress, although they'd surely be disappointed with their threepenny haul if she was set upon. Only one of the mean crumbling houses had an upper floor accessible from the outside. The stone staircase was covered with green slime and she lifted her skirt to climb the steps. At the door, the foulness of the passage was overlaid by a sicklier odour.

'Hello. Is anyone there?'

She heard violent coughing and the sound of phlegm being discharged from the back of a man's throat. The man must be sick himself.

'Hello?'

Hester pushed open the door and entered a large room lit by a single foul tallow candle smoking in one corner. A man was sitting beside it, puffing on a pipe, his eyes half closed.

'Doctor Bant?'

The physician leaned back in his chair at her words. She now recognised the smell – the sickly aroma she was used to inhaling when she visited the local paupers who congregated outside a warehouse in the bowels of Bristol docks. She was also familiar with the ravages wrought by opium on patients at the hospital she attended. One look at those poor souls would have been enough to put anyone off the foul substance. But an addict is an addict, she knew, and she must make the most of the fact that he was at least conscious. If she delayed her visit to another time, he might be comatose or agitated by awaiting his latest pipe smoke.

She shut the door behind her, looking for a jug of water to give the man, but found only a beaker with a fur of mould growing inside. On the table was a sheaf of papers that bore the brand of three balls suspended from a bar. Doctor Bant was a habitual user of the pawn shop, it appeared.

'If I could have a minute of your time. I've come to talk to you about a patient at Southwell Union.'

The man moved slightly.

'I only go if the master or matron send for me.' His words were slurred and lumbering as if the effort of speaking were making him ill. 'I don't get paid otherwise.'

Hester crouched beside him.

'It's not a current patient I want to talk to you about. It's one you treated in the past. A woman with a baby in the dormitory for the undeserving poor.'

He moved his lips and Hester was forced to bring her head towards his rotten mouth to hear his words.

'Which one?'

'A woman a little older than me but with my features. Her name was Mercy.'

'Mercy?' The name amused the man. 'You don't get much mercy at the Union.'

Hester, repulsed, willed herself to stay calm.

'She died. I've heard it might have been cholera, but another account gives it as childbed fever. Do you know which?'

The man coughed with laughter.

'I've treated no one for cholera at the workhouse recently.'

So Kitty had been right.

'A fever, then? Do you remember her at all?'

The man shrugged. 'Childbed's a woman's task. Why are you asking me?'

'The baby lived when it was born, but it's there no longer. I wondered if you might have been called to attend to it.'

He stared at her, his pupils pools of black.

'I remember no child. Why don't you leave them in peace?'

'I need to know what happened to the baby.'

The pipe dropped out of the man's mouth and he stared at her, a stench emitting from his fetid jaws.

'God rest its soul,' he said. 'God rest its eternal soul.'

Hester thought mention of the child might shake him from his torpor. She saw a spark flare behind the doctor's glazed eyes, a hint of the intelligence that he must have possessed to become a physician. But she watched aghast as, with trembling hands, he poured a drop of dark brown tincture into a smeared glass and swallowed the lot in one gulp. When his eyes turned to her, his pupils were pinpricks and the spark had gone. She'd lost him to the netherworld.

From the physician, Hester went directly to the workhouse, conscious her clothes might reek of opiates. The doctor had given her no useful information but had added to her sense of Southwell as a town gone awry. It was an odd feeling. Bristol was a city full of people of all ages and cultures. It attracted both the ambitious and the destitute, yet Hester had never felt the continual prickle of fear she was experiencing here.

She passed the road sweeper, still at the same spot, who put his finger on the tip of his tongue as a reminder. She nodded and hurried on. At the end of the pauper's path, the workhouse porter, his face as pugnacious as ever, was at least civil if not welcoming as he poked his head out of the booth.

'You're back, I see.'

'I am, Mr . . .'

'Heggs.' He looked behind her. 'Your friend not coming with you?'

'What friend?' Hester turned to follow the porter's gaze over her shoulders, but the landscape was empty except for a woman in the kitchen garden pulling out potatoes. 'Who do you see?'

Heggs narrowed his eyes. 'I thought you'd brought a friend with you. The sun is casting shadows, that's all. It doesn't matter. You're to go to the deserving women's day room. Some of the inmates will join you there. If you're to come, you can at least make yourself useful.'

Smiling, despite his flat words, Hester entered through the front porch. Out of the back window, she saw a lone inmate at the pump, her muscular arms filling a wooden bucket. A couple of women were in the kitchen, one filleting a heap of fish while another lifted a pan of hissing broth off the range. In the deserving women's day room, an inmate was on her knees, applying beeswax to the floor with a brush.

'Is it all right if I take a seat here? I'm being joined by some of the women.'

The girl looked up at her.

'Do what you like.'

Hester saw it was Little Pinch, her tone no more polite than during her previous visit. She pulled out a chair and sat down, the girl giving her a curious glance as she carried on with her task.

'Don't be expecting any visitors. The master's furious he's got to accommodate you.'

Hester got the impression that Little Pinch delighted in Mr Kirkham's displeasure.

'He's said we're allowed to talk to you, but we'll be in for what for if we spill any details of our life here.'

'Will anyone come to talk to me?'

The girl looked over her shoulder. 'Doubt it.' She picked up her tin and left before Hester could question her further.

For half an hour, Hester sat, humiliated, furious that this was how she was to spend her days. Sitting in an empty room with no one to talk to. Around her, she could hear muted sounds of activity. The thump of wood hitting animal bones, crushed to provide feed for the surrounding fields. The roar of a cow being milked by inexperienced hands. Everyone with a task except her. It would be good revenge for Mr Kirkham to humiliate her so, and the only thing to rectify it would be another letter from her mother to the board of guardians. Mr Kirkham would have had his fun and she'd have been put in her place, reminded who was in charge of the workhouse.

She'd just made up her mind to leave when she heard footsteps along the corridor and two women trooped in as if they were regulars in the army. Mrs Kirkham brought up the rear, stuffed into a brown striped dress that revealed every bulge of her ample body.

'Sit down, ladies.'

Both obeyed, keeping their eyes lowered to the floor. One woman was very old, unfit for any kind of physical exercise, the other pregnant, probably nearing her term. She could have been aged anywhere between twenty-five and forty and looked sickly, her complexion ashen.

'Miss Goodwin will be visiting us on Monday and Thursday mornings. There's bedding to be mended and I'm sure she'll be happy to help us in our endeavours.'

Hester winced, remembering the hash she'd made of the stockings when talking to Susanna. A couple of men brought in the laundry basket, a heavy wicker thing. One of them cast a glance at the ashen woman, but she didn't raise her eyes to acknowledge his presence. Hester selected a blanket with a hole that needed darning. She thought she might fare better with wool. It needed a less delicate hand and soon she had her head bent over the task, working alongside the women in silence. Mrs Kirkham left them to it and she could hear the woman's voice shouting orders from the laundry room across the way.

'How long until your baby's due?' Hester kept her voice low.

'A couple of weeks at most, I think.'

'Your first?'

The woman shook her head.

'I don't have any alive. I want a girl this time. My last two were boys. Maybe girls live longer.'

Superstition, but if you've already lost two, you must cling onto any hope, Hester thought.

'Perhaps being in the workhouse will help. Mrs Kirkham has an admirable attitude towards cleanliness.'

'It's us who do the work, though. But you're right. There are worse places.'

'Do you have a husband?'

'Yes. You saw him just now. There's a promise of a job helping with the apple picking. We'll be gone once the baby is born.'

'There was a girl the last time I was here. Elisabet. She was in the undeserving women's dormitory. What happened to her?'

'Stuck to her bed. The baby's nearly due and she has the sickness.'

'Sickness?'

'She shakes and has convulsions. Mrs Kirkham thinks her case is hopeless.'

Hester placed her darning in her lap.

'There's no such thing as hopeless. She should be attended to by a doctor.'

'Old Bant? She'd be better off leaving it to nature.'

'Perhaps I can help.'

The girl stopped sewing.

'You can't just go up there. We were told . . .'

'Told what?'

'Ordered to talk to you about nothing much.'

Hester looked at the two women, their heads bowed over their work.

'What are the Kirkhams afraid of me finding out?'

'It's nothing. We've been told not to talk about the undeserving women, that's all. Life is hard enough for us here. We don't need Quakers making it more difficult for us.'

The elderly woman put her hand to her forehead and Hester saw drops of sweat from exhaustion.

'I don't understand why I'm to be kept apart from that dormitory. Surely that's where my work would be better fitted. You all seem content. Are you treated well?'

'We're never hungry,' offered the pregnant woman. 'The rations are good. Meat and potatoes in the evening. I have nothing to complain of myself, except I can't be with my husband.'

'What about the undeserving poor? Do they have something to complain about?'

'Not for the food. Their rations' the same as ours.'

'What then? Why am I to be kept apart? What is Mrs Kirkham worried about?'

The woman looked at the door and moved her chair a fraction nearer to Hester's.

'She found out you've been asking about the pale lady. Proper furious she was when she found out. All of the girls who met you on your visit went without their food that evening. Little Pinch, Elisabet and Ellen.'

'Who told her we'd been talking about the pale lady?'

The girl shrugged. 'I don't know, but it got back to matron.'

Apart from her conversations with Edward and the Francombes, the only other person in Southwell she'd mentioned the pale lady to was Reverend Flint. She remembered his fury and decided he must be the culprit.

'Mrs Kirkham's fair worked up about it,' continued the girl. 'Says it's nothing but gossip and fancy.'

'If that's all it is, why's she so upset?'

'I don't know.'

'And have you heard stories of the pale lady?'

'The women don't like to talk of her. They say she steals babies, only she won't take mine. I'll be gone before then.'

'Elisabet called her the angelmaker.'

For the first time, the woman looked up and frowned at Hester.

'The angelmaker? I've not heard her called that.'

Hester heard a bell sound in the distance and the two women put their mending to one side.

'Is it time for lunch already?'

'We have to be at our tables prompt or we miss out.'

All she'd been given was ten minutes with these women.

'Fine.'

Hester threw the mangled blanket back into the wicker basket. She went out into the passageway and followed the sound of Mrs Kirkham's voice, leading her to the laundry, where the stench of musty blankets mingled with soap.

'It's time for me to leave, I see. There's something I need to ask you, though.' She looked round. 'Away from these women.'

Mrs Kirkham, frowning, took her to a corner of the courtyard, the eyes of the inmates on them.

'Well, what is it?'

'I was told a story by a former resident here that my sister's child lived.'

Mrs Kirkham hadn't been expecting this. She started, her cheeks, already in high colour, deepening to puce.

'Nonsense. Who told you this? One of the women you've been speaking to?'

'No, not them. A resident who has moved away.' She could see Mrs Kirkham's mind working furiously, but she wouldn't give up Kitty's name. 'Well, is it true?'

'The baby died just after your sister. What of it?'

'How long after?'

'A day,' the matron conceded, her coal-black eyes on Hester. 'Is that why you've asked to return? To mither me and my charges? Because if that's the case—'

'And were they buried together?'

'It's what I told you, wasn't it? Are you calling me a liar?'

Hester let the silence grow. She wasn't sure who had the upper hand. She was here on sufferance, but surely the matron didn't have the power to bar her entry.

'Next time, perhaps I might be allowed to visit the undeserving women. All of God's creatures are equal in His eyes.'

'Is that what you think?' Mrs Kirkham stepped back to let Hester pass. 'You'll learn.'

# Chapter Twenty-Three

'You spent the afternoon moping around the house yesterday, Hester. I think, given your recent bereavement, the workhouse isn't the best place for you to visit.'

Dorothea was at breakfast in a morning cap and robe, which Hester tried not to gape at. Amos would have had a fit if his wife or daughters had appeared in such clothing. Dorothea was buttering a slice of toast with her gaze on her.

'Are you sure your visits are strictly necessary?'

Hester frowned. 'Has Caroline said anything? I'm perhaps not the companion she was hoping for.'

'Nonsense. I have to write to your mother tonight to tell her how you're settling in. I know she'll be getting a letter from you, but daughters don't tell their mothers everything, do they?'

Hester swallowed.

'So I thought, why not have a trip out today so Ruth can see you're keeping yourself amused here? I've even managed to persuade Caroline to rise early.'

'A trip to where?'

Caroline, also wearing a morning robe, came into the room yawning as she took her seat at the table. She looked like a ruffled chick forced into the open air.

'I was just telling Hester about our planned trip,' said Dorothea.

'Do you like Byron?' asked Caroline, pointing to her teacup for the maid to fill.

'The poet? I'm afraid—'

'I know, your father wouldn't let you read him.' Caroline yawned again. 'Or did that extend to all poetry?'

'My father didn't think reading, music or any form of the arts a worthy pastime. He thought they contributed to puffed-up human vanity.'

'Did he now?' Caroline ignored the warning glance from her mother.

'We did study Wordsworth at school, however.'

'Oh, Wordsworth.' Caroline sniffed. 'Byron was no Wordsworth. Wait a moment.' She went out of the room and returned with a thin leather-bound book. 'Why don't you take a look at these and see what you think? We've a trip planned to Newstead Abbey, which was Byron's ancestral home. Edward will be taking us.'

'He can afford the time away from his patients?' asked Hester.

'He can if it means spending time in your company.'

Dorothea looked up.

'Caroline, please, none of your matchmaking. Edward will be here at eleven. Perhaps, Hester, you can look at Lord Byron's poems while we dress.'

Hester flicked through the book and was immediately pulled into Byron's dark heart:

Rayless, and pathless, and the icy earth
Swung blind and blackening in the moonless air;

He's calling out to me, she thought, and stayed at the breakfast table after the others had left, falling into his words. The hour went quickly as her friends dressed, Caroline making it down first, wearing a dress of pale blue topped by a bonnet that would have caused a stir in any city, let alone this small town.

'Well, what do you think of our local poet?'

'May I keep it during my stay here? He has a sense of darkness that I understand.'

Caroline looked down at the leather-bound book in Hester's hands.

'Do you? Well, you are full of surprises, aren't you, Hester? Let's wait on the steps for Edward to arrive. You must see his carriage.'

Edward was drawing up in his physician's phaeton as they opened the door – he was clearly proud of the glossy green carriage pulled by a single horse but making an effort not to show it.

'But we won't all fit in that.'

'Of course we won't. Don't be ridiculous, Hester. We've hired a carriage from The Black Griffin for the day. It's waiting for us over there.'

Hester followed the direction of her gaze and saw the landlord standing by two horses, pulling affectionately on their ears. He caught her eye and turned away. He could hardly call out insults like Quaker Jane to her when she was in such distinguished company. Strange, though, that he'd thought to bring the horses direct to them rather than leave it to an ostler.

Edward gave the landlord his phaeton and took the reins of the carriage, bringing it up to the front door.

'Matthew Alban is as unfriendly as ever, I see. He keeps a fine stable, though.'

His voice was loud enough for Matthew to hear and she saw him tense as he led the horse and phaeton away.

Dorothea emerged to join them on the steps.

'We're all here? Then let's go.'

Hester hadn't realised how low in spirits she'd become after her first visit to the workhouse until she was in the carriage flying through the Nottinghamshire countryside. This, she was sure, was what her mother had envisaged for her when she'd agreed to let her come to Southwell, rather than the disheartening visit to the Union.

When Newstead Abbey came into view, Hester understood a little of the darkness at Byron's heart. It was a former abbey, but there was nothing calming or peaceful about the ruins. The building was square, grey and austere. Long mullioned windows reflected their arrival in their tiny panes of glass as the coach drew up at the entrance. The forbidding exterior failed to dampen Caroline and Dorothea's high spirits. The wind had positioned Caroline's ridiculous bonnet at a rakish angle, which a final gust stole away.

'My hat. Edward, please.'

Edward shared an exasperated look with Hester and chased after it, handing it solemnly back to Caroline.

'We could look around the gardens. It's a nice day,' said Dorothea. 'You'll have to keep your hand on your hat, Caroline. Unless you'd prefer to see inside the house. I could apply to the housekeeper.'

'Oh, let's get out of the wind,' said Caroline, steering Hester towards the main entrance.

They were led into a cool hall which, despite its luxurious furnishings, reminded her a little of the workhouse anteroom. The sun cast its shadow on the floor without providing any warmth. Hester was aware of a fifth person in the room standing in the shadows but saw that her companions noticed nothing amiss. Not her sister, but the other shadowing. She could make out, for the first time, a female form. So, the other shadowing was a woman. She tucked the piece of information away to consider later.

A door opened and the housekeeper appeared.

'Colonel Wildman and the family are away at the moment. I can show you round, if you wish. Is there another?'

Dorothea shook her head.

'The maid thought you were five. No matter.'

They made a tour of the downstairs rooms – chambers far grander than Hester had seen but with that same chilled air. Caroline concentrated on the paintings of family members, assessing the fashions of the ladies with a keen eye. In a large sitting room, they interrupted a maid blackening the fireplace – a dirty job that she undertook with vigour. The application with which she scrubbed the metal reminded Hester of Little Pinch applying beeswax the previous day. This maid started in surprise at their appearance. She'd probably been told that she should make herself scarce when visitors were present.

'Sorry, ma'am.' The words died on her lips. 'No, no!'

She stared, ashen, at them, her mouth open with horror. Clutching her chest, she paled and collapsed to the floor in a dead faint.

She can see the spectre, thought Hester, and I shall have to pretend I'm as confused as the others.

The housekeeper, rather than going to maid's aid, hastened Hester and her friends out of the room.

'Don't worry about Dorcas. She's a nervy sort. I train them up well enough, but you can't get past their personality. Can you make your own way out? I'm going to have to calm the poor girl down.'

'I'm sure we can,' said Edward with a backwards glance at the door. 'Are you sure I can't take a look at the girl? I'm a physician. I could just check—'

'She doesn't need a doctor – she needs a new set of wits. You leave her to me.'

The episode cast a pall over the day. The sun had retreated behind a cloud and once they were in the garden, Hester felt the squeeze of longing for Bristol in the days before Mercy had left. How compelling the past was, calling her away from her mission.

Aware of the enormity of the task that faced her, Hester realised she could never get to the bottom of the mystery without some help.

Dorothea and Caroline were admiring a gaudy bunch of chrysanthemums in a bed, their heads bent together. Either of them might make a confidante. Dorothea with her air of sympathy, Caroline with her worldly manner. Then there was Edward. A physician could be a reassuring ear if she set out the mystery of her niece who had drawn a breath, at least for a moment. But as he went up to join the Francombes, Hester was aware of how much of an outsider she was. From the clothes she wore to the shadowings that hounded her, she had nothing in common with any of them. No, she'd have to carry on alone.

# Chapter Twenty-Four

When Hester wasn't in the workhouse, the days passed in a blur of day trips and visits to the assembly rooms with Dorothea and Caroline, where they were occasionally joined by Edward. Even when the bad weather obliged them to stay inside, Hester enjoyed the novelty of reading a book without having to slip it under a cushion to hide it from Amos. Ruth sent letters from Bath, her tone lighter than Hester could remember. Susanna wrote too, complaining about the cranky stove she was forced to cook on and the unremitting drizzle in the town. She'd picked up on Edward's presence in their company and her notes urged Hester to say more.

> You tell of this Doctor Holland, or Edward as you've come to call him. Do tell all. A surgeon? Well, Amos would have approved of his profession, but your reticence suggests he's not a Friend. Oh, well. Times are changing and Amos is no longer around to forbid such a match. Hester, you must write more about him.

But what more was there to tell? Edward remained equally attentive to all three of them, although Hester sensed his interest in her. She trailed down the stairs, Susanna's letter in her hand, thinking of what to compose in reply. She stopped at the entrance. Dorothea was slumped on the couch, her hand covering her eyes.

'Dorothea! Is everything all right?'

Her host made an effort to straighten herself.

'I'm sorry you found me like this. Was there something you wanted?'

'I was going to write a letter at the desk.'

'Then don't let me stop you.' Dorothea stood, smoothing her skirts.

'But what's the matter?'

'The days do occasionally weigh heavily on me after Mr Francombe's death. Let's not talk about that now. You've had your mail, I see. Is all well in Bath?'

'Ruth's enjoying herself with the family.'

Caution made her reticent about Susanna's letter. Would Caroline write to a servant? It seemed unlikely and she doubted Dorothea would approve, either.

'Well, I shall write to her myself this afternoon and heap praise on your stay here.' She paused. 'Would you like me to mention Edward? He seems to have made rather a favourite of you.'

Hester refused to look embarrassed.

'He's very good company, but I don't think I'd describe myself as a favourite.'

'Nonsense. Well, I might just mention his name. It's best to do these things slowly. Ruth's nobody's fool. I shall mention his mother was a Friend and leave it at that. I shall expect a barrage of questions in Ruth's reply.'

'Are his parents in Southwell?'

'Well, no. They moved to the outskirts of Nottingham a few years ago.'

'But they visit him here?'

Dorothea hesitated.

'There's been an estrangement. Not Edward's fault. His father has a rather fixed view of the world. I'm sure you'll understand that. Now, let's change the subject. How are you getting on at the Union?'

Hester was surprised. Dorothea had shown little interest in her workhouse visits thus far.

'I've still not managed to meet the undeserving women on my visits. They're determined to keep me among the respectable poor.'

'And what's wrong with that?'

'They don't seem particularly unhappy. They'd rather be elsewhere, of course, but they're clean, well fed. I wonder what purpose I'm serving there.'

'It was you who asked to go, wasn't it? What were you expecting?'

'Not oakum picking.'

Dorothea laughed as Hester showed her fingers, red from separating fibres.

'I'm not surprised you're feeling disheartened. It's the antithesis of industry. You do a day's work for an hour's pay. That's the point of workhouse tasks. You can't make a profit, otherwise you're taking work from the town traders. So you do loss-making work.'

Hester enjoyed sitting with the women in an alliance to industry, but none of them had been able to tell her any more about the pale lady, nor give her any more information about Mercy's baby. Deserving and undeserving poor were kept apart with little mixing during mealtimes or exercise. Soon, October would be over and she'd be no nearer to finding out what happened to Mercy's child.

'I don't know what to do.'

Dorothea looked at the letter in Hester's hands.

'Write them a note and say you'll make a complaint to the board of guardians unless you're allowed to visit the truly desperate. That might do the trick. Now, you must excuse me.'

Hester, unconvinced by Dorothea's excuse for distress, put Susanna's letter to one side and set to the task at once.

> You kindly agreed for me to visit the women of Southwell Union,
> but I see I am denied access to the undeserving poor. I would partic-
> ularly like to speak to the women who find themselves abandoned
> with child. Surely these lost souls are as in need, if not more, of
> my companionship.

Hester, aware of the hypocrisy of her words, sealed the letter and
placed it in the tray.

The response came on Monday of her third week, when Hester
was escorted by Little Pinch not to the day room, but up into the
women's dormitory above.

'You've been meddling again.'

The girl kept her eyes to the floor, but Hester heard laughter
bubbling in her voice.

'Have I upset Mrs Kirkham?'

'She's furious.'

Mrs Kirkham was waiting for them, tapping her foot as they
entered the room. She felt it again, that strange undercurrent of
unease, the sense of time thinning out. *Mercy, where are you?* she
silently asked, but the room was still. The same women as on
her first visit to the dormitory were present, Ellen standing to
attention while Elisabet lay on the bed.

'You said in your letter you wanted to meet the undeserving
poor who have found themselves compromised with child. Well,
here we are – although I fail to see what help you can give them.'

'Just these two women?'

Mrs Kirkham inclined her head.

'They share a room with the other undeserving poor who can
at least work to earn their keep. Little Pinch, you can go now,
although I'm sure your time will come when you're confined to
this room like these two.'

The girl didn't need telling twice, disappearing with a clatter down the stairs.

'Little Pinch is expecting?' asked Hester.

'Oh yes, although she's hidden it very well. To be fair, she probably didn't know when she came to us for help. At least she can work. These women here' – Mrs Kirkham pointed a fleshy finger at the two – 'are undeserving and currently unfit for work. They can talk to you this morning.'

The two girls slid their eyes towards Hester and Ellen winked at her.

'I'm not sure what you'll be wanting to say to them. Read them the Bible, perhaps.'

'That wasn't my plan.' Hester kept her voice even in the face of Mrs Kirkham's scorn. 'I'd just like to talk to them, see how they're faring.'

Mrs Kirkham shrugged and left the room, her back erect as she passed into the corridor. Hester could feel some of the tension dissipate as the matron left. Elisabet's pregnancy hardly seemed to have advanced in the month Hester had been away, while Ellen was now in full sail, a picture of ruddy health in contrast to the clearly ill Elisabet.

Hester coughed. 'I came here a few weeks ago because my sister was one of your number. You might remember me.'

'Of course we remember you,' said Ellen. 'How many visitors do you think we have?'

'Shall we sit down? The beds will suffice. Elisabet, stay where you are. You're clearly ill.'

'We ain't supposed to sit on the beds when the matron isn't here.' Ellen kicked at the cot. 'They're bloody uncomfortable anyway.'

'Well, Mrs Kirkham knows I want to talk to you and there isn't anywhere else.'

Ellen plopped on the bed, giving her a sly glance of amusement as the springs groaned under her weight. Elisabet remained listless. Hester had been told she had a fever, but it looked spent, leaving the girl with a yellow complexion.

'Elisabet?' asked Hester.

The girl raised her head.

'Don't you think you should be in the infirmary if you're sick?'

'It's nothing but the sickness of child. I'll be even sicker if I enter the infirmary. Besides, I can hear the sound of the children next door. It gives me comfort.'

Hester paused. She noticed, among the sounds of the workhouse, the babble of young children not old enough for the schoolroom.

'Who looks after them?'

'Other inmates,' said Ellen.

'But not you?'

'No sense in mixing with children. They don't like to encourage the likes of us. We're not supposed to be happy we're having a baby.'

The bitterness of the girl's words pierced Hester.

'I know this is a place that no one enters voluntarily, but I wanted to see if I can help you in any way.'

Ellen bit a fingernail, looking up at Hester through hair hanging in thin hanks.

'I don't want no charity.'

'I just want to understand a little about your situation.'

This got Ellen's temper up.

'Now you listen to me. I'm not giving my bloody life story to someone who doesn't know her fanny from her donk.'

Elisabet gasped in horror at Ellen's words and Hester felt her face stain in shock.

'Don't mind her,' Elisabet said, suddenly courageous. 'Come and sit next to me. I'd welcome the company.'

Hester moved over to the girl's bed while Ellen looked on.

'Do you remember what you told me the last time I was here?'

'I remember.' The girl spoke hardly louder than a whisper. 'You told someone that I'd mentioned the angelmaker, didn't you?'

'I didn't realise it was such a secret, Elisabet. I'm so sorry.'

'I heard you'd come back here. One of the girls at dinner said you'd been asking after me.'

'I wanted to see if you were well.'

'Well, I'm as you see. This baby is eating away at me from the inside.'

'Then you need to see a doctor.'

The girl shrank. 'Not I. Doctor Bant isn't touching me with his fumbling hands.'

No, thought Hester. That I can understand.

'Why did you come back here?' Elisabet asked.

Hester was propelled by a need to protect this frail girl who looked as if she'd had all of her life force pushed out of her, but wasn't sure how much she could trust Ellen, who was listening intently.

'We have family friends here. When I knew I'd be spending the month in Southwell, I thought I'd pay you a visit.' She found Elisabet's hand and gave it a squeeze.

'She was very annoyed,' said Ellen.

'Who? Mrs Kirkham?'

Elisabet nodded. 'Among her airs and graces, she has a terrible temper on her. Then, when you wrote again this week, she tried to get Mr Kirkham to refuse your visit. Keep you downstairs.'

'Why didn't he?'

'He was overruled by the board.'

'Elisabet. Can't you get in touch with relatives? You said you came over with your uncle's ship the first time. Write them a letter to say you're not thriving here. Children are born on ships. It'll give you a new start, too. You don't have to tell them you weren't married.'

'But I was married. I'm a widow.'

'You were married?' Hester stared at the girl. 'Then what are you doing with the undeserving poor?'

Elisabet stared at the floor.

'When I met my husband, we went back to his village. But there was no work there and any money I earned in the fields, he drank.'

'How did he die?'

'Found dead in a ditch last winter. They think he tripped on his way home from the hostelry and banged his head. He was stiff as a board in the morning.'

Hester frowned, remembering Matthew Alban's flippant words about the drinkers in his inn. They, too, left widows behind who might end up on the parish like Elisabet.

'But—'

'I had nowhere to go, so I moved in with my husband's brother. I already knew I was expecting, but I tried to keep it secret. When he discovered my condition, he turned me out. He didn't want to bring up another's child, even his own nephew. So, there I was. An immoral woman.'

'That's what happens,' piped up Ellen. 'They have their way with us and then we're out on our arses.'

It could have been Susanna sitting in Ellen's place, with less ripe language.

Hester dropped her voice. 'Listen, Elisabet. I need you to tell me more about the angelmaker. She and the pale lady are one and the same, aren't they?'

Was it Hester's imagination or did Ellen freeze?

'Do you remember?'

Elisabet shrank into the bed. 'I remember.'

'Who is she?'

'She's the ghost of a woman who comes at night and steals your babies.'

'A ghost? Do you believe in spectres, Elisabet?'

The girl looked up and nodded. 'And so do you, don't deny it.'

Hester swallowed and nodded. 'You're right, I do. But ghosts don't take real live babies, do they?'

'They do,' she insisted. 'Take them away whether the mothers want it or not.'

Hester looked to Ellen. 'Well?'

'You'll get nothing out of me. My trap is shut. I fancy a hot meal tonight, for a start. Anyhow, no bugger is getting my baby.'

'And Mercy's? What about hers?'

The girls froze.

'What do you mean?' asked Ellen.

'Mercy's baby lived. Don't deny it. I've been told by a former resident.'

The room was silent.

'Well?'

'The angelmaker took her,' whispered Elisabet. 'I wanted to tell you last time, but perhaps it was for the best.'

'Where did she take her?'

'We don't know where they go,' said Ellen. 'So there's no point asking us.'

Hester stood.

'She's not a ghost, is she? She's a living woman who takes children.'

'No,' said Elisabet. 'No.'

'I also learned that Mercy died of childbed fever, not cholera. Why lie about it?'

Ellen shrugged. 'They always say cholera when inmates die suddenly. People don't ask too many questions.'

Hester could have cried in frustration. The girls hinted at so much yet revealed nothing definite.

'You also called her the pale lady. Why this name?'

'She's shrouded in a pale light, but I know what she is. An angelmaker,' said Elisabet.

'No one else calls her that,' said Hester. 'I've heard her called the pale lady but not the angelmaker. Why that name?'

'Watch it,' hissed Ellen. 'You've got nothing to worry about, Elisabet, so why don't you keep your trap shut?'

Confused, Hester glanced at Ellen, but she was looking not at Hester but at Elisabet.

'Why does she say you've nothing to worry about?'

Elisabet grasped her sleeve.

'None of us are safe, despite what she says. I'm in this wing, aren't I, along with the others? Undeserving, they call me, so I'm at their mercy. There's nothing you can do, miss. When the pale lady comes, your baby is taken from you.'

Hester felt the coolness on her cheek. *Ask*, whispered Mercy. *Ask*. 'But who is the pale lady?'

The two girls looked at Hester.

'I don't know, but she's the most fearful thing you'll ever see,' said Elisabet finally.

# Chapter Twenty-Five

The highlight of Hester's stay was to be the apple fair. Southwell was famed, she learned, for its apples, especially the Bramley variety, which was becoming renowned throughout the country as perfect for pies and dumplings. As anticipation grew, everyone at Guy House from Dorothea down to the scullery maid had an opinion on whether or not the day would be fine.

The morning, as it turned out, was overcast, with rain pitting the window, but by midday, the sun was drying the cobbles of the street, to the relief of the servants, who were to be given an afternoon off. Caroline, who had naturally missed the morning's showers, complained that the field where the fair was to be held was a mire.

'What shall I wear? Last year I ruined a good wool dress along the hem. Mud seeped into every fibre. I shan't be doing that again.'

'You could always wear dark grey,' said Hester, aware of her limited wardrobe. 'The mud won't show then.'

Caroline glanced at Hester to see if she was joking.

'I don't want to depress myself. I'll find a dress from last year that will be suitable. Which reminds me. Mother's asked for me to look out some dresses to pass down to you. Do you have any colours in mind? Please don't say grey.'

'If I'm to keep them, they'll have to pass muster in Bristol. Light brown or a pale lavender, perhaps.'

'I'm sure I'll be able to find something. Leave it with me.'

Dorothea had woken with a slight fever and said she couldn't accompany the pair of them, trying hard to hide her disappointment.

'I've been every year since I was a child. I don't suppose a break this year will make any difference.'

Hester was shocked to see dark circles ringing Dorothea's eyes. As she'd got to know her hostess, she agreed with Ruth's assessment that widowhood was unlikely to suit her, as right now she showed every sign of continuing to grieve for her dead husband.

'Would you like me to ask Edward to visit you? Perhaps a tonic will help.'

'No, Hester, I don't think that'll be necessary. I didn't sleep well, that's all.'

They took the trap to the field. Hester would rather have walked with the steady stream of pedestrians making their way to the fair, but Caroline was adamant she didn't want to be out in the damp weather. Her chosen dress was light coffee brown with huge leg-of-mutton sleeves.

'That's unlikely to hide any stains,' commented Hester.

'I don't care. It's last year's.'

Caroline drove the trap with the same confidence as her mother, ignoring the stares as they passed. As they approached the field, she happily queued with the other carriages as the crowds passed them in high spirits. When they reached the main gate, Caroline handed the carriage to a waiting boy and gave Hester a friendly shove.

'Go on. If we lose sight of each other, we'll meet under the oak. Do try to let your hair down.'

Hester was assailed by a riot of music, cries of pleasure and the babble of the crowd. The fair might have been held to celebrate apples, but the stalls groaned under the weight of pies, loaves of bread and huge shanks of ham. While trading was brisk, the people had come not only to stock their larders, but also to play games. The first she encountered involved a pig running up and down a pen while men tried to catch it. They were ineffectual, grabbing at it helplessly while it squealed with displeasure.

'They grease the tail,' whispered Caroline. 'Whoever catches the pig wins it, but it's no easy task.'

Hester pulled a face, making Caroline laugh.

'Do you like horses?' asked Caroline.

'Not especially. Why?'

'There's racing at the bottom of the field. Shall we take a look?'

They moved past a chestnut stand, where roasted nuts were being distributed in small paper cones.

'There's Edward,' said Caroline, but he'd already spotted them, weaving through the crowd towards them. 'Not with your patients today? They shall feel neglected, I'm sure.'

'Most of my patients are here,' he said, smiling. 'So why shouldn't I be, too?'

He looked younger out in the open air, his manner more relaxed.

'Quite right,' said Caroline. 'Come with us to see the race.'

It was the most popular attraction, the crowd cheering as hooves clattered and money changed hands.

'Are you all right with a wager?' asked Edward. 'I know Quakers don't approve of such pleasures.'

'Of course. As long as you're not hoping I'll place a coin on the horse myself.'

Hester smiled to soften her words, but her eyes were on the figure she hadn't expected to see. She'd assumed Matthew Alban would be busy at the inn, but he was following the progress of a dark grey stallion racing towards the finishing line.

Becoming aware of her scrutiny, he turned and glanced at her companion, his expression hardening. Neither of her friends noticed him, their eyes on the next group of horses to race. She moved away from them, refusing to let Matthew's scowl over-shadow her day. While most of the fair-goers had their eyes on the race, in the distance stood a figure – the woman who had asked Hester to find her baby while grasping the very child she was seeking. Seeing the girl, Hester could have cried with relief. Here, at least, was proof the girl wasn't a shadowing. She was flesh and blood, standing apart from the crowds. Seeing Edward and Caroline still transfixed by the horses, Hester slipped away and approached the girl.

'Remember me?'

The girl's eyes were unfocused as she turned.

'Do you have news?' She took a step back. 'Do you have news of my baby?'

Hester saw that, once more, the child was in her arms.

'It's there.' Hester pointed at the child. 'The child you look for is there.'

'No,' whispered the girl. 'Not her.'

Hester frowned. 'Did you have another child?'

'Taken away and slaughtered like the innocents.'

Hester swallowed, her mouth dry. 'Slaughtered? What do you mean?'

The girl moved in closer, holding on tighter to her baby.

'I've heard she's buried in the potter's field with the others, but I can't find them.'

'Potter's field?' asked Hester.

The girl spun round on her heels, the baby rocking precariously.

'I'm sure it's around here. A girl mentioned the apple fair. I think the potter's field is just beyond. Can you help me?'

Hester looked at the crowds to the east of her and the wide fields stretching into the distance. The music of the fair had dulled, the piper muted and the drummer quietened.

'I can't see anything.'

The girl looked bone-weary, her lank hair stuck to her face. She shook her head in defeat.

'What's your name?'

The girl shrank back. 'Lizzie.'

'Were you in the Union? Is that where your baby was taken from?'

The girl's eyes focused and she took in Hester's appearance.

'You keep away from my baby. You won't have him. You stay away.'

'What—?'

A crowd of revellers approached, one waving an apple branch, and Lizzie was subsumed into the throng. Hester tried to keep her eyes on the wraithlike girl but lost her as she was carried away. Lizzie was a living spectre, not one of the dead, she realised. Never before in her sightings had one of the visions spoken to her.

She returned to Edward and Caroline, who were cheering the runners, although both admitted to losing their stake. Caroline spotted a friend and took her leave of them.

'Edward will show you the rest of the fair. He won't mind.'

And with that, she was gone.

The physician flashed Hester a look of exasperation at Caroline's knowing tone.

'Let's enjoy ourselves, shall we? There will be no gambling, but you are allowed to have fun, aren't you?'

'Of course.' Hester's mind was still on Lizzie. 'I've seen a girl around town holding a baby, asking where her other child is. A pauper. Do you know of her?'

Edward made a face. 'Possibly. I might have seen her on the street. She's not causing you trouble, is she?'

Trouble? Trouble was already here.

'It doesn't matter. Let's explore. Now, I've always been fascinated by tales of the Aunt Sally. Do you think they'll have one here?'

'I'm sure of it.'

The game was more macabre than she'd anticipated. A lifelike head had been modelled out of a turnip to resemble an old woman complete with clay pipe. As Hester threw a stick at it, she was reminded of the elderly woman at the workhouse and felt a wash of shame. The pleasure in being out in the late-summer sun with an attentive companion, however, chased away any melancholy. Edward was recognised by everyone, raising his hat continually but remaining attentive to Hester. Only when the mayor passed, recognisable by his chain of office, did he stop and Hester took the opportunity to admire a stall filled with an assortment of birds in gilt cages.

'Fancy a sparrow, Quaker Jane?' asked a voice in her ear.

She refused to give him the satisfaction of showing surprise.

'I prefer them in the fresh air.'

'So do I. Shall we set them free?'

'No.' She turned in alarm and saw the look of amusement in Matthew's face.

'I'm only jesting. I should be up before the magistrate if I did that. Are you enjoying your visit here?'

'Some of it,' said Hester, turning to check on Edward, who was still speaking to the mayor.

'I see you've made the physician's acquaintance.' Matthew looked over to Edward, his face unreadable.

'He's a friend of the Francombes. Do you know him?'

'Of him, I do. He was cast out from his family, I heard.'

Hester frowned. 'Cast out? I heard there was an estrangement. Do you know why?'

'Just rumour.'

Hester waited for him to elaborate, but his eyes were on the mayor.

'I don't know him well, so it might be idle tittle-tattle. I've no need of a doctor and, if I had, it wouldn't be him.'

'Why ever not?'

Matthew smiled. 'Too expensive.'

Hester couldn't tell if he was teasing.

'Tell me. How well do you know the workhouse?'

She saw his face close and he moved away from her.

'Hasn't your business there finished?'

'In relation to my sister, yes. But I've been given permission to visit.'

'Visit?'

She saw him take a step back.

'What the hell do you want to visit there for? I knew you were up to your do-gooding.'

Hester felt her temper rise.

'I'll visit whoever I want.'

'You don't know what you're meddling with.'

'Then tell me. What am I meddling with? Is it the spectre of the pale lady?'

He scowled at her, all humour gone.

'Spectre? That's the least of your worries. Stay away from . . .'

He stopped as Edward approached them.

'Sorry to desert you, Hester. The mayor does like to monopolise my attention.' He turned to Matthew. 'Mr Alban. I'm surprised the inn isn't keeping you busy.'

'It is.'

Hester watched as he stalked across the field and back towards town.

# Chapter Twenty-Six

It was the thing Matthew dreaded most and it came around three in the morning. A loud hammering on the front door of the inn. He wasn't asleep. The Quaker girl's news that she was visiting the Union workhouse had crawled under his skin and left him restless in his bed. He knew he wouldn't be able to sleep, which meant he'd left the inn open longer than usual, a card game of euchre taking place in the corner extending well past midnight. Doctor Bant had drunk too much ale and had begged a bed for the night, which Matthew had reluctantly given him, helping the old sot up the wooden stairs and onto his bed.

Matthew pulled on his breeches at the sound of the knock and threw on a jacket that still smelled of the fair. He kept his weight behind the door as he opened it and a knife in his unseen hand.

'Who is it?'

'Heggs, the porter at the workhouse.'

Matthew gripped the knife tighter and held fast to the door.

'What do you want?'

'The doctor. He's not at his rooms. The woman who lives below said he was drinking here.'

'What's the problem?'

There was silence behind the door, the man possibly wondering how much to reveal.

'A girl. Found hanging. She still breathes.'

Matthew swung open the door.

'Take a look at the physic and see how much help he'll be for you.'

Heggs followed on his heels as Matthew retraced the steps he'd taken an hour or so earlier. Matthew opened the door and indicated the physician sprawled on the bed.

'Think he'll be much use?'

'Jesus.' Heggs kicked the man. 'The girl's already half-dead – this one will finish her off.'

The physician let off a hefty snore.

'I'll leave him.'

Matthew followed the man back down the stairs.

'Would the Kirkhams consider another doctor?'

He thought with distaste of the man who had accompanied the Quaker girl that day.

'They won't want anyone else inside the building – too many questions.'

The men's eyes met.

'There's Edward Holland.'

'I've heard he'll go where there's money,' agreed the man. 'But that's not the case here, is it?'

Matthew opened the door and the cold night came rushing in.

'Will the girl live without medical help?'

Heggs shrugged. 'Who knows. She put the rope around her neck herself. The outcome of these things is never clear.'

'Was she with child?'

'Still. There are two lives to try to save.'

Matthew looked at the man. 'I have no medical training. I can't help. Perhaps a midwife . . .'

Heggs glanced in the direction of the workhouse. Impossible to see in the dark night.

'She'll probably already be dead, stupid bitch. Come all this way from Sweden, too, and she ends up at the Union. Not much of a new life.'

'Why do you think she did it?' asked Matthew, his throat dry.

The man shrugged. 'Don't make sense. She was a widow – the bairn would have been looked after.'

'What do you mean?'

Heggs shook himself. 'Never mind me. Thank you for your time.' Tipping his hat, he was off.

# Chapter Twenty-Seven

Hester was dressing when a maid appeared in her chamber, clutching a note.

'From The Black Griffin, ma'am. A young boy brought it round.'

Hester frowned in the mirror where she was fixing her hair.

'A note for me?'

She opened the envelope and saw the words written in Joan's hand:

> A girl is dead in the workhouse by suicide. The child she was carrying is lost, too. Matthew will kill me if he finds out I've written. They're burying her this morning.

Hester pulled on her boots and wrapped the warmest shawl she possessed around her for the journey to The Black Griffin. The courtyard of the inn was busy. A lumbering wagon had arrived and its goods swayed perilously as the horses were changed. Hester slipped past Matthew to find Joan in the kitchen, peeling turnips for the pot.

'What made you write to me?'

'Matthew was in a foul temper after seeing you at the fair. Said you'd been visiting the women there. I thought you'd want to know about the death.'

'Do you know which girl it is?'

'She was from Sweden, the porter said.'

'Elisabet.' Hester dropped into a chair. 'How did you find out?'

'The doctor slept here last night. Couldn't stand on his own two feet. The girl was alive then, of course. By the time he'd sobered up, it was too late.'

'Doctor Bant? I can't imagine him able to do much while sober. Did he eventually go?'

'Aye. Not much point, but he went this morning. Was back within the half-hour to say the girl had died.' Joan looked over her shoulder and lowered her voice. 'So I wrote you the note.'

'When Matthew told you I'd been visiting, did he say why?'

'Interfering, according to him. I've heard you've been asking about the women with babies.'

'How do you know that? I never said that to him.'

'He might not know. It's inn talk I've overheard. You go to the workhouse and you have a special interest in the women with child.'

So, she was the topic of discussion at the inn. That didn't bode well, as it seemed the Kirkhams had their ear to the ground when it came to town gossip.

'My sister went a similar way,' said Hester. 'Not by her own hand, but her baby supposedly died with her.'

Joan pulled a chair from the table and sat next to her.

'What's going on?'

'I don't know. The women talk of a pale lady – a spectre, they say – who takes their babies.'

'Nonsense.' Joan's chin wobbled in indignation. 'You don't believe that.' She paused at Hester's face. 'Do you?'

'I'm not sure. There are children at the workhouse – I've heard their babble. But at the same time, the women are scared of someone. It's probably a real person. Ghosts can't actually take babies, can they?'

'They say the Swedish girl's mind was gone. She was in desperate straits by all accounts.'

Hester remembered Elisabet's conviction that she was being eaten from within.

'She was terrified of her child being taken. I wonder if the illness affected her mind.'

'Well, she's at peace now.'

'I hope so.' Hester drew her shawl tighter. 'How did you know they were burying her today?'

'The gravedigger was in here as soon as we were open. He likes to fortify himself against the dead before he starts digging.'

'What time's the funeral?'

Joan snorted. 'Funeral? They'll open up a grave, put her in the ground and that's it. There won't be no funeral.'

'Then I'll go to the church.'

'She won't be buried in the main plot. That's consecrated ground.'

'Then where will she lie?'

'At the boundary on the north side. The vicar's a strange one and that's no mistake. I keep a wide berth from him. But he allows everyone a burial in his grounds. Suicide or not, she was a lost soul and she deserves her eternal rest.'

'There's no potter's field where they bury suicides in the town?'

Joan looked at her in astonishment.

'Potter's field? Suicides? Who'd have thought a sober-looking girl such as you would have such an imagination. She'll be buried in the churchyard within sight of everyone else.'

Joan sent word to the driver of the death cart that he was to pick up a mourner at The Black Griffin and, within half an hour, the wagon came into view. The cart carried a single shrouded body lying on a layer of straw.

'They've surely not brought her here.'

'There are to be two burials today,' Joan said. 'Quicker to put them in the ground at the same time.'

Hester followed the corpse to the workhouse, the ancient horse taking its time through the streets. Was there ever anything more depressing than an autumn burial? wondered Hester. At least in winter, the weather matches your mood. No such fortitude on a cool autumnal day with only a hint of melancholy in the air. The weak sun blinded her vision as she picked her way to the gate of the workhouse.

'Wait there,' the man said over his shoulder as he disappeared towards a small building where Elisabet's body must have been laid to rest.

Hester stopped, glad to be on the periphery of the workhouse grounds. She pressed back against a tree and watched as a woman beat a large rug, clouds of dust exploding into the air. Through the haze, a child came coughing. No, not a child but Little Pinch. Hester gave a low whistle and the girl looked around her in surprise.

'Over here. It's me, Hester.'

The girl looked over her shoulder and came to join her.

'You'll never guess.'

'Elisabet is dead, I know.'

Little Pinch gaped at her. 'How did you find out?'

'A servant at The Black Griffin sent me a note. The porter went there to look for the doctor who was sleeping off his sore head. Why do you think she did it?'

The girl tapped her head. 'Lost it, hadn't she? Thought her baby would be taken, but it was never going to happen to her.'

Hester frowned. 'Why not?'

The girl stepped back.

'Stands to reason. You just ain't worked it out yet.'

'Tell me!'

But the girl had hurried off at the sound of the death cart, which came into view with the slight figure of Elisabet wrapped in a workhouse-branded sheet next to the original corpse. The driver whipped the pony past her.

'Wait,' Hester shouted after him. 'I'm coming with you to the church.'

They entered the gate of the churchyard and Hester saw the sexton already there, his gravedigger's shovel over his shoulder. At the sound of the cart, the parson emerged from the porch and came over to meet them. In the outside air, Reverend Flint had lost some of his malevolence but none of his decrepitude. His off-white surplice was stained with egg yolk and coffee spills. The cart stopped in front of a large pit and the corpse from town was taken from the cart.

The parson was determined to get through the ceremony quickly. Hester was unfamiliar with the words that slipped over his tongue but, in any case, they were meaningless in his bored monotone. When he'd finished, the cart moved on to the per-imeter of the graveyard. There was no boundary wall – just a small ditch to represent the edge of consecrated ground. Elisabet, wrapped in a winding sheet, was lowered into a single grave. The priest said nothing. No full burial rites for a suicide. In her head, Hester incanted a phrase she knew well: The truest end of life, is to know the life that never ends.

The driver of the death cart departed, his job completed, as the sexton moved in to fill in the grave. Hester, desperate to avoid a view of the hole in the ground, moved away and called to the parson.

'I'm still looking for my sister's resting place. I'd like to say a few words over it.'

The parson stopped but didn't turn.

'Still asking your questions. Talk to the sexton if you must.'

She watched him limp back to his congregation of straw.

The sexton had stopped infilling Elisabet's grave and was listening to the conversation.

'Well?' she asked him. 'Did you bury a girl from the workhouse last month?'

The sexton leaned on his spade.

'She's over there . . .' He nodded at a patch of grass, unmarked except for undulating hollows. 'I buried her myself. We don't get many workhouse deaths in September. It's the cold season that finishes them off.'

'Over here?' Hester stepped through headstones to where the sexton was pointing. 'Are there many others buried here, too?'

'Of course, but your sister's in there at peace. I couldn't choose a better spot myself.'

'Was there a baby buried with her?'

'Baby?' The man licked his lips. 'I don't know anything about that. She were shrouded. I don't look too closely.'

'There will be a burial record for her in the church, though, won't there? It'll say if a child was buried, too.'

'I don't know anything about that, either. Records aren't my province.'

'No, of course they aren't. I'm sorry.'

Hester looked down at the grass, wondering if Mercy held a child in her arms, like Lizzie at the apple fair. If she did, then Hester would let them rest in peace, ignoring the sly rumours of the pale lady. It was a mystery she was unlikely to solve by herself, she saw.

A gust of wind swept across the graveyard and Mercy stood opposite, her face stricken.

'Is she there?' Hester whispered.

'I just told you – I buried her myself.' The sexton sounded put out.

'I'm sorry.' He must think her mad. 'I'd like to order a gravestone. A small one will suffice. Can you direct me to the right person?'

The sexton began throwing earth back in again with his spade, his flagon of ale no doubt calling to him.

'There's a stonemason in town. Do you know The Black Griffin pub?'

Hester nodded. 'I know it.'

'Go down the alley next to it. The stonemason can be found to the rear of the premises.' He looked her up and down. 'Do you have a man to accompany you?'

'I do not. I shall go by myself.'

'As you wish.'

The sexton clearly felt he'd done his Christian duty by warning Hester and he picked his way across the graveyard to the inside of the church.

Disheartened, Hester gave her sister's resting place a final look and headed back to town.

# Chapter Twenty-Eight

Hester trudged towards the main street, across the quagmire marked by horse dung stinking in the sun. It soiled the bottom of her dress – she'd need to give it a wash, as Caroline hadn't donated any of her old gowns as promised. Feeling filthy and sweaty, she arrived at The Black Griffin to see Matthew in his shirtsleeves sweeping the pavement outside.

'Good to see you doing that yourself,' she said, unable to stop herself. 'I thought it might be a job for a stable boy.' I sound like Amos, she thought.

'I'm not afraid of hard work, if that's what you mean. What's the matter, Quaker Jane? You look in a bad mood.'

'I've been to a burial, so I've no temper for your insults today.'

Matthew stopped brushing.

'The girl who died at the workhouse?'

'Elisabet, yes. I hear you were roused in the night to try to help.'

'The porter wanted the medic – or as much use he'd be to the girl.' He paused. 'Who told you she'd died?'

'A note was sent. It came as a shock.'

At least she was able to keep Joan's secret.

'Do they know why she did it?'

Hester shook her head. 'She was ill in mind when I last saw her. She couldn't answer any of my questions.'

'Questions?' Matthew's voice was sharp. 'What questions were you asking?'

Hester looked at him, wishing she hadn't used that phrase.

'Just about how everyone is treated.'

She saw him relax slightly.

'Anyhow, what can we do for you inside The Black Griffin today? Have you come to sample our ale?'

Hester, bone-weary, ignored his mocking tone.

'I'm looking for the stonemason at the rear of your hostelry. I want him to do a small job for me.'

'Old Henry? His workshop is over there . . .' He nodded to the passage next to the inn. 'You're not planning on going there alone, are you?'

'Of course. If you're concerned, you can stand guard to make sure no one follows me down.'

He was at her side in an instant.

'It's not who might follow you down that I'm concerned about, it's who might be already there. You'll see for yourself.'

Together they entered the dank, foul-smelling alley, where drunks lay in various states of inebriation.

'Why do you serve them ale if you know they're going to end up here?'

'What would you prefer me to do? Only serve customers who I know have a warm bed to go to? What's happened to your egalitarian principles, Quaker Jane?'

'I've seen enough families ruined by beer.'

'Have you now.'

His voice mocked in her ear.

'Well, if it wasn't for my inn, it would be another. That's the point. They can't help themselves.'

They'd reached the end of the passage and entered a room where the air grew less fetid, infused with the scent of sawdust and flint. The man who turned to greet them was hideously disfigured, one eye pulled down into his cheek and the skin on his neck aflame with the unmistakable markings of a burning. Hester slid her gaze away, but not before spotting that one of his ears had fused to the side of his head. She felt Matthew's hand on her back, urging her forwards.

'He's a good man. He can't hear very well, that's all. You'll have to shout.'

Hester looked round. There was a small, mean window at the top of the room and she stepped towards it so the man could see her face. She took off her bonnet, aware that her hair was stuck to her scalp from her walk from the church.

'I'd like to order a gravestone to be placed in the churchyard near the workhouse.'

The man could lip-read, she saw.

'A stone? I thought Quakers shunned all grave markers.'

'Times are changing,' she answered, with a glance at Matthew. 'I'd like it simple, though. Plain stone with just a name.'

'Limestone is a good choice,' said Matthew behind her. 'It carves easily and looks honest.'

Hester turned to the stonemason.

'Limestone sounds what I want. It won't be expensive, will it?'

The man shook his head. 'I'll do it for you at a good price.'

'The sexton will direct you to the plot of land where my sister lies. Ask him where he buried the Quaker's sister. He'll know what you mean.'

'Try to catch him when he's sober,' said Matthew.

'It'll be an approximation of where she's buried, but I'd like the grave marked. Can you do it before I leave? I'd like something to tell my mother about when I return.'

'When do you go?' asked Matthew.

'Before the month is out.'

'Good.'

He really was infuriating.

'Will there be an inscription?' asked the stonemason.

'My sister's name was Mercy Goodwin. She had a baby. Only . . .'

'Only what?' asked Matthew.

Could she say? Could she tell these two men in this fuggy room with the smell of rot just outside the door the secret she was holding close to herself – that the baby might not be in the shallow grave? She shook her head.

'I was told the baby was buried with my sister, but I have no name.'

'I can put Mercy Goodwin and child.'

Hester hesitated then nodded.

'Thank you.'

She shook the man's hand and he sighed.

'Always girls,' he said.

Hester moved away from the window into the darkness so they wouldn't see her face.

'What do you mean, always girls?'

Henry came forwards and laid a hand on hers, his touch surprisingly gentle.

'Other girls. Gone.'

'You mean they've died?'

Matthew moved forwards.

'Pay no attention to him.'

'Then what did he mean?' Hester asked. 'Henry, what other girls?'

Hester saw a look pass between the two men and to her frustration, Henry shook his head.

'Nothing. Bad place for women, that's all.'

He would say no more.

'What happened to his face?' she asked Matthew after they emerged into the passage.

She could see he was anxious to leave. He'd made sure she was safely in and out of the stonemason's but now he wanted rid of her.

'He was doing a job on a church. There was a fire that started above ground and the damage you see is the result.'

'Is that his main work? Making headstones?'

'He's employed by the minster. The church will employ him, but builders prefer him not to work on houses. They say he brings bad luck. Superstitious rubbish. The dead, however, can't complain, can they?'

No, they can't, Hester thought, but they can have someone complain for them.

# Chapter Twenty-Nine

Hester hurried back to the Francombes' to change before the afternoon's music recital. It would be a new experience. Amos had considered such pastimes not only a grievous waste of anyone's time, but also an act close to consorting with the Devil. It should have been an exciting trip, but Hester could summon no enthusiasm for the afternoon.

She was beginning to understand the wide gulf between the life the Francombes led and that of those confined to the workhouse. It had never occurred to her before. In Bristol, her own life was one of pared living and self-sacrifice. When she visited the poor, she never felt that she might be an affront to those in need.

When she arrived in her chamber, two dresses had been laid out on the bed. One was a lavender and another a more severe navy. Hester felt an attack of conscience when she saw the care that had been taken to choose the gowns. Both were muted and sober and would do her well when she returned to Bristol. She wondered if it was the hand of Dorothea or Caroline behind the choice. After washing, she tried on the navy and, although a little long, it made her other clothes look like rags.

Dorothea came in and clapped her hands.

'My dear, it fits you like a glove.'

'It's very kind of you.'

'Think nothing of it. Navy, I can see, suits you far better than me. Only . . .'

'Only what?'

'You've dressed a little early. The recital isn't until four. You've missed lunch, but I'll get a tray sent up to you and you can rest before we leave.'

After she'd left, Hester groaned. The thought of staying in her room for a few hours was intolerable. Whenever she shut her eyes, she was assailed by images of first the grave and then the foul passage to the stonemason's. She'd never sleep. As she expected, silence descended over Guy House, Caroline and Dorothea resting after their lunch and the servants tiptoeing about their business. Giving up on rest, Hester rose and changed back into her drab grey gown and sensible boots to take a walk around town.

Once out in the street, she was paralysed by indecision. There was nothing more depressing than an aimless walk. She struck away from her usual route past The Black Griffin to the workhouse, heading instead towards the south of the town. She was unsurprised to see she was in one of the wealthy streets. The rich, she found, looked after their own and huddled together. Even the passages and side streets were immaculate, swept clean that morning and swabbed down with water from the river.

Her pursuer was back, she saw. A shadow following her, more noticeable when she strayed off the main street. It wasn't just the sensation this time, but also an echo of footsteps heard just behind her. Twice she stopped and the tip-tap of clogs also stilled. It was a sound she only heard in the workhouse, where the metal soles clanged on wood and concrete.

*Is it you, Mercy?* she asked, but she knew it couldn't be.

Mercy appeared beside her, not on her trail. This was a lost soul, telling her she mustn't give up her quest.

After an hour or so, she realised she was lost. Even the minster was out of sight and she had no landmark to gain her bearings.

She wondered what the time was. The clock had struck two thirty as she was leaving the house and she must have been wandering for nearly an hour. She'd miss the recital unless she hurried. She passed a row of tall town houses that radiated solidity and affluence. Outside one was Edward's phaeton, recognisable by its glossy green carriage.

She hurried on, crossing to the other side of the street. She didn't want him to see her loitering as if she were following his movements. She'd hoped she might manage to avoid detection, but the front door opened and Edward emerged, hat in hand as he took leave of a woman weeping into her handkerchief.

Hester saw only a glimpse of the woman's face, suffused with grief. Someone must be sick in the house, although the woman's cries weren't of anguish but hysteria. A sudden accident, perhaps. Hester pushed onwards, taking a turning towards the river and hurrying to return to Guy House. She heard the sound of hooves approaching and Edward's gig pulled up beside her.

'This is a surprise. Why did you rush away when you saw me?'

'I decided to take myself for a walk but I got a little lost. I didn't want to impose on your professional life.'

'Why don't you climb up? I'll take you home. That's what happens when you wander around town unaccompanied.'

He reached down a hand and pulled Hester up beside him. She felt his body heat – the temperature of a fever – but she didn't dare ask him if he was poorly. The horse trotted over the cobbles, swishing its tail in contentment.

'The lady of the house seemed upset.'

He glanced at her. 'I can't discuss my patients, Hester.'

Hester flushed, rebuked.

'Of course not. I'm sorry.'

'It's no matter, don't worry. Nothing that a trip to the countryside won't cure.'

'For the lady?'

'Exactly. Just what the doctor ordered.'

He seemed amused at his joke but didn't share it with Hester. He dropped her at Guy House without coming in, which put Caroline, who had been watching from the window, in a temper.

'I hope you don't intend to monopolise Edward during your stay. You may have caught his eye, but I need companionship, too.'

'We met in the street, that's all. He gave me a ride as I was running late.'

Her words didn't mollify Caroline, who remained in a foul mood despite the attempts of the players at the recital to lull them with Schubert. By the end, Hester was bored. She'd often lamented the fact that she wasn't allowed to attend concerts and now she realised what she'd missed – nothing. Music allowed too many thoughts of past hurts to intrude. Amos's blows, Ruth's refusal to stand up to her husband, her own suppressed visions. Above all, sitting in that ornate room, the hurt of Mercy's leaving came back to her.

Hester recalled the shock of abandonment when she realised Mercy had run away. It wasn't the same outrage at the elopement that had afflicted Amos and Ruth. It was the fact that Mercy hadn't trusted her enough to tell her of her plans. She'd left without saying goodbye, and that was almost impossible to bear. And yet, the old alliance and affection held firm. Even if Mercy's shadowing hadn't appeared, Hester thought she'd still be here in Southwell.

They returned to Guy House in the dark, the horse splashing rainwater up at her new dress. Caroline pleaded a headache, saying she needed to lie down. Hester, not cowed by her friend's bad temper, sat in the drawing room reading until she was joined by Dorothea.

'What's the matter with Caroline? She seems to be out of sorts,' asked Dorothea.

Hester laid down her copy of *Ivanhoe*.

'I'm to blame. Edward gave me a lift home today and it upset her. I'll refuse next time.'

'You'll do nothing of the sort. Caroline doesn't like to be left out of things, that's all. Where did you see Edward?'

The words were issued casually, but Hester thought Dorothea was listening intently to her answer.

'A street towards the south of the town. Trinity Place, I think its name was. I'm afraid I got lost. When I saw the phaeton, I tried to pass by unnoticed, but Edward saw me.'

'Edward's a very observant young man. Trinity Place? Well, I know that Edward is the physician to Mrs Hill. She must still be having the crying fits.'

'There was a woman crying.'

'Don't distress yourself, dear. Mrs Hill has been the same after each of her children.'

'They died?' asked Hester.

Am I ever to get away from dead children? she thought wearily.

'Don't be morbid, dear. Of course not. Some women simply fall to pieces after childbirth.' She paused, glancing quickly at Hester. 'I wasn't too well myself.'

'A depression?'

'Something like that.'

'And her children are well?'

'Of course. Sent out to the country to be weaned. Her youngest will be sitting on a healthy peasant's breast as we speak.'

'She's crying because she misses them, perhaps.'

Dorothea sighed. 'I wish sometimes I had your view of people. I don't think Mrs Hill is in any hurry for her children to return. Of course, they'll have to come back once they start to speak. Mrs Hill won't want her children with country accents.

'It's different for the lower classes, of course. Married women keep their babies with them, although unwanted children of single women have to be found permanent foster homes to enable the mother to continue to work. There are arrangements that can be made. A poor family in need of extra income might be persuaded, with the promise of regular fees, to take in another's child. It's accepted all around the world, especially in the Low Countries. What's the matter, dear?'

'Permanently foster in the Low Countries?' Hester frowned.

'Have I said something?' asked Dorothea.

'It's nothing.'

Hester smiled at her host, seeing again the signs of weeping. But her mind was working furiously at an idea that had planted its seed in her head.

# Chapter Thirty

The nightmares were back with a vengeance and, for the first time, Hester dreamed of the two terrors in the same night. When she slipped into a shallow slumber after turning out the light, she was in the pit. It wasn't a nameless grave, however, but one that belonged to her. Dug ready for her body.

She jerked awake as the first clod of earth hit her face, fumbling for the candle to bring a sliver of light into her darkness. The sound of activity from the servants in the house reassured her that it wasn't yet properly night and she'd fallen back to sleep, grateful she'd done battle with her dark demon early.

But much later, her second night terror came. The fire, the burning flames and the searing pain. As she scrambled awake, she realised she'd forgotten to blow out her candle, which had reduced to a useless nub. The deep blackness of the autumn morning provided no reassurance.

Lying in bed, she formulated a plan. The days were speeding by and soon she'd have to make plans to return to Bristol. Despite her desolation in the churchyard, she decided she owed Mercy one final effort to discover what had happened to her baby, and she'd start by paying a surprise visit to the workhouse. Saturday wasn't her day for visits, but she was tired of the orchestrated meetings.

The porter, Heggs, gave Hester a hateful look as she passed his booth, slamming the door with the toe of his boot. She crossed the hall to the kitchen, where Little Pinch was doing battle with a pile of pigs' trotters. Hester felt her stomach somersault at the sight.

'Good morning.' She didn't know the girl's first name and she couldn't bring herself to call the girl Pinch. 'I see you're hard at work. Are you well?'

'No. Found out I'm expecting, haven't I.'

'I heard. Mrs Kirkham told me.'

Little Pinch shot her a look of disgust.

'You're in the best place for your situation. Perhaps we could talk once I've visited the women in the dormitory.'

'No point going upstairs. They ain't there.'

The girl brought a cleaver down on one of the hooves.

'What do you mean?'

'It's roll call, ain't it. Every morning we's all lined up and given our tasks for the day. Those who are fit for it, I mean.'

'Roll call?'

'That's right. I've heard some workhouses count 'em at dinner, but we can't do that here on account as we have no dining room.'

'Where do you eat, then?'

'In the day rooms and the central hall. It's a fault with the building, the master says. Badly designed. Anyway, when they want to do a head count, everyone goes outside near the stables.'

'Why have I not noticed the roll call?'

'You come afterwards, don't you. By ten o'clock, everyone has been counted.' She stopped and placed the cleaver on the table. 'What's you doing here on a Saturday, anyhow?'

Hester hesitated, wondering how much to confide.

'There's something I want to ask the women. How long will the count take?'

'As long as it takes.' Little Pinch winked at her. 'You'll just have to talk to me, won't you?'

'You didn't have to join them?'

Hester took off her bonnet and settled next to the range, feeling its heat on her back.

'I'm counted. They know I'm here and someone has to prepare the food.'

'Pigs' trotters for lunch?'

'Don't be daft. Meat's for evening. It's pea soup for lunch, which ain't popular. The young ones don't like peas. They'd rather have kettle stew.'

'Kettle s—'

'Hot water. Anyhow, they can't have it. It's pea soup or nothing. Some of them choose nothing.' She picked up the cleaver and regarded the bloodied blade. 'Then there are them who don't like a decent trotter, either. No pleasing some people.'

'How old are you, um, Little Pinch?'

'Fourteen.'

'And your real name?'

'Little Pinch is what I've always been known as.' She lifted the blade for the next blow.

'And how did you get here?'

'I'm an orphan. Lost my father in a weaving accident. Got his arm stuck in the machinery and he bled to death. My ma died of the coughing sickness. Consumption. I was fourteen – old enough to work, but no one decent would have me on account of my height.'

'It doesn't stop you doing jobs, does it? I've seen how hard you work here.'

'Try telling that to the housekeepers where I was trying for work. They saw me as unlucky. Deformed. So if a decent household wouldn't have me, I had to go somewhere less respectable.' She stopped. 'My old master was responsible for this.' She pointed to her stomach with the tip of the cleaver, causing Hester to wince. 'That's what you wanted to know, wasn't it? Who got me in this way?'

There was no accusation in the girl's words.

'You don't mind being branded undeserving by the rules of the workhouse?'

Little Pinch shrugged. 'Deserving, undeserving. It's all the same to me.'

'But the dormitory?'

'What about it?'

'A coldness, the stifling of all air. It suffocates me to be there. Don't you feel it?'

Little Pinch picked up a pile of prepared trotters and dropped them in a bowl.

'Maybe.'

'And the pale lady?'

Hester had expected more tales of spectres and lights, but Little Pinch took her question seriously.

'Seen her twice. Never want to see her again. When a baby is born, I shut my eyes tight and stuff my ears. If the lady wants to come, so be it, but I ain't looking.'

'Aren't you scared for when your time comes?'

'She'll get nowhere near my bairn. I've got plans.'

The girl contemplated the blade of her knife.

'A cleaver doesn't frighten spectres. But she's not a ghost, is she?'

'Don't know what you mean.'

'I think she frightens you and you've every right to be scared, but she's not a ghost. Who is it who takes the children? Is Mrs Kirkham the pale lady?'

'Her?' scoffed Little Pinch. 'The only thing I'm frightened of is the back of her hand.'

'Listen.' Hester looked around to see if any of the inmates had returned from the count. 'When the pale lady takes the babies, what do the mothers do?'

'They wail, scream. What do you think they do?'

'Are they crying because they don't want their children taken or are they frightened of what'll happen to them?' Hester remembered Mrs Hill's tears. 'There are some women who send their children out to the country to be fostered while they're weaned. They come back to their own homes when they begin to speak.'

'I know that.'

'For working women, the arrangement is more permanent. Children taken to be fostered until they're of age. Do you think that's who the pale lady might be? A woman taking children to a better life?'

'What? Out of the kindness of her heart?'

Hester recoiled at the harshness in Little Pinch's voice.

'No, of course not.' She remembered Dorothea's words. 'The children are fostered in return for a payment. Have you heard of this?'

'And where would they get their money from? We're paupers, aren't we?'

Little Pinch turned away, but not before Hester saw the flash of fear in her face.

'But you have heard something. What if someone sent you money, in an envelope, for example?'

Hester was beginning to think this was exactly what Amos had done. Susanna had spoken of taking a letter addressed to Nottingham. Amos hadn't completely given up on his daughter but had sent money to Mercy so that she could give away her child. He'd have seen it as an act of charity.

'You think that's what happened with Mercy? But her child's dead. Buried alongside her, that's what Mrs Kirkham told us girls.'

'Her child lived for a while.'

Hester turned her face away at the crack of a trotter's knuckle as Little Pinch wielded the knife.

'So what?'

'Did the pale lady appear on the night that Mercy died?'

Little Pinch screwed up her face, trying to remember. Finally, she nodded.

'I heard Mercy's cries and then she became silent, but they were replaced by those of a child.'

'And then you saw the pale lady.'

'I told you, I screw my eyes so tight I see nothing.'

'So how do you know the pale lady appeared?'

'I heard someone cry out in terror next to me.'

'So, tell me, what would a lady who steals babies want with a dead child?'

Little Pinch stared at her, her mind working.

'The child was alive and she wanted it for her own means.'

Was alive or is alive? wondered Hester. Was there a woman in the Nottinghamshire countryside with a child to her breast, paid to look after the baby using money given to her by Amos?

'If I wanted to find a woman who would take a child, where would I ask?'

Little Pinch put her hands to her face.

'Oh, I don't know, miss. Maybe I've heard of such acts, but it feels against the order of things. Please don't ask me anything more.'

'Who, please? Who? Can you find out for me?'

'Oh, I don't know. It's no use. The pale lady either wants your child or she don't.'

'What do you mean? I keep hearing these sentiments. How is it preordained which child is taken?'

But Little Pinch had talked enough.

'Don't go berating me. I don't know much and I know I'm not telling. Speak to the parson. He knows. He's in on it. Ask Reverend Flint.'

# Chapter Thirty-One

Hester found the church empty of both Reverend Flint and his congregation of straw. She passed the stone angel, turning her face from its shrouded body, and called on the large house next to the church. Peering through the smeared front window, she saw a large brass cross on the sill next to a cat cleaning its whiskers.

She raised the heavy knocker, listening to the sound echo around the house, followed by a shuffling. The door opened to reveal the parson, who turned a battered face to her, his yellow-grey hair covering one side of his sallow and pockmarked cheek.

'What do you want? I thought I told you not to come round here again with your prying ways.' He peered over her shoulder. 'You still have your follower, I see.'

This time Hester didn't turn. That the parson could also see her follower was a surprise but of no consequence.

'Your sister's in the ground. Leave me in peace.'

'It's not my sister I want to talk to you about.' Hester swallowed, getting ready to deliver the story she'd concocted during the walk. 'A girl I know is in trouble.'

'If she's in the workhouse then it's the Kirkhams' business. Everything goes through them.'

'Not the workhouse. It's a woman from a respectable family who finds herself in difficulty. I heard you might be able to help.'

'I see.'

He opened the door a fraction wider.

'May I come in?'

'No, you may not.'

From behind him, she could see shapes in the dark hallway. Dear God, did he bring the figures inside the house with him?

'Can you help me at least? This lady is quite desperate.'

He grinned at her. 'It's you that be needing me, is it? No point in hiding it. You're no better than your sister. Stay here.'

He closed the door and she waited in the cold for him to return. He took so long that she thought he'd decided to leave her stranded on his doorstep. She was about to turn away, when the door opened and he thrust a card in her hand. She read the script:

Mr Quare – Surgeon and Man-Midwife

PREGNANT WOMEN, whose situation requires them to put their infants out to nurse and be humanely taken care of. Tenderness, honesty and secrecy are the basis of this concern. He flatters himself that ladies will find, on application to him, the greatest attention and most profound discretion.

Letters (post paid) to 5 Rope Walk, Southwell.

'Who is this Mr Quare? I thought there were only two doctors in Southwell. Is it his real name?'

'Ah, well, that I can't say.'

'Surely you know if there's a doctor in the town named Quare?'

The parson shrugged. 'He tells me that is his name. Who am I to argue?'

'He? There's not a woman, too?'

'Questions, questions. I'll take the card back.'

He made to snatch the card from her and she shrank from his yellow fingers.

'I'll contact him. What will this person do with the baby?' asked Hester.

The priest tapped his nose. 'Don't ask, don't need to know.'

'How can you be part of such a thing?' Hester looked at the card, stifling the urge to rip it to shreds. She put it in the pocket of her dress to study later. 'You represent the Lord here on Earth and you condone this? Allowing babies to be taken from their mothers?'

'There's plenty who take the card like you. Don't forget that. They don't want scrawny brats suckling their breasts.'

Hester turned her face. 'The angelmaker is part of this, isn't she?' she asked. 'Someone mentioned that fostering of babies is popular in the Low Countries. I'm sure it's true for Scandinavia, too. A woman in the workhouse told me the angelmaker takes away the babies, because it's a phrase she used in her own country.'

'*Änglamakerska*,' the man said, smacking his lips. 'You're right – it's common practice in Europe, and thankfully becoming popular here. A little angel comes and takes your baby and all is solved.'

'And if Quare isn't the angelmaker, who is?'

'The woman who collects your baby.'

'Where does she take them?' Hester's voice rose and she saw the display of emotion repelled the parson.

'They go to the country to be weaned.'

Hester exhaled. 'That's all? You're sure? Why did you tap your nose before?'

'You have one of your fancies. That's all,' he wheedled. 'All it involves is weaning the baby in exchange for money.'

'Then why do the women fear her if they're giving up their children by choice?'

The priest's ravaged face worked as Hester stared at him. She saw the glint of madness in him as she looked into his eyes.

'Not all of them make it,' he whispered.

'What do you mean? How do they die?'

Reverend Flint shook his head, as if aware he'd said too much.

'Tell me where they're buried,' Hester urged. 'Where will I find these children?'

He shrank from her words, taking a step backwards.

'Stay away from the place. The Devil lives there.'

'No he doesn't,' said Hester, drawing herself up. 'The Devil lives here.' She pointed to his chest. 'He lives right inside the person responsible for this.'

'You're right,' he whispered. 'You're right.' He lifted a hand and pointed it at her. 'The Devil lives inside womankind. You bring the sin into the world and then take it away.' He spat at her. 'She-devil!'

## Chapter Thirty-Two

Hester looked down at the card again. Mr Quare was the person she needed to find. She'd met two physicians since her arrival – the repulsive and incompetent Bant, and Edward. Surely neither of them could be masquerading as Quare. Edward, for one, didn't live in Rope Walk but in his smart rooms on Church Street. Nor did he give off the whiff of seediness suggested by the words printed on the card. Rope Walk might refer to a river trade and it was this part of town where Doctor Bant had his lodgings. The passage she'd entered had no signage, but she'd taken directions from the road sweep. He'd know if it went by the name of Rope Walk.

The boy was busy brushing the cobbles when Hester found him. A recent fall of straw from a hay cart littered the road and had the scavengers out filling their pockets with the stuff to replenish their bedding.

'Are you going to take some for yourself?' she asked. 'You're clearing the street for the benefit of others.'

'Been paid thruppence to tidy it away,' puffed the boy. 'The lady across the road saw it happen and gave me the money. She likes the street outside her house kept nice.'

And the honest boy was working hard for it, she thought.

'You gave me directions last time to the physician, Bant. Do you remember?'

'I think so.' The boy stopped and wiped his forehead. 'You need to see him again?'

Hester shuddered at the thought.

'What was the name of the passage he lives on? You pointed it out to me but never told me the name.'

'Doesn't have a name,' said the boy. 'Just the passage.'

'It's not called Rope Walk?'

'Rope Walk?' The boy frowned. 'I don't know no Rope Walk. Who told you there was a place round here with that name?'

'Another physician lives there. A Mr Quare.'

The boy shook his head. 'Means nothing to me.'

Giving the boy another penny, she then made her way up the passage towards Bant's house, holding her breath against the foul stench. The rain hadn't improved the slimy staircase and she hung onto the rail, trying to ignore the foul liquid seeping into her gloves. She pushed open the door and the familiar smell of opium wafted towards her.

'Hello?'

The man was hunched in the corner, his head to one side and a faint trail of saliva trickling down his chin. He was catatonic and she saw this time she'd get no sense out of him. She crossed to the table. The pile of pawnbroker chits was still there and she found an inkpot with a quill at one angle. She lifted it, intending to leave the man a note, but the ink had congealed and the quill was blunt.

She looked at him in disgust and felt the ground shifting beneath her. She had no choice but to ask the other doctor in town. She'd show Edward the card that evening and ask his advice.

Caroline was in the little sitting room, tapping her feet on the floor, when Hester returned from her morning walk. Hester saw immediately that she was in a capricious mood. For a moment, she wondered if now was the moment to confide in Caroline. She clearly loved a scandal and, in this world of abandonment and childbirth, Caroline's worldliness would be a comfort. But she held back. Caroline didn't give a fig about the plight of the women in the Union, and her disdain was more than Hester could bear. She put aside thoughts of Mercy and Elisabet and stepped into the room.

'Oh, there you are. I wondered when you'd be back. You are going to change, aren't you? You've got the touch of the grave about you.'

Hester frowned. The visit to the churchyard had been a whim and she surely couldn't smell of the place.

'I'll put on another dress, I promise.'

Caroline grunted. 'So, what do you want to do this afternoon? I'm so lethargic. Autumn always brings on the melancholy for me.'

Hester searched around for inspiration.

'We could go to the market. It was busy when I passed through. Plenty enough for entertainment.'

'Of course. I'd forgotten it was Saturday.' She paused, her eyes shrewd. 'Where have you been? It's not a day for visiting the Union.'

'I went for a walk.'

Caroline frowned. 'Oh, you and your walks. All right. Let's go and see if there's anything to amuse ourselves at the market. There was a talking bird for sale there once. Which reminds me . . .' She wagged her finger at Hester. 'A little bird tells me that Edward has a rival for your affections.'

'A rival? Whatever do you mean?'

'There's a note for you that arrived this morning. It looks like a man's hand. It's been put in your room.' She smirked. 'You can look at it in private.'

Hester hurried to her bed chamber, passing a startled maid on the stairs. The envelope had been left on the small chest of drawers and she tore it open, her hands trembling with anticipation. The note was brief:

We will not tolerate any more meddling in matters that do not concern you. End your inquiries or you shall be sorry.

Hester dropped the letter as if it were on fire, retrieved it and carried it to the window where the light was better. The message was unsigned, of course, and as she looked more closely, she wondered why Caroline had automatically assumed it had come from a man. She studied the envelope, which revealed only her name and address. Did it look like the writing of a male? Hester wasn't so sure.

The message was similarly oblique. 'We' in the first sentence. The likelihood was that it had been written by someone at the workhouse, although the message wasn't delivered on the cheap notepaper she'd seen before. Here, the paper was a respectable linen white.

The odd thing, thought Hester, was that the note validated many of her actions. Up to now, she'd been scrabbling around in the dark, a little like the mouse she'd heard the other night inside the bed chamber wall. The note told her she was making progress. That something terrible had happened and that, despite her inquiries being met with silence and indifference, she was heading in the direction of some truth. Her actions in the last day or so had unsettled someone. The likely suspects were Mr or Mrs Kirkham, perhaps both.

She wouldn't give up her investigating, of course, and in any case, thought Hester as she tucked the letter in a drawer out of sight, she didn't feel in the least bit scared. The warning could be safely ignored. All she need do was come up with a writer of the note to satisfy Caroline's curiosity. Something to put her off track immediately. If she were left with any impression that Hester had an admirer, she'd never hear the last of it.

Hester stripped down to her underwear and, hesitating, removed that, too, wondering if she did smell of the grave. Once the notion that she stank had been sown, she couldn't rid herself of the fear. She gave herself a quick wash in cold water – there was no time to call for a jug of hot. Dressing in the blue gown Dorothea had given her, she joined her friend in the hallway. Hester was struck again by how sophisticated Caroline looked. No one would ever shout Quaker Jane to her. She had a worldly elegance about her, from the ribbon threaded through her underskirt to the dainty pink shoes.

'Well?' said Caroline.

Hester made a show of sighing in disappointment.

'A note from an acquaintance of my father asking if there's anything he can do while I'm here.'

'Who? We know all the Friends here.'

'Not a Quaker. He knew Father through the bank.'

'Oh.' Caroline sounded bored. 'Never mind, then. He sounds deadly dull. How depressing. I was sure I'd have to tell Edward there was a rival for his affection. Let's go out.'

The temptation of the market was impossible to resist, the heightened excitement reminding Hester of the apple fair. They idled around a few of the stalls, Hester spotting one run by Friends where there were fixed prices next to the goods. Friends didn't barter – a sure way to godlessness and avarice, according to Amos. Hester, used to this way of trading, purchased a bar of soap and was pleased to see that their stall was as busy as those surrounding it.

When she turned to show Caroline her purchase, she realised she'd lost her friend in the activity of the market. A mass of people was passing across the cobbles, sweating and jostling each other with good humour. Stepping away from the stall, she found herself being carried in the opposite direction to where she wished to go. She gave herself up to the crowd, resistance futile, until she found herself wedged between two men, one burly, the other lean, who ignored her as she bounced between their flanks.

She saw she was being carried towards the minster. Perhaps, she thought, it would be quieter there. She tried to overlook the proximity of the two men. Watch out, Mercy hissed in her ear. The gap closed between the men, squeezing the breath out of her until she fell, conscious of a boot trampling over her, and then another.

# Chapter Thirty-Three

When Hester opened her eyes, she was in a bed chamber lying on top of an uncomfortable mattress. Not her room at Guy House or, she thought, the workhouse, although the whitewashed walls reminded her of the place. A fly was buzzing in the window, its little body tapping against the pane. Hester became aware of a weight of pressure in her chest, the pain exploding when she sat up.

'Don't move. The doctor's coming to see you when we can find him.'

Joan swatted the fly and flicked it out of the window.

'Am I in The Black Griffin?'

'Heavens, no. We'd never have got you across the square with that crowd. I've brought you to my rooms while we wait for the physician.'

'Can you help me to sit up? I'm in agony.'

'You'd be better staying still. I'm worried about those ribs of yours.'

'The pain is terrible as I lie flat, please believe me.'

'As you wish.'

Joan manoeuvred herself around Hester and pulled her up with a groan. She left the room and returned with a tin cup of water.

'Drink some of this.'

'How did I end up here? The last thing I remember was falling.'

'I was nearby when they carried you to the gate. I heard some-one cry "the Quaker lady has tripped", and I thought it might be you. It's easy to lose your footing in the crowd. You wouldn't have been the first death from crushing at the market.'

Hester thought of the two men who had, she was sure, jostled her to the floor. She looked at Joan's concerned face and decided to take a chance.

'I don't think it was an accident that I fell. There were two men walking beside me, taking me in a direction I didn't want to go.'

'Robbers,' said Joan, her voice clotted with disgust. 'The market is awash with them.'

'Has my reticule gone?'

'You were brought in as you are. I saw no reticule. Was there much money in there?'

Hester shook her head. 'A few coins, that's all.'

She was sure she'd fallen to the ground clutching her bag. Had one of the men bent down and scooped it out of her hand, or was it the work of an opportunistic thief taking advantage of her distress?

A foot on the stairs made them both turn their heads. Edward stooped under the worm-riddled beam to enter the room. Hester saw that his hair was damp as if he'd recently emerged from bath-ing. He crossed the room, his eyes on her.

'I must ask my female patients to stay away from the market at midday. You're my third fainting this week.'

'I didn't faint. I was pushed to the floor.'

Joan, who was patting her cap to improve its shape in front of the doctor, nodded.

'I told her about the robbers who prey on ladies, especially those looking a little lost, if you don't mind me saying.'

'I wasn't lost, though. I couldn't get to Caroline and I ended up near to the minster gate.'

'I think she might have bruised a rib or two,' said Joan, still not satisfied with her cap.

'Take a deep breath in,' ordered Edward, putting his hand on her chest.

Hester obliged, gasping as if her lungs were filled with shards of glass.

'Painful, is it? Your breathing is steady, so hopefully a few broken bones is all you've sustained. I'll take you back to Guy House. Caroline is beside herself with worry.'

'Are you sure?'

Hester couldn't stop the words from coming out and she saw Edward smile.

'Beside herself is perhaps a little strong. She is worried about you, though. Can you stand?'

Hester felt his arms around her as she was lifted off the bed. The pain made her legs buckle, but standing, her lungs felt freer.

'I'm much better now I'm upright.'

Flanked by Joan and Edward, Hester tottered down the narrow steps. She saw Joan's rooms were in a side street not far from the market square where the crowds still thronged. Climbing up into Edward's coach was agony and she concentrated on making sure her body stayed upright. As they moved out of the darkness of the street, she saw a man in a doorway watching them. Small and lean, he lit a cigarette as they passed, turning his head away so she couldn't get a good look at him.

'Trot on.'

With a flick of the reins, the phaeton sped away.

# Chapter Thirty-Four

Matthew listened to Joan's account with growing anger. She'd slipped out to the market for more potatoes and disappeared for over two hours, leaving him to deal with two chaise-carts on his own. Annie had been worse than useless, tipping boiling stock over the floor.

'I knew it would come to this. The Quaker girl's got no sense whatsoever.'

'Anyone can fall victim to one of those rogues. They choose market day because everyone is concentrating on buying and having fun.'

'You think that's all it is?'

Joan frowned. 'What else could it be?'

'She's been going to the workhouse. She's a girl with a head full of questions, none of which she keeps to herself.'

'Well, they don't like her visits. So what? You think those thugs might have been employed by Mr Kirkham to keep her away? I heard he's harsh, but he's not a criminal.'

Matthew turned away.

'Matthew!' Joan's voice was sharp. 'What do you know that you're not telling me?'

Matthew was in no mood to talk, aware of his busy inn and the four o'clock mail coach due.

'Don't mind me. I've got a bad feeling, that's all. Something is in the air.'

Joan sniffed. 'We're coming up to All Hallows' Eve. It's a time for your fears to rise. You sure there's nothing you want to tell me?'

Matthew turned to her.

'I just wish the dead would stay buried.'

# Chapter Thirty-Five

Edward came to see Hester on the Sunday morning. The house was quiet, the only sound that of servants moving around downstairs. A maid entered, pulling back the curtains to announce the doctor's arrival.

'Would you get rid of the chamber pot under the bed, please?' Hester pulled herself up, wincing at the ache in her chest. 'I'd rather Doctor Holland didn't see that.'

After the maid had left, Edward came in, bringing with him a blast of icy air.

'The morning is cold,' he said after noticing that Hester had pulled her shawl tighter around her. 'How are you feeling today?'

'Better. My chest is still sore, though.'

'I still think it's likely you've fractured a rib. Rest is what you need. None of your long walks.'

'Of course.' She saw that he was restless, picking up objects on her dressing table and replacing them. 'Is everything all right?'

He turned and she saw signs of strain under his eyes.

'I'm exhausted, that's all. I doctor to the farmers around here, too. My physicking lasted into the night yesterday.'

'But you're up so early.'

'I wanted to see you before the day starts. Are you sure you're well?'

She hesitated and he spotted it immediately.

'What is it?'

'There's something I want to show you.'

She pulled the card given to her by Reverend Flint from underneath her pillow. It was fortunate that she'd put it in her pocket rather than her stolen reticule. He looked at it, his mouth curling in disgust.

'Where did you get this?'

'Reverend Flint handed it to me. He was under the impression I might need it when I was simply asking about Mercy.'

It was a lie, of course. She'd deliberately misled the parson, but Edward's agitated manner inhibited her.

'I know of such physicians, of course, but I prefer to have nothing to do with them.'

'You don't recognise the name?'

'I don't. Nor the address, and I know this place well. As I told you recently, there are only two doctors in this town. Me and Bant.'

'There's no point printing cards if the place doesn't exist.'

Edward sighed. 'I know. May I take this? I could ask some questions. The rogue won't be hard to track down. Now, have you told me everything?'

'There's something else. I received a note yesterday.'

'Where is it?'

'In the drawer of that chest. I had to hurry out to market, so I put it in there for safekeeping.'

Edward crossed to the chest and opened it.

'The drawer is empty except for clothes.' He lifted some garments to check.

'Are you sure? Try the next one.'

She heard the sound of the drawer opening.

'Nothing there, either.'

'Gone.' Hester exhaled. 'Who could have taken it?'

'A maid, perhaps. Surely neither of the Francombes would rifle through your things. What did it say?'

His agitation, she saw, had turned to anger.

'That I'd been meddling and I was to stop.'

'You were threatened. That's outrageous. What were they referring to?'

Hester hesitated. 'I've been asking the women about the pale lady who appears to them. The first woman I met at the workhouse, Elisabet, called her the angelmaker. I think she might be connected to the services offered by this Mr Quare.'

Edward tucked the card in his pocket.

'You need to leave this to me. You're still injured. Allow me to make inquiries. If I draw a blank, I'll give the card back to you when I see you next, I promise.'

Hester nodded but fretted after the doctor had left. The card was her sole proof that something was going on in Southwell.

Hester made it down to dinner that evening and noticed Dorothea giving her quick glances. With a lurch, she realised that Edward had confided in her host, Caroline remaining oblivious to her mother's concern. She was on tenterhooks all evening, expecting Dorothea to ask her about the card, but she proved to be discreet, winning at cards and retiring early to bed.

Hester's ribs still ached when she returned to the workhouse the following day. At the entrance, she saw Little Pinch scurrying across the kitchen garden, her miniature feet tripping over themselves in her haste to be indoors. She shouted a greeting but the girl hurried on. Hester frowned and made to follow but was brought up sharp by the porter.

'You can't go in.'

He stood at the entrance of the porch, his arms folded across his chest. He'd been waiting for her, she realised, with the satisfied manner of a man about to deliver bad news.

'I'm sorry?' Hester looked towards the girl, who disappeared round the side of the house.

'I have my orders. No callers today.'

'But today is my day that I visit.'

'You came Saturday.'

'But I didn't get to see any of the women. You mean I have to wait until Thursday?'

'You can't come then, either.'

'But it's been agreed with the board of guardians.'

'Not any more.' The man's voice dripped with satisfaction. 'There's been an outbreak of cholera. No one is to enter or leave without the master's permission.'

Hester took a step back.

'Are you sure? I heard this place had its own water supply.'

'Very sure. It's been certified by Doctor Bant.'

'May I speak to Mrs Kirkham? I just need to—'

'Didn't you just hear me? Be off with you.'

He stepped through the front door and slammed it behind him, leaving Hester in the drizzle, looking towards the wing she was barred from entering.

The exertion of just getting to the workhouse had exhausted her and the effort of putting one foot in front of the other to return to Guy House was more than she could bear. She briefly contemplated getting a restorative cup of coffee at The Black Griffin, but the thought of Matthew's taunts stopped her. Reluctantly, she turned her back on the workhouse and began the long walk back to the Francombe residence.

As she passed the graveyard, she saw the sexton at work, digging a single grave.

'Has someone died?' she asked.

He didn't look up from the task.

'Old Mistress Spence in town.'

'You might be in for some extra work. I've heard there's an outbreak of cholera at the Union.'

He straightened and glared at her, his bushy eyebrows knitted into a single brow. 'Nonsense. Who told you that?'

'The porter. He told me there was an outbreak and I wasn't to enter.'

The sexton laughed, his voice mirthless.

'That's what they tell all the visitors when they don't want them inside. There's no cholera outbreak. Never has been as far as I'm aware. They just don't want you near.'

'You're sure?'

He grinned, showing his two teeth. 'Very sure. Mr Kirkham and I have a laugh about it sometimes. Tell them we have cholera, and that'll keep the do-gooders away.'

Hester leaned against the wall, exhausted. If she could have summoned a coach to speed her back to Bristol, she'd have stepped into it and left this miserable town. She was to be denied access to the workhouse and there was little she could do if they said there was cholera. It was the disease everyone shrank from, striking fear into the hearts of every resident. Just when she felt she could drop to the ground, she felt the presence sidle up to her. Not Mercy, the other.

'Oh, go away.'

The sexton looked up. 'Pardon?'

'Never mind.'

She felt a shove on her side, pushing her towards the church door. What did the spirit want? Another confrontation with Reverend Flint?

'Is the parson in today?' she asked the man, who had resumed his digging.

'Called to Nottingham on Church business. He's had to leave all of his *friends* behind.'

She caught the note of mockery in his words.

'You mean the figures? You know about them?'

'Takes 'em into the church every morning and back to his house at night. They're having a rest today.' He wheezed with laughter.

Hester felt another shove towards the door. She wasn't to see the parson, then. She tried to imagine what else might be in the church for her to see. A glimmer of comprehension broke through.

'Can you direct me towards the churchwarden? I want to look inside the parish registers. It's he who is responsible for them, isn't it?'

'Keeps 'em under lock and key. Three keys, in fact, it takes to open the chest in the church. What would you be wanting with them?'

'I want to see my sister's burial record.'

'I told you, I put her in the ground myself.'

'I'd like to see if there's a name for the child she was buried with.'

The man hesitated and Hester realised that here was another who couldn't read.

'It doesn't matter. Where can I find the churchwarden? He can unlock the parish chest for me.'

'Oh, I know where the keys are kept.'

'You do?'

'In his pocket.'

Hester sighed.

'But there's another set hanging under the table in the vestry.' The sexton tapped his nose.

'Would you open it so I can consult the registers?'

He led her into the vestry behind the altar. Hester, used to plain meeting houses, found the church frigid and unwelcoming. Plaster was coming off the wall in shreds and the place reeked of damp and mildew. The vestry was slightly better. It had the air of a room where activity took place. The parson's surplice was thrown over a chair next to a candle nearly down to its nub and the remains of what looked like a glass of wine.

The sexton retrieved the keys and deftly opened the three locks. He'd clearly done it before, probably because his palm had been greased with a coin. Hester could spare him half a crown, which he took with a nod.

Hester picked out the book of births and a second that recorded deaths. The marriage register was of no interest to her. She opened the pages of births, scanning the entries for the previous two years. Eight babies had been born at Southwell and baptised at the church. Some born in wedlock with the names of the parents there to see, but the parson had no problem with illegitimate children, either. The baseborn son of a local woman had been baptised only last week. Hester frowned, flicking through the pages. No baseborn children from the workhouse, though. Had he denied them baptism or had they already been taken by the pale lady?

Hester closed the book and opened the register of deaths. Only four baby entries over the last year, and not one who had died at the workhouse. One of the children had been a day old and yet its burial had been recorded. If Mercy had been buried with her child, then the entry would be in this book. It was blank. Mercy lay alone in the grave, she knew now, but there was a bigger mystery. If the children had died as Lizzie and Elisabet had claimed, they must be buried elsewhere.

# Chapter Thirty-Six

When Hester arrived back at Guy House, an embarrassed maid said that she was to go and see the mistress as soon as she returned. Hester gave the servant her coat and went into the sitting room. Dorothea had her back to Hester as she entered. She was at the mantelpiece, reading a note, which she folded and tucked under the clock when she saw her guest. She got straight to the point.

'I'm extremely concerned, Hester, about the events that took place on Saturday. If it had been an accident, it would have been bad enough, but these things do happen. However, Edward tells me you were deliberately attacked.'

'It was just an impression.'

'Nevertheless, you did receive a note threatening you, did you not? Why didn't you show it to me?'

'I . . . I don't really know. I suppose I wanted to prove to Edward that the attack wasn't a figment of my imagination.'

'But you say the note has now gone?'

'From my room, yes.'

Dorothea sighed. 'I've spoken to the servants and they deny all knowledge of it.'

'But—'

Dorothea raised her hand. 'I believe you. Edward, however, is very concerned about your well-being, and so am I. I've written to your mother that I think you should return home.'

Hester went still. 'You're sending me away?'

'In her last letter, your mother told me that she was considering returning to Bristol a little earlier than anticipated. There are some affairs of your father's to sort out.'

'She never mentioned it to me. I'm to go to Bristol?'

'I think it's the best course, don't you?' Dorothea made an effort to smile. 'I've so enjoyed having you here, but I think your mother would appreciate your company. There are creditors, I believe.'

Hester could do nothing but nod, her face burning with indignation. She saw it was useless to argue. She could hardly claim a close friendship with Caroline to keep her here.

'I'm sorry that my visit is to be cut short. May I ask you a question? Why did you write to invite me here? Caroline and I are very different people.'

Dorothea looked at her. 'Do you have any idea what it's like to lose your husband? Your mother has been plunged into widowhood and must now fend for herself, relying on handouts and goodwill from friends and family.'

'Father's finances are shaky, but we'll manage. We've been left with some means.'

'And how would you know that, Hester? Have you asked your mother exactly how she's placed? Down to pounds, shillings and pence? Do you know what you and your brothers will live on over the coming months and years?'

'We discussed me finding work and Ruth said that it hadn't come to that. There were other options.'

'There are other options, Hester, but they're very limited when you're a woman. I'd rather hoped that you and Edward might form an attachment, but his attitude towards you is more physician and patient. Perhaps' – Dorothea made an effort to smile – 'you could come back some day and renew the acquaintance.'

Her words lacked conviction. Hester wouldn't be returning to Southwell.

'That would be nice,' said Hester dully. She looked towards Mercy, who had appeared near the fireplace. *I've failed you*, she told her sister. 'When am I to leave?'

'There's a coach from The Black Griffin tonight at eleven. That'll give us plenty of time to get your things together.'

'So soon?'

'If you've made enemies here, Hester, I'd rather you left at once.'

Strangely, it was Caroline who came to say goodbye to Hester when the big clock in the hall chimed ten. Clearly, Dorothea felt she'd said her farewells in the little sitting room. Caroline came down the stairs as Hester was waiting for the trap.

'I hear you're leaving us. I'll be sorry to see you go.'

Hester, red-faced and furious, turned her head.

'It's supposed to be for my own good. I'd prefer a say in the matter.'

'We don't get a say. If it's not our fathers telling us what to do, it's our mothers.'

'We could have waited until Ruth replied.'

'But, Hester, you were threatened and you tried to keep it all to yourself. If Edward hadn't mentioned it, we'd never have known. I was so sure you'd just fainted in the market. What have you been doing?'

'Nothing of any import.'

Caroline kept her eyes on her. 'He also showed me that card with the surgeon's name on. What possessed you to give it to him?'

'What . . . what possessed me?'

'For goodness' sake, Hester. Edward's a physician, but he was also your suitor. Heavens knows what he must have thought when you gave him the card.'

'I don't care. I trusted him and he's told both you and Dorothea.'

Caroline sighed. 'Your naivety is both touching and infuriating but, as I said, I'll miss you. And I never saw you with coloured ribbons in your bonnet.'

Hester managed a weak smile.

At that moment, Mercy appeared, her expression distraught. Hester glanced at Caroline to see if she'd noticed anything amiss, but she was fiddling with her hair in the looking glass. Caroline paused and turned.

'What is it?' asked Hester.

'That's strange. I thought I saw something in the mirror. It's nothing.'

# Chapter Thirty-Seven

It had been a day of back-breaking toil. One of the ostlers, a dopey lad with his head in the clouds, had received a kick from one of the four horses on the midday mail coach and had been carried off screaming in agony. It left Matthew one man down, and the other stable hands were subdued. They were a superstitious lot who disliked accidents around the inn. He'd been glad to see the back of them, leaving him with only Joan to help with the evening diners.

He heard the trap enter the courtyard – a passenger for the night coach heading to London. It was an unfriendly hour and he'd be happy when he was safely in his bed. He went out to meet the carriage and was astonished to see Hester sitting upright, her eyes fixed in front.

'Leaving already? I thought you were here for the month.'

She didn't look at him. 'So did I.'

So that was what had come to pass, he thought. He lowered his voice. 'You're better off away from this godforsaken place.'

She turned to him. 'Southwell?'

'The town, the people, the workhouse. The whole damned lot of it. It's not for the likes of you.'

'What *am* I like?'

Innocent, he nearly told her. Untouched by the taint of deceit and something much, much worse.

'You don't belong here,' he muttered instead and helped her down from the trap.

She followed him into the dining room. It was a quiet night now the regulars had stumbled off into the darkness. Joan was sweeping the floor when she caught sight of the pair of them, giving the lass, Matthew noticed, a wide smile.

'You're finally leaving us, then.'

'Unfortunately.'

Matthew saw she'd been crying, her eyes rimmed with pink and a high colour in her cheeks. Perhaps it was the thought of leaving her physician friend that was upsetting her. The idea made Matthew savage.

'I told her she's better off away,' he said, his ears straining for the sound of horses' hooves. He looked up at the clock, which showed a quarter to the hour. 'Would you like a drink while you wait? Coffee, perhaps. You'll not sleep anyhow on the journey south.'

'No, thank you.'

Hester sat and composed herself. There was work to be done at the back, but she was also looking at him with a beseeching gaze.

'All right. What is it?' He pulled out the other chair in front of the dampened fire.

'There's a child.'

Matthew felt a rush of nausea in his nose. Of course there was a child.

Joan had stopped sweeping and was listening intently.

'My sister, Mercy, was the mother. I was told she was buried with her baby, but I now know that's not the case. The child was taken and the trail has gone dead. I want to find where my niece has gone. There's something else. I have a name. A Mr Quare. He lives in Rope Walk. Do you know him?'

The name rang a distant bell, but Matthew couldn't place it.

He shook his head. 'Why do you ask?'

'He's a man who takes unwanted babies and humanely places them with other people. The card I was given said his name was Quare.'

Matthew looked up at Joan, who shrugged.

'It means nothing to me.'

'I intend to find this man.'

Hester stared at him, her face defiant.

'You'll have difficulty doing that from Bristol.'

Matthew's fear had made him sarcastic, but he saw the girl wasn't cowed. However, for all her bravery, she wouldn't be involving him, that much was for sure.

'I'm not getting involved in your business and nor is Joan.'

'I'm not asking you to.'

It took the wind out of him.

'So, what *are* you going to do? Employ a man to look into it for you?'

'A man? A man is the last thing I need.'

Joan snorted and came to join them. It was she who had cottoned on to the girl's plans before him.

'You can't stay at mine. There's no privacy. That whole court would know you were there within the hour. I'd have you in a blink, but it won't work.'

'That's kind of you, but I won't impose. How much are the rooms here?'

So, she did intend to bring trouble on them. Matthew stood up.

'You're not staying at The Black Griffin.'

'I won't leave Southwell. I'd rather stay in a place where I know it's respectable, but I'll find a bed for the night elsewhere if you turn me away.'

Matthew looked at her determined face and silently swore.

'If you're to take a room, it needs to be where you can remain hidden from my patrons. They'd spot an attractive young girl and drink makes for loose tongues. You need to remain hidden.'

'Is there a room away from the balconies?'

'There's the attic,' said Joan.

'I know. I know.'

He could feel his temper rising. There were three rooms at the top of the inn. The smallest was used by the maid, Annie, and he had the largest facing the street. But there was another tucked under the eaves, which was what Joan had in mind, but how would he feel having this girl so close?

'It's not fit for a gentlewoman.'

'I don't mind. It's more important I remain hidden.'

He shook his head. He'd have no peace with her in the room next to his.

'There's another room on the first floor. It faces front but doesn't lead on to the balcony, so it's unpopular. It's at the end of a passage, which means no one will pass your room. It's large – there's a table for you to have your meals. You wouldn't need to come here.'

'You'll let me stay?'

Matthew hesitated, knowing that once he'd said yes, he was being plunged into a deception with high stakes. Far higher than Hester knew. But into his misgivings came again the sound of the girl's shriek he'd heard that evening earlier in the year. The animal cry of a woman subjected to some unnamed horror – and not the first time he'd heard such sounds.

'You can stay,' he said. 'How much money do you have?'

'Enough for a room, I think.'

'Never mind about the room. I don't care about that. We'll need to bribe the driver. I know him. He'll keep his mouth shut, but it'll cost.'

'He'll say he's taken me south?'

'He will, and what's more, he'll tell me who is asking.'

'Will five shillings do?'

Matthew snorted. 'You need to learn the price of bribery. On second thoughts, I prefer you as you are. Half a crown will be enough. You leave that to me.'

# PART THREE

## THE BLACK GRIFFIN

*It is an honour to appear on the side of the afflicted.*
Elizabeth Fry

# Chapter Thirty-Eight

A shadowing came to Hester that night, but it was a dream, nothing more. Not the nightmare of the fire or the pit. This time, she was in a large house, some of it dilapidated. In her dream, she tried to identify its location, but the name drifted from her as if it were thin wisps of mist.

In one of the rooms, a workhouse girl stood, her hands blackened from cleaning the fireplace, one finger pointing at the person behind Hester. She twisted round to see who the girl was accusing, but the action jerked her awake to the sound of the birds tweeting the start of the day. She heaved as she sat up, the pain in her ribs causing her to catch her breath as daybreak crept into the room through the slats in the shutters.

The coach south had departed without her, and only Matthew and Joan knew she was staying at the inn. The Francombes, living on the edge of town, rarely ventured up this way on foot and she should be able to avoid detection as long as she kept indoors on market day. Edward would be harder to avoid. He was a prominent physician in the town, as she'd seen his phaeton in the distance a few times during her stay at the Francombes'.

Hester lit the candle. One possibility was that she visit Edward and take him into her confidence as she had done Matthew and Joan. He'd professed his dislike of both the workhouse and Doctor Bant often enough, so surely he had no issue with her remaining in the town for a few days more. There was also the matter of the note with the name Quare, which he'd promised to investigate. Perhaps he'd send a letter to Bristol with any discoveries but, more likely, he'd let the matter drop now she was supposed to have left.

She was torn with indecision. Although she hadn't sworn him to secrecy, he'd nevertheless told Dorothea about the threatening note. Had it been an act of charity? She wasn't sure and she saw she couldn't rely on him. In fact, she couldn't trust either him or the Francombes. She remembered her dream, the location of the house, so elusive while she'd slept, coming to her.

She lay in bed thinking. The inn was waking up. Matthew clearly locked up at night, unusual for a coaching inn. She needed a plan of action. Dorothea would have written to her mother to say she was on her way, which meant that by tomorrow, Thursday at the latest, the hunt would be on for her. She must do as much as she could before then. She dozed for a while until she was roused by a knock at the door. Joan entered, carrying a jug of hot water.

'Plenty for you to wash by. And I've brought you these . . .'

Over her arm, she had a serge dress in a light brown with a matching bonnet hanging from chocolate-brown ribbons.

'For me?'

'You can't wear your Quaker dress. You stand out in your outfit.'

'I have others. Dorothea gave me two gowns.'

'I've seen them. I had a look in your trunk while you were asleep. They're too smart for here. You'd be spotted the minute you left the inn. This dress is an old one of mine. You'll blend in well enough.'

The gown was of a fashion a decade or so earlier. It must have been Joan's best dress, as the cloth showed little sign of wear.

'Are you sure you can spare it?'

'You can give it me back when you leave. It needs letting out for me.'

Hester held the dress against her. There was a small looking glass over the washstand and she could just see the fawn fabric against her neck.

'It'll be a change from grey.'

'Don't you mind wearing the same colour every day? It's not like you can't afford anything finer.'

Joan opened the shutters to let in the cold October air.

'I've never known anything else. While my father was alive, we stuck to a very strict code. It was a sign of simplicity and godliness.' Hester thought of the glamorous Caroline and her elegant mother. 'But times are changing. The rule is more relaxed now. I might even persuade my mother to let me wear my new gowns.'

'Your father is dead?'

'Yes. Yes, he is.'

A note in Hester's tone must have given her away, as Joan gave no condolences.

'I'll leave you to it. The straw bonnet is of a fashion that will conceal much of your face. Do you have a plan?'

'I hardly know where to start, but I've remembered something.' There was no point telling Joan about the dream. 'I want to go out to Newstead Abbey.'

'Newstead?' Joan stared in astonishment. 'I thought you were here to discover the goings-on at the workhouse. Why do you want to go there? It's not a day for trips out. Even Lord Byron left that rotting pile to live in Southwell with his mother.'

'There's someone I want to see. It might be nothing. Is there someone who will take me? I can pay for the trip.'

'I'll see what I can do.'

When Joan returned with the breakfast porridge, she said, a note of surprise in her voice, 'Matthew will take you himself.'

'You sound shocked. Does he not normally venture out of town?'

'Not when there's work to be done here. You're honoured. Either that or he wants to keep an eye on you.'

Hester stiffened. Having finally escaped the confines of the Francombe household, she hoped she wasn't going to be chaperoned everywhere by Matthew Alban. She needn't have worried. He was waiting for her at the seat of a dog-cart pulled by a surprisingly strong-looking horse.

'Don't dawdle. If you keep fannying around, someone will spot you.'

'Thank you, as ever, for your concern,' said Hester, climbing aboard. 'I want to go to—'

'Newstead Abbey. Aye, I heard.'

For the rest of the journey through town, he remained silent, keeping his head bent low over the reins. Once they were out on the open road, he relaxed, putting the horse into a canter.

'That's a strong-looking horse for the cart.'

Matthew snorted with what sounded like a laugh.

'You mean it should be a nag pulling this contraption?'

'I—'

'Oh, don't mind me. This is Merlin. Finest horse in Southwell. He comes from the same stock as the ones I rode as a child.'

'So what's he doing pulling a cart?'

'You wanted a ride to Newstead, didn't you? It was this or sitting on the saddle behind me. A fine sight that would have looked.'

Hester turned her face and she heard him chuckling next to her.

As the house came into view, he dropped her off at the edge of the parkland.

'I've business to attend to three miles from here. I'll pick you up again at half past twelve. Don't wait on the roadside – I'll come up to the house.'

Hester nodded and watched the mismatched horse and cart

disappear into the dust. The recent rain had turned the track to the house into a mire and as she picked her way through the clods, she was conscious of the mud splashing up her petticoats and soiling Joan's dress. By the time she reached the house, she was too ashamed to go in through the front entrance as she had done with Edward and the Francombes. Instead, she made her way round the back, slipping through an open door that led to the kitchen rooms. A scullery maid looked up in surprise at her appearance.

'I'm looking for the maid who sweeps the downstairs fires. It's not a bother, she'll know me. I think her name was Dorcas.'

'That's where she'll be now. She told me she was going to do the east wing a few minutes ago. She won't have finished yet.'

'May I make my own way there?'

'I'll have to let the housekeeper know we have visitors.'

'Of course.'

The maid hesitated at Hester's confidence, clearly at odds with her more humble attire.

'Of course, it might be more bother than it's worth,' said the maid, winking at her.

Hester climbed the stairs, the house alive with repressed activity. From behind closed doors she could hear the sounds of curtains being swished as the rooms were opened up for the day. The girl she was seeking had a dirtier job, the cleaning of the fires and, after trying a few silent rooms, she found the maid laying kindling down. She turned to Hester as she entered, her expression alarmed.

'Please, carry on. I just wanted a quick word with you. We can talk while you work.'

'What do you want with me?'

The girl had a strong Nottinghamshire accent, her expression sullen as she continued with the fire.

'We met before. I came here recently – a group of four of us when you were blackening the fire in another room.'

The girl stopped sweeping.

'The Quaker. I remember.' She turned to Hester. 'You're dressed differently. Those are ordinary clothes.'

'My circumstances have changed.'

Hester had only said the words as an excuse for the fact that she was no longer dressed in the garments of her faith, but the effect on the girl was remarkable. She threw her brush down into the grate and clambered to her feet.

'Oh, miss. I'm terribly sorry to hear that, but I can't help you.'

Hester swallowed. Like the parson, the girl had got the wrong end of the stick but had revealed a glimmer of truth in doing so.

'Do you know who can help me?'

'No. I don't want to get involved in such matters. My advice to you would be to get away from this place.'

'Does the name Quare mean anything to you? I believe he's based in Rope Walk.'

Dorcas stared at her, mouth agape.

'Quare? Who's he?'

'I was given his name in connection to the pale lady. I believe they're associates.'

'I don't know the name. Never heard of him.'

'The pale lady means something though, doesn't it? I need more information about her, Dorcas. It's important.'

Dorcas approached Hester. Hester could smell sweat and the carbolic soap the girl was using for cleaning.

'The Devil is conjured when a baby is born. You and your baby need to be gone before the child is a day old. Do you hear? Have the baby here if you must, but leave as soon as you can. And, whatever you do, stay clear of the workhouse.'

Dorcas picked up her mop and bucket and was hauling it out of the room.

'Dorcas!' Hester grabbed her arm so that she couldn't leave. 'When you say the Devil, who do you mean?'

The girl cried out. 'I don't know who. The Devil takes many forms. Don't you forget about that.'

'But you recognised someone, didn't you, from my companions. Remember? When I came here before, you were frightened of someone I was with.'

'I'm frightened of everyone. That's what that place does for you.'

'Did you recognise the doctor, perhaps? Doctor Holland? He must have visited the workhouse.'

'Him? We never saw suchlike. If one of us was sick, there was an old sawbones who would come and finish us off. Nothing like that gentleman. Now, if you'll excuse me.'

The girl tried to push Hester away, but she held on tight.

'The Francombes, then? Dorothea Francombe or her daughter, Caroline?'

'I've never seen them before.'

'So why did you cry out when you saw us?'

'It was you in the grey dress. I was scared. I thought the pale lady had come to get me. Maybe she isn't just in the workhouse but in this place, too.'

Hester stared at her. 'The pale lady? She wears Quaker grey?'

Caroline had made a joke of it on her first evening at Southwell. Had she unwittingly hit on the truth?

'The woman who steals them children wore grey. It was you who scared me. Now, leave me alone.'

Hester stumbled away from the house, aware she'd got more than she'd bargained for. She'd unjustly had her suspicions of Edward and the Francombes when it was she who had scared the girl. She was back waiting at the gate when Matthew's cart appeared in the distance. His face was grim as he drew up beside her.

'Is everything all right?' she asked.

Instead of jumping down, he held out his hand and pulled her up beside him.

'I've heard some news about a farm for sale, that's all.'

He didn't elaborate, flicking the reins at the horse. Once the horse had settled into a rhythm, Matthew turned to look at her.

'Find anything out about your sister?'

'Not about my sister, no.'

'Do you believe her baby to be alive?'

'I'm not sure. When he gave me the card, the parson suggested some babies are taken to the countryside. It's possible that Mercy's child was given that chance. What do you think?'

'I don't think I have the same belief in the goodness of people as you, Hester.'

'A girl told me the baby was alive after birth. I have to hold onto that. The card said that babies given to Quare would be humanely treated. I feel I'm still grasping at straws.'

She paused, waiting to feel the presence of Mercy, but felt nothing other than the wind on her face.

# Chapter Thirty-Nine

Hester found the confines of her chamber intolerable after the visit to Newstead and was glad she hadn't pushed the option of the attic room. Even in this decent space tucked away at the end of the passage, the walls felt as if they were closing in on her. Worry, however, had cleared her mind and the next step was evident – she must find a way of accessing the workhouse, however difficult that might be.

At a knock on the door, she hurried to unfasten the latch. Joan was carrying a tray laden with a casserole, stewed fruit and a mug of water. It was honest fare, although Hester's appetite had departed her and she knew she'd have trouble eating it.

'Leave it on the table. I'm not hungry yet.'

'Don't let it go cold. Congealed rabbit won't help your appetite.'

'It smells delicious.'

Hester thought back to the foul meal she'd eaten on the first visit to Nottinghamshire. The gin-soaked innkeeper and his equally grogged wife had been a disgrace to the coaching profession. Matthew might have his rough ways, but he was a sober landlord who kept respectable rooms.

'Is the inn busy?' Hester poured cold water from the jug into the bowl and dipped her hands in.

'Quiet now, but there's a coach due at nine. A private party, so they'll want the best of everything. We'll put them in the small room to the side. I've done all the food. It's up to the maid to make sure nothing burns or boils over.'

Poor Annie – there'd be a multitude of hissing pots and crackling pans to watch over. A telling-off was coming her way, Hester was sure.

Joan made a show of plumping Hester's pillow.

'Were you wanting something, dearie? I can spend five minutes. I know it must be lonely up here for you all by yourself.'

'It's nothing, really. I've been wondering how you came to be working here. Where did you meet Matthew?'

Joan gave Hester a brief look and smiled.

'Meet him? I've known him since he was a baby. He's my cousin's son. We're family. When the old innkeeper wanted to sell up, Matthew made him a low but decent offer. The old fella had got sick of the trade and was keen to go.'

'Matthew has money, then?' Hester tried to keep the surprise out of her voice.

'He's not gentry. Well, I don't need to tell you that – you can see for yourself – but the farmers are rich enough around here. His family have orchards near Linby. The trees yield a decent crop and there's always plenty of apples on the menu at The Black Griffin.'

'He didn't want to be a farmer?'

'Oh, he wanted to, all right. If you're brought up on the land, it's hard to shake off. It's the father who's the problem. Silas Alban is as violent as you get. There are three sons, Matthew's the eldest, and they've all flown the nest. Matthew's lucky he was willed some money from his grandfather on his mother's side, otherwise he'd be a wandering pedlar or general labourer. Mind you . . .' Joan paused, her eyes on Hester. 'He'd have made good whatever he decided to do. He's clean and sober, unlike most of his father's family.'

'Your last name is Alban, too?'

'It is, dearie. The Albans are known enough around here. So, what else did you want to know?'

Hester made a face. 'I hope you didn't think I was prying. I was just—'

'Interested. I know. I think you being interested in things is going to bring you a whole heap of trouble, but you've already worked that out for yourself, haven't you?'

'You don't know what's going on, do you, Joan? There's not anything you're not telling me?'

'I promise you, dearie, if I knew anything, I'd tell you – not least so as to stop you from getting yourself in trouble. But I don't know. The workhouse looms over this town like a citadel. It's the model, people say, of workhouses all over the country and I pity every place that has one just like ours. But what goes on behind those closed doors, I have no idea.'

'No one's ever spoken to you about it?'

Joan stopped and gazed at her, hesitating.

'What is it?'

'Hester. The people who end up in the workhouse have got as low as low can get. Do you understand? None of us have money here. We live from day to day, week to week. There's no one who could earn a living elsewhere who voluntarily goes into the workhouse. It's the desperate and the destitute who end up there and it sounds as if your sister was both.'

Miserable, Hester nodded.

'Then I'll be leaving you. There's roast fowl for the private party and Matthew will have my guts for garters if it's overdone. And we all know how slapdash Annie is.'

After Joan had left, Hester was left alone with her copy of *Ivanhoe*. She tried to concentrate on the familiar words, but the adventures seemed dull after her own recent escapades. Eventually, she put the book down when she realised she'd read the same page twice without taking in a single word. She crossed to the window to look out for the coming private carriage. Stagecoach journeys were expensive enough, but owning your own coach suggested wealth and privilege.

A young ostler who she didn't recognise was filling a trough with animal feed for the coming horses. He turned at the sound of wheels on cobbles and Hester followed his gaze as two handsome black stallions turned into the courtyard, the roof of the coach only just fitting under the archway.

Matthew came out to greet the arrival, looking ill at ease. He rubbed his hands on his trousers as if trying to dry his palms. He wasn't required to help with the carriage. A servant, who must have had a chilly journey, jumped off the back and opened the door for the occupants.

The man was first to disembark, dressed in a flared frock coat as styled by Prince Albert, set off by a gold necktie. His luxuriant moustache was just visible under his top hat. The woman who followed took Hester's breath away. She was dressed in the most impractical colour for travelling – an off-the-shoulder lemon dress with a bell skirt that got stuck in the carriage door as she tried to disembark. Hester saw Matthew exchange an amused glance with the stable boy before he ushered his guests into the building.

Her evening's entertainment over, Hester was about to return to *Ivanhoe* when she heard the sound of a horse approaching – not a carriage but a solo rider. They were unlikely to get a warm welcome, she thought. All the effort inside the inn would be focused on ensuring those wealthy private guests wanted for nothing. Unannounced lone riders and pedestrians often ended up eating their food in the kitchens as it was. They'd be lucky to manage a bowl of broth with Matthew, Joan and Annie busy.

When the rider came into view, Hester saw with a jolt that this man wouldn't be consigned to the kitchen table. Edward had come to the inn. Had he discovered that she was staying here, her trip to Newstead been spotted by someone who knew her?

Unlike the earlier visitors, Edward didn't make his way immediately to the front door. Instead, he dismounted and walked over to where the horses were being stabled. An ostler was rubbing down the two from the carriage. Matthew's mare would be there, too, and a change of horses for the mail coach. She watched as Edward took a good look around the yard and then disappeared into the stable.

'Quiet night,' he shouted to the stable boy when he emerged.

The boy shrugged and Edward said something that Hester couldn't make out but saw it drew a laugh from the lad. Hester smiled at the pair and wondered if she dared go down and see Edward. Surely her suspicions had been false. The maid had said she didn't recognise him and he must have only been trying to do right by her by mentioning the letter to Dorothea.

In the end, she stayed put. If the Francombes were to hear she was here, she'd be sent for and put on the next coach home. No, she'd stay up in her room, watching.

Hester sat in silence for over an hour, her ears straining for any tread on the board to prove that one of the maids had been indiscreet or inn gossip had brought to Edward's ears the lone female guest. But the upstairs rooms stayed silent, only the sound of doors opening and closing in the distance.

Finally, the horses were harnessed back onto the carriage and the wealthy couple emerged from the inn. The woman looked as elegant as before but out of temper, her cheeks high with colour. The gentleman's expression she couldn't see, but she noticed that Edward had come out of the building as part of their party. He seemed in high spirits, replacing his top hat and laughing heartily. He watched the carriage depart before mounting his own horse and riding away. It wasn't until he'd finally left that Hester realised she'd been holding her breath.

# Chapter Forty

From the banging of the pots and pans in the kitchen, Matthew could tell that it wasn't just him who had overheard the conversation in the private dining room. Joan was in a temper and from experience, he knew it would take her at least three days before she regained her good humour.

He didn't blame her. The conversation that he'd heard in snatches – he, too, knew where the gaps in the wall were – had confirmed all of his suspicions. He'd never trusted Edward. He looked too rich to be a simple country town physician and now he had a good idea where some of that extra money was coming from.

After clearing away the empty flagons and glasses, he left the sweeping up of the room to Annie, whose calm expression suggested she at least had been spared the details of the conversation.

'They treat you well, Annie?'

The girl bobbed her head. 'Yes, Mr Alban. The woman was ever so beautiful, wasn't she?'

Matthew grunted. The room still stank of her perfume – a cloying, sickening fragrance.

'The physician was friendly, too. He doesn't usually frequent this inn, does he?'

No, he bloody well doesn't, thought Matthew, so why the hell did he choose it tonight? A thought struck him.

'He didn't ask any questions, did he?'

'He only asked if we were busy. I said not at the moment, although we had a few guests staying.'

Matthew went cold.

'Did he ask about any in particular?'

'Oh, no.' The girl turned her face away from him.

'Are you sure?'

Annie jumped at his raised voice.

'I'm sure.'

'That's all right, then.'

Taking a deep breath, Matthew joined Joan in the kitchen.

'It's a hanging offence, what he's up to,' said Joan.

She didn't look at him, her arms immersed in a deep tub of water. If she wasn't careful, he'd have no more plates left to serve his food.

'I know.' Matthew didn't want to get into the morals of it.

'Do you think it's connected to . . .?' Joan jerked her head to the ceiling, indicating one of the rooms on the upper floor.

Matthew had no doubt who she was referring to.

'I don't know. Probably. Too much of a coincidence for it not to be.'

'Can't you prohibit him? Stop him from conducting his filthy business in this inn? It's not like you, Matthew, to put up with such things.'

'If he's here, I can follow what he's up to. Otherwise, Hester's going to walk into a hornets' nest.'

'You think she's in danger?'

'As you said, it's a hanging offence. If he's connected to the workhouse, he's not giving cough syrup to the women, is he? He was asking Annie about our guests here, too.'

'Oh no. What did she say?'

'Nothing according to her, but I want you to check, Joan. Can you do that? She wouldn't meet my eye.'

'I'll speak to the girl before she goes to bed. Sly devil, picking on her. He's evil.' Joan wiped her hands on a towel.

'Perhaps.'

She stared at him in astonishment. 'You don't think he is?'

'There's evil around. I can sense it. I wonder, though, if there isn't someone else more dastardly than Holland.'

# Chapter Forty-One

Hester found Joan tight-lipped the following morning when she brought in the breakfast. She was civil enough but didn't want to talk, which suited Hester after a disturbed night. She'd dreamed of fire – that old dream where she was engulfed by flames in a burning building. As beams cracked and timber fell, she heard the sound of horses stampeding, desperate to get away. The dream was so vivid, she woke with the smell of fire in her nostrils and hurried to the window to see if the inn's stables had caught alight in the night. The yard was empty except for a farrier going about his business.

'I see Edward was here last night. Did he have business here?'

Joan put the tray down on the table with a bang.

'How would I know?'

Hester turned, surprised by Joan's temper.

'Have I done something to upset you?'

'Not you, dear, not you. Take no notice of me. You'll find your dress hanging in the closet. I spent an hour brushing the mud off the hem this morning.'

'Joan, I'm sorry.'

'Oh, don't worry. We're all like bears with a sore head this morning.'

Hester took a mouthful of the bread and conserve from the tray. From outside, she heard a burst of shouting, Matthew's voice filling the morning air. She crossed to the window and saw him bawling out a sobbing Annie.

'What's going on out there? Has something happened?'

Joan crossed the room to join Hester at the window.

'Annie's getting a telling-off. Don't worry about it. Matthew's bark is worse than his bite.'

'What's she done?'

'Nothing to worry about.'

Hester stared at Matthew, who looked about to cuff the maid.

'Are you sure?'

'Of course I am. Discretion is the most important thing when it comes to the running of an inn. Annie's young – she'll learn.'

Hester turned at the note of doubt in Joan's voice.

'What is it?'

'Nothing to worry about, dear, only . . .'

'Only what?'

'Matthew thought it better you stay in your room today. There are coaches coming and going and it's best you're not seen.'

'Of course,' she said, fuming.

Another man telling her what to do. Well, she had to put up with it with Amos, but Matthew was a different matter.

After Joan had returned to the kitchen, Hester left the rest of her breakfast and dressed in haste. Feeling like a thief, she went down the stairs with her boots in hand, slipping them on her feet once she reached the door. She pulled her bonnet down over her face and set off, looking for a street hawker to question.

On the other side of the street, she saw a girl selling matches.

'I'm looking for Lizzie. She carries a baby around with her but asks after another. Do you know who I mean?'

The girl's eyes were huge as saucers in her thin face.

'I know who you mean, but I ain't seen her this morning.'

In frustration, Hester carried on. She returned to the spot of their first meeting, outside the milliner's, and then to the place where she'd passed the girl from Dorothea's gig. Both spots were empty save for wisps of mist from the autumn morning. Stumped, Hester moved into a doorway as the lamplighter came along to extinguish the flame on the lamp at the street corner. She kept her head down and called out to him.

'Have you seen the girl with the baby who is often on this crossroads?'

'I saw her standing on the edge of the field hosting the apple fair. Try there.'

He moved on, uninterested.

The field of the fair was empty, but Hester could still conjure the sounds of that day in her head, from the music of the players to the shouts of the crowd. She crossed the field, her boots sinking into the mud up to her calves. She could well imagine Joan's face when she saw the state of her dress again.

When she reached the far end, where the races had taken place, she stopped, debating which way to turn. Lizzie had mentioned the potter's field when they last spoke – a biblical reference Hester knew well. There were enclosed areas to either side of her, one filled with gorse stretching into the distance, the other with a copse of trees in the middle.

As she was considering, Mercy appeared, her mouth gaping in terror as she looked towards the field Hester had passed through.

'What is it?'

She turned and was blinded by the low sun. Putting her hands to her forehead to shield her eyes, she saw two figures making their way across the field towards her. Farmers? There were no livestock in sight and these two men were closely watching her as they approached.

As a cloud inched across the sky, covering the sun for a moment, she was able to study the men more carefully. She recognised the rotund form of one of her attackers from the market, along with the slighter figure of his accomplice.

'Mercy, help me!'

Panicking, Hester lifted her skirts and began to run.

They were on her at once. They had advantage in both speed and attire. She tripped over the hem of her dress, regained her balance and lost it again, falling face first into the scrubland. The burly man picked her up by the shoulders and the other had her feet.

'Take your hands off me!'

One assailant picked up a stone and, with a sickening crack, she felt the blow on her head, and everything went dark.

Hester was in her nightmare. In a pit in the ground, the cold earth chilling her body and the damp seeping into her dress. The two men stood over her, throwing lumps of earth on her face. She let out a moan, lifting her hand to wipe the soil away.

'She's not dead yet,' said one, surprised. 'You're supposed to kill them before they go in the grave.'

'You do it. You struck the first blow. I've not killed a woman before.'

'You'll take your share of the money easily enough though, won't you? Pass me that stone at your feet.'

Hester rolled onto her side, trying to stand, but the blow had left her groggy. In an instant, one of the men was in the grave.

'Watch out for the corpses,' shouted the other. 'They give off foul fumes. I've heard of men being overcome and then joining them in the grave.'

In terror, Hester tried to crawl away.

'Now don't be like that, my Quaker friend.'

He approached her, rock in hand, lifting it to strike the blow.

'Do you have my baby?'

Both Hester and her attacker shrieked at the sound of the voice above them.

'Jesus, who's that? It's a spectre.'

The man at the top of the pit took a step back.

'I'm looking for my child. Did you kill her?'

Hester saw the girl, who did look like a phantom in the mist. The baby in her arms let out a wail like a banshee, which mingled with the thin air, turning Hester's blood to ice. Her attacker dropped the stone and scrabbled out of the grave muttering curses, which failed to hide his horror. Hester heard the pair squelch off quickly into the distance, shouting oaths at each other.

Hester rolled on her side, wincing at the earlier injury to her ribs, and tried to stand. She lifted an arm towards the girl.

'Can you help me, please?'

'I'm looking for my baby. Is she down there with you?'

Hester grasped clumps of grass and, inch by inch, hauled herself out. She refused absolutely to look at the shapes at the other end of the pit.

The girl kept her distance. The baby's shrieks had turned to rasping sobs and its mother rocked it, her mind elsewhere. On all fours, Hester vomited, shock and terror convulsing her body.

'Please, help me to stand. I have to get back to The Black Griffin inn.'

'I can't leave.'

'Why not?'

'My baby is here somewhere, I'm sure of it.'

Hester looked up at the girl.

'If you help me, I promise, I give you my word that I'll help you to find your child.'

There was silence and blood had begun to trickle down Hester's face and into her eyes. Without help, she'd be left here to die and the men would have achieved their aim, she was sure of it. Just as she was deciding to lay her cheek on the cold, hard ground, she felt an icy hand touch her wrist. She grasped the girl, who pulled her upright.

Hester learned that morning that you sometimes have to rely on another, less strong than you, when times are desperate. They stumbled across the field as Hester's legs wobbled and the baby shrieked. The girl knew the way – she might have lost some of her wits, but not all of them.

She got them to The Black Griffin, where they burst into the dining room. Annie was stoking the fire and she let out a piercing shriek, bringing Matthew and Joan rushing into the room. They both made to catch Hester, but it was Matthew who got there first. He grasped her around the waist and began to haul her up the stairs.

'The inn is busy. I need you out of sight. What happened?'

'I was attacked. The two men who stole my purse on market day. They were following me when I went out this morning.' Hester's head swam.

'Christ.'

'How do they know that I didn't leave? Have they been watching the inn?'

Matthew swore again.

'Annie told your friend Edward last night that there was a lone woman guest here. He must have guessed it was you.' With a heave, he shouldered open the door to her chamber. 'Where's Joan?' he shouted over his shoulder.

Annie was hovering behind them.

'She's seeing to the baby.'

'Get some hot water from the kettle and some linen. I need to clean Hester up. Get Joan up here, too. You look after the baby. You know how to do that, don't you?'

'Oh yes, I'm the eldest of nine.'

'Well, run off then, and keep your trap shut if any of the guests ask you what's the matter. This is your fault.'

With a wail, the girl fled and Hester felt herself being lowered onto the bed.

# Chapter Forty-Two

Matthew disappeared while Joan peeled off Hester's bloodstained shawl and began to bathe the wound on her head. They could hear him pacing the passage outside the door, his boots marching across the splintered floorboards. When she'd finished, Joan took the small looking glass from the wall and brought it over to Hester.

'There's only a small mark. It'll be the blow that caused any damage, not the cut.'

Hester stared at her face, rubbed raw after Joan's cleaning, and saw a thin gash on her temple. Joan handed her a muslin cloth.

'Hold that over the wound. How's your headache?'

'My brain is fit to burst.'

'I'll soak some brown paper in vinegar, that'll do the trick.'

The thought of the old cure made Hester want to retch again, but she was too tired to argue. As Joan hurried away, Matthew took her place, his face set as he pulled up a chair.

'You look terrible.'

'Thank you very much.'

Hester wished she didn't look so weak in front of this man. She had to make him believe in her competence if she was to be allowed to stay and carry on. Lying with a cloth to her head was hardly achieving that.

'What the hell were you doing creeping out of the inn before breakfast? I knew there was danger afoot.'

'Oh, did you? And you never thought to tell me yourself? You left it to Joan to inform me that I was to keep to my room.'

This infuriated him further.

'I don't need to hide behind women's skirts. If I'd seen you, I'd have told you myself. I was going to at least wait until you were dressed. How are you feeling?'

'As I look. Terrible. And before you suggest it, I'm not leaving.'

He snorted. 'No, I didn't think you were. You're not in any fit state, anyhow, to make the journey.'

Hester was aware of the quiet of the inn, the baby's bawls gone.

'Where's Lizzie, the girl who helped me here?'

'Taken fright and left. Wouldn't let Annie have the baby even to clean it up.'

'Poor girl. I doubt she accepts help from anyone. She saved my life. If it hadn't been for her asking about her baby, they'd have killed me.'

'I have no doubt about that. Can you describe them?'

'One large and round, the other smaller and thinner. I think they had fair hair. The mist was bad, so I can't describe their faces. Do you know them?'

'Not immediately. I shall look out for a pair fitting their description. I'll tell Joan and Annie to keep their eyes peeled, too.'

Hester pressed the muslin more firmly to her wound, her head still pulsating with pain.

'Are they likely to seek me out again?'

Matthew stood and went to the window.

'Do they know you're still alive?'

'I'm sure they do. One jumped down into the pit to finish what he'd started.'

'Then they'll come back here and watch the pub. I can't see anyone at the moment but, if they're in the employ of Edward Holland, they'll know you're staying here.'

'Edward? He's surely not responsible for the men. He was all concern for me after my last attack.'

'Well, who else is responsible?'

Hester jumped as Matthew's voice rose.

'I don't know.'

'All right, have it that your Doctor Holland is whiter than snow. I'm not in the mood for arguments now. All I'm saying is that while your attackers might have taken fright in a field, they'll be more confident in town. We need to take care.' He patted her like he might a horse. 'Try to get some rest.'

She dozed that afternoon and the headache eased. She wasn't sure if it was the mush of soggy brown paper reeking of vinegar or whether the blow had done less damage than she feared. She even managed to eat some supper, taking sips of the warming soup Joan brought up. That evening, however, as darkness fell, Hester was truly afraid. She knew that her life was in danger and there was little she could do to protect herself.

Matthew made a performance of shutting up the pub once the midnight coach had left. She heard him go from room to room, closing the shutters and finally locking and barring the side door. Annie came in to do the same with Hester's window coverings, closing off the sound of the street so that all she could hear was the muffled noise of horses' hooves and cries from the night pedlars who would find no customers here at The Black Griffin. A private coach had attempted to book a meal at half past midnight – the message had come from a rider sent ahead and Matthew had declined the much-needed business.

As the inn settled for the night, with Joan back in her house and Annie finishing the last of the cleaning tasks in the kitchen, Hester felt well enough to throw a cloak over herself and creep downstairs. Matthew was sitting near the fire contemplating the dying embers, the dog snoring at his feet. A boy was scraping dirt off a pair of boots, the swishing of his brush the only sound to be heard.

'That's enough. You can sleep indoors tonight. Will the fire in the dining room do you?'

The boy didn't need asking twice. With a grateful look at Matthew, he picked up the boots and scuttled off.

'I'd rather the doors remain shut now. I don't want anyone injured.'

'You think they might try something tonight?' Hester reached down to pat the dog.

'It's possible. If they've been hired to kill you, then they won't have earned their fee yet.'

'You're sure you don't know who the men are?'

He shrugged. 'Some ruffians. Their names don't matter – they're hired to do the job. Try to get some sleep. We're secure for the night at least.'

Back in her chamber, Hester waited in the silence, refusing to undress in case she needed to flee. There was a lock on her door but no key. She dragged her portmanteau in front of the entrance, which would do little more than slow an attacker. She heard Annie's cough and saw the light of her tallow candle as she passed her door. In the attic, she heard a door shut and the inn was quiet. Matthew must be keeping watch downstairs, as she didn't hear another climb the stairs.

Hester blew out her candle and lay in the darkness wide awake. She felt the mattress sag as if a person were sitting on the bed.

'Mercy, is that you?' she whispered.

No reply, of course, but she felt the room expand and some of the tension leave her.

In the street came a sharp cry, turning her insides to jelly. Moments later, she heard a creak on the stairs and, in desperation, she reached for the candlestick and grasped it. The person knew which door to knock.

'Who is it?'

'Me, Matthew.'

Hester got up and pulled her portmanteau away from the door. Matthew was standing outside, holding a lamp, which dazzled her eyes.

'May I come in? Don't light the candle. I'm not a pretty sight.'

He kept the lamp high so she couldn't see him clearly. She reached out to steady herself on his arm and gasped as she felt a sticky thickness attach itself to her fingers.

'You're injured?'

'Not me. This isn't my blood.'

She took a step away from him. 'What—'

'Someone tried to get in. A stealthy fellow, but he tried both the side and kitchen doors. They were secure enough, so he made a watch on the pavement opposite. He never saw me coming.'

'Just one man?'

'For now. I didn't kill him, if that's what you're worried about. I grew up on a farm. I know what wounds kill and what maim.'

'Is he still out there?'

'I sent him off, limping into the night. He won't be back.'

'And his friend?'

'He'll be assuming he's got a night off. Probably drunk in another inn. For tonight, at least, we'll be all right.'

He pulled the chair away from the table and lowered himself into it, resting the lamp on the floor.

'Now, listen. There's a stagecoach heading south at ten in the morning. If there's not space inside, the days are fair and you can ride outside. It's not ideal, but I can give you my coat. It'll get you to London, where you change at The Swan with Two Necks. There's a coach to Bristol that evening. I know you don't want to go, but the minute you're out of Nottinghamshire, you'll be safe.'

'I'm not going anywhere,' Hester hissed.

He grabbed her arm, his fingers digging into her skin.

'Don't pretend you're not afraid, because I can smell the fear coming off you.'

'Another thing you learned on the farm?'

'No, I've learned it as the landlord of The Black Griffin. I've heard more tales of woe, of despair, of thievery and blackguardery than any man should hear. I've learned to smell fear and act on it. You don't have that skill, Hester, which is why you need to be away from here.'

'If I leave now, I'll have failed, don't you see? I need to know what happened to Mercy and the child.'

'What's the point? You know the way of the world from your do-gooding. There *is* no justice. Some are rich, some poor. Some live, some die. There isn't any reason behind it. Is there something else that propels you?'

She felt utterly weary. He wanted rid of her and she couldn't blame him. But with him reeking of the butcher's shop, it was a night of confidences. She told him first of her dreams. He listened with his eyes on her.

'There's plenty that lay a lot of store on dreams, but I'm not one of them. So, one of your worst came to pass today. It means nothing.'

'There's more.' Hester searched around for the words that would explain everything but wouldn't having him packing her off to the asylum. 'I see spirits. People who have died. I have done ever since I was a child.'

She'd shocked him, she saw. His eyes widened and he turned his face away.

'I can see you don't believe me. No one does, except my maid, Susanna. I've spent most of my life having to pretend they don't exist. It made my father froth at the mouth and I was forbidden to talk about it – Mercy was the same. She, too, told me it was stuff and nonsense, and the matter came between us a little.'

'They're here with you now?'

She remembered the pressure on the mattress and the sense of Mercy lying beside her. Her spirit had fled at the sound of Matthew's knock.

'They come and go.'

'What do you mean by they? Who do you see?'

Hester massaged her aching temple. 'My sister, Mercy, has been alongside me ever since she died. There's another, too, who started following me around the same time. Much harder to grasp. While I was in Bristol, I felt someone else walking behind me.'

'Friend or foe?'

Hester felt a spark of hope at the question. He didn't regard her as insane.

'I'm not sure. I sense despair, but it's hard to hold onto the sensation. I sometimes feel my grasp of reality shifting. Until today, I thought the girl with the baby was a spirit, as no one else seemed to see her.'

'That's because she doesn't want to be seen. It seems to me you have a knack not just of seeing spirits, but also the living who normally prefer to remain hidden.'

Hester laid her head against the bedstead and groaned.

'What are we going to do? I'm staying here, but I cannot remain in this room forever. I need an ally and it seems it'll have to be you. Can I ask you to help me find out what happened to Mercy's child?'

# Chapter Forty-Three

Matthew looked at the girl and considered his options. Hester wouldn't take the carriage home, he saw that. If he were unlucky, she'd slip away from the inn and find herself another room in which to do her meddling. He hadn't liked using the knife this evening. He preferred keeping it for animals already dead. Skinning a rabbit, for example, or carving up a dead game bird.

There had been the sickening sound of steel meeting bone when he'd plunged the blade into the man's thigh. The villain had bled so much, Matthew wondered if he'd severed an artery, but the speed with which the man had hobbled away convinced him that he'd done what he'd set out to do. He'd maimed the man enough to get relief for the night.

Tomorrow would bring the other assailant and he'd be unlikely to be able to creep up on him, too. Perhaps if he told the girl at least part of the truth, she'd know how much danger she was in.

'So,' he said, the chair creaking as he shifted his weight. 'Tell me what you *do* know.'

'It all centres around the pale lady, which Elisabet, the Swedish girl in the workhouse, told me about the first time I arrived here.'

Matthew kept his expression neutral as he thought back to the previous time when she'd arrived on his doorstep and he'd called her Quaker Jane. What an oaf he must have seemed to her.

'Some of the women think she's a ghost who comes to take their babies away. Because of my shadowing, at first I thought she might be a spirit, the type I see. Or perhaps just a rumour, a kind of hobgoblin conjured by the women to frighten each other. Now, I don't.'

'You think the pale lady is a flesh-and-blood woman who takes away babies?'

'Yes, that's what I believe. Elisabet called her an angelmaker. The Scandinavians use it as a term for women who are charged with collecting babies from mothers and delivering them to other women to raise in return for a fee. The mothers send money for their child's keep when they can. Even in the workhouse, it's possible to scrabble together a few coins.'

'So, the pale lady comes to collect them. If the women have given up their children willingly, why are they so afraid of her?'

'Because I don't think all of the women at the workhouse do give them up voluntarily. I also suspect that some of the children never reach their destination. Some live and some die. I can't find the pattern in how they decide.'

'Money?'

'Money is one possibility, but I think some children die even when coins have changed hands.'

'You think children are killed in this town and no one knows about it?'

She had her eyes on him. 'I think you know something.'

'Me?' Confound the woman, he thought.

'You've never liked me going near the workhouse. Are you now going to tell me why?'

Matthew hesitated. It was hard to articulate prejudice and mistrust, but he guessed, after all she'd told him, that this was a girl who would understand instinct.

'This is an inn. A crossing place, if you will. Apart from my workers, no one stays long. I'd trust those in my employ with my life, but the people who use the inn, I just watch and listen.' He looked down at his bloodied coat. 'There have been tales.'

'Of what?'

'Women dying in childbirth. Not so odd, perhaps. It's a dangerous condition, but they're not looked after well in the workhouse. Then there's the babies.'

'You do know something. What is it?'

'To take a baby from the Union, you need a coach or cart. I've had mine hired at odd times in the past. They feel like furtive transactions – I don't like them.'

'Who hires them?'

'They don't show their faces. Whoever they are, they send servants, and rarely the same one.'

'But didn't you ask who their master was?'

'Of course I asked. They weren't telling. Then I noticed the hiring coincided with births at the workhouse and I wanted nothing more to do with it. The inn shuts at night now.'

'So, where do they get their carts from? Another inn?'

'I assume so.'

'And that's it? Just the carts made you suspicious?'

A wave of fury welled in him. How could this girl look so deep inside him?

'There are the women, too. The mothers left behind without the child. The girl who brought you here—'

'Lizzie.'

'She cries at night. She stands outside the milliner's shop and wails like a banshee. It goes right through to my bones, although I've tried to shutter the window to drown out the sound. That isn't a woman who has voluntarily given up her child.'

'Are there others?'

He shrugged. 'There must be.'

'And you think Edward Holland is involved in some way. Is it because he was here the other night?'

He wondered how much to tell her. He could have explained it to a farm girl. They knew all about copulating and what the result of it was. Hester knew it in theory. Her sister had experienced what happened when you chose the wrong mate. But how much did she actually know of the mechanics of it all?

He took a deep breath. 'When you're expecting and you don't want the child, you have options.'

'Like the angelmaker.'

He could have sworn. No, not the damned angelmaker, he wanted to say. Much worse.

'No, before they're born.'

He saw her pale.

'I've heard such tales. Herbs and tinctures to bring on early labour.'

'The midwives are expert in that. But when they fail? What then?'

She shook her head. 'I don't know.'

'There are men and women – mainly women, I thought, but men, too – I know who will aid the surgical removal of the child. Edward Holland is one such man.'

# Chapter Forty-Four

Hester wasn't as naïve as Matthew thought. She knew of such women able to rid you of babies. She'd seen what happened when it went wrong. A woman taken to Bristol Infirmary, her insides on fire. An infection, her mother had told her, but Hester had listened to the idle chatter of people around her and had understood. Babies were disposable if you knew the right person. But the calm and respectable Edward . . . Could he really be responsible for such acts?

'The couple who came in a wealthy carriage. They weren't husband and wife?'

'Lord Pulley has no wife, but he's engaged to the daughter of an earl in Wiltshire. He wants no bastard getting in the way of that match.'

'You overheard the discussions.'

'No, Hester, I didn't overhear. I was listening in, although none in the room were aware of me. I like to know what goes on in my hostelry.'

'The lady is pregnant?'

'She is.'

'And Doctor Holland agreed to help her get rid of it.'

Matthew made a face. 'I'm not sure if he'll commit the act himself. Men such as he don't get their hands dirty. Perhaps he knows of a woman who will carry out the procedure.'

'A midwife?'

'Our town's midwife is respectable. She'd never touch such a thing. But there is a person I've heard of. I don't know how they learned their butchery and I don't want to, either, but they'll be contacted via Doctor Holland.'

'Then Edward must be Quare.'

'I said he's not a man to get his hands dirty.'

'But the woman's life will be in danger. Isn't there anything we can do?'

'We're all in danger. I need to think what to do next.'

Hester, still frightened after her day, gathered her courage.

'Today, when I was attacked, I was in a field near the apple fair. I was looking for Lizzie, the girl who rescued me.'

'To what end?'

'To question her.'

'But her mind is gone. I hear her screams at night. If I could shut out her cries with new windows, I would. It's a call from the dead.'

'The pit I told you about hadn't been dug for me.' Hester swallowed. 'There were bodies already in it.'

'A churchyard?'

'No, of course not. A field, I told you.'

'And where is this place?'

'I don't know exactly. I was trying to find it when I was attacked. Near where we met on the day of the fair.'

'That's church land. They take a hefty rent for the annual fair.'

'There's a field beyond there. The women call it the potter's field.'

Matthew frowned. 'There's no potter out there.'

'It's a biblical name. From where Judas' thirty pieces of silver – the profits he earned by betraying Jesus – were buried. After that, it was a place for burying strangers and outcasts. The women call that piece of grassland the potter's field.'

'Why?'

'There's a grave there. I was nearly buried among the dead myself.'

He stood, towering over her. 'This isn't your imagination, is it?'

'It is not.' Groaning, Hester slid off the bed. 'If you don't believe me, I'll take you there myself.'

'At night? You're injured. We'll wait till morning, then I'll take a look.'

'Morning will be too late. They know I've found it. The pit will be filled in by then, I'm sure.'

'I know what dug soil looks like. I'll find it.'

'And my attackers? They'll be looking for revenge on you.'

Matthew stood, grimacing. 'I'll go at dawn. I can slip out and be back before the first coach. Describe the place to me.'

'I want to come with you. Please.'

Matthew regarded her and perhaps saw the resolve in her face.

'Aren't you frightened after what happened today? You nearly joined the dead.'

'I have to carry this to the end.'

Matthew came for her at five, the moon still low in the sky. Hester had washed and redressed in Joan's gown and saw he was wearing clean clothes.

'Joan will have a job getting my old coat clean. Are you ready?' he asked.

'I am. Do you have a lantern?'

'We walk by moonlight.' Matthew took her arm. 'You hold on to my jacket and we'll find the field together. I can guide you as far as the church land and you must tell me there where you think the field is. A lantern will attract too much attention. I'm well known around Southwell. Keep your head down. If we see the nightwatchman, we'll move into the shadows.'

The town was silent as they slipped out of the inn. Hester looked across to where the man had stood and saw only a dark liquid on the floor. Matthew pulled her along.

'Don't dawdle,' he hissed.

They hurried across cobbles, through narrow passages until they came to the field that had been such a riot of sounds only days earlier. Her foot sank into the mud and slime as they crossed to the far boundary.

'Which way now?' asked Matthew, keeping his voice low.

'I was carried a short distance. I think Lizzie helped me through two fields on my return.'

'The land to the east is exposed. There's nowhere to hide a grave. The western field has a small copse. An ideal place for a burial. We'll try there first.'

Hester stumbled after Matthew, aware of her pounding head. The boundary between the church field and the common ground was only a small ditch, upon them before Hester realised, when she felt her boot fill with water.

'I crossed this field – I remember the ditch.'

'Then we carry on.'

They continued their trudge until they reached the copse. Matthew let out a retching cough.

'Jesus, Hester. How can you come back here? I can smell the dead in my nostrils.'

'What?'

'Can't you smell it? We go no further together.'

'But—'

'You stay here and I'll look near the trees. If one of us is to fall into an open grave, it might as well be me. We keep talking.'

'Why?'

'Noxious fumes can kill a man. If I stop speaking, it means I've been overcome. You then run back in the direction we came and wake one of the ostlers. Do you hear me? You don't come after me or you'll be as dead as I am.'

'I understand,' said Hester, although she didn't.

She couldn't see that if Matthew stopped talking, she'd run away from him. But she knew he wouldn't leave her unless she agreed. In the moonlight, she saw him swoop down and pick up a fallen branch which he used to stab at the ground in front of him before he took a step forwards. Presently, he moved out of sight and she was forced to wait in the night, where only foxes foraged and, in the distance, a coach approached the town. She heard Matthew talking, although his words were now indistinct. Then, all of a sudden, silence.

'Matthew?' she called.

To her relief his harsh voice carried across to her.

'I'm all right. Stay where you are.'

She saw the flare of a match and then another. Finally, the figure turned and made its way back to her, the stick discarded.

'What did you see?' she asked.

He drew a breath and she could smell the fear and the fury.

'There were women. Babies, too. It was like hell. Hell on Earth.'

# Chapter Forty-Five

Matthew was silent on the way back to the inn. Only when he'd unlocked the side door and bolted it behind her had he extracted Hester's promise to say nothing to Joan.

'I need to think what to do.'

'How can a place be hidden in plain sight?'

Matthew shrugged. 'It's private land. Well away from the town.'

She saw him still trying to fathom what he'd seen.

'There's something else, isn't there?'

He sighed. 'Not much gets past you, does it? I didn't see any signs of soil to infill the grave. There should be a heap of earth ready to be placed back on the bodies.'

'I felt soil land on me when I was lying in the grave.'

'There is some, but not enough to cover the whole area. I think the pit is always left open.'

'What?'

'It's common enough. Saves them digging each time.'

'Do you think there'll be another body soon?'

'Hester, I don't know.'

Back in her chamber, she made a decision. Whatever Matthew's plans were, she didn't think it involved her staying in Southwell. He'd insist that she leave on a coach, and she'd be helpless. There was also the complication of Ruth, who would already have received Dorothea's note to expect Hester's return. Susanna would have been despatched to meet the London coach and would have returned home each time without Hester. If she was lucky, her lack of appearance might be put down to a miscommunication. Ruth might wait a day before sending a letter back to Dorothea or she might write immediately. If that were the case, by tomorrow, Dorothea would already know she hadn't left Southwell.

Unless, of course, it was Dorothea who was in cahoots with Edward, but that made no sense. Dorothea had appeared upset at having to send Hester back to Bristol. Caroline might conceivably know about Edward's character, but she showed little interest in the workhouse.

Thinking about the various possibilities made Hester's head ache even more. She had a small window of time to act and it was the note of fear in Matthew's voice that had convinced her that the time had come.

She shouldn't have slept, of course, but she was so weary and sore that she plunged into oblivion as soon as she pulled a blanket over her. It was around three in the afternoon when she woke, roused by the rattling of a key in the lock. Annie entered, carrying a tray.

'Who locked me in?'

'Matthew said it was for your protection but that you wouldn't like it. It took him ages to find the key.' The girl giggled.

'Where's Joan?'

'In the kitchen. Busy.' The girl looked out of the window. 'Why, there's the midwife hurrying along.'

'What do you mean?'

The girl strained to follow the woman's progress.

'I wonder where she's going. She isn't half in a hurry. Somewhere out of town.'

'The workhouse?'

'Maybe. I dunno.' Annie wasn't interested.

'Will you tell Joan I want a word with her? Don't tell Mr Matthew.'

Joan was up immediately, full of curiosity. She'd picked up the atmosphere of the inn that morning and Matthew had proved to be tight-lipped. Hester, deflecting her questions, told her what she wanted her to do.

'I can probably manage it. Those clothes do show up around town. You're sure you want to do this?'

'I'm sure, and don't say anything to Matthew.'

Joan nodded. 'He'll have my skin when he finds out.'

'It's my only chance. Please, do what you can.'

Joan appeared around teatime with a bundle of rags which, when unwrapped, revealed themselves as the clothes of the workhouse. They'd been stamped with the message 'stolen from Southwell Union' in advance of their theft as if the board of guardians was well aware of the disreputable nature of its inmates. They were very clean. Hester had noticed how each woman, even among the undeserving poor, was not only dressed identically, but also smelled of carbolic soap.

'It's the washing,' said Joan as she tied Hester's apron around her.

It was long with deep pockets, although what the pauper women kept in them Hester couldn't fathom.

'They make the inmates wash in the morning, before every meal and at night,' said Joan. 'Cleanliness is next to godliness, I suppose, although I personally think God would prefer kindliness if it's a toss-up between the two.'

'I think any form of kindness is sadly wanting inside the Union.'

Joan spun Hester round and surveyed her.

'I think you'll do. You'll not fool anyone, of course, if they see your face. But, from the back, you'll pass as one of them. What's your plan?'

Hester moved over to the small mirror on the wall, its glass pitted with brown spots. She'd lost weight since arriving at the inn, despite the efforts of Joan to feed her three big meals a day.

'I don't have any plans. I'll slip into the women's wing and wait.'

'But why tonight?'

Hester stared at her reflection.

'Because a baby is about to be born.'

# Chapter Forty-Six

Dusk was falling when Hester passed through the workhouse gates. It was dinner time and, in the distance, she could hear the sound of spoons scraping against bowls, hungry diners trying to squeeze the last morsel from their meal. The porter, as she'd suspected, had slipped away for his evening draught. He'd be at Matthew's inn right now, wondering why Joan, who had never previously given him the time of day, was suddenly interested in his army experiences fighting Napoleon.

Hester could well imagine the weariness of the people having their evening meal. Men tired of breaking bones, their arms heavy. Women, thinking about their straw beds after a day of laundry. Even Mr and Mrs Kirkham would be tired. Keeping people controlled with an iron will required effort, too. Hester hoped the workhouse, just for tonight, would be slumbering enough that it might keep everyone off guard.

She crept around the west of the building, passing three women leaving the cowshed, who paid her no attention. The door to the yard at the back was open and she entered the long, silent corridor and climbed the stairs, her eyes darting around as she approached the undeserving women's dormitory. As she pushed open the door, Ellen shot upright, her lips working with fear.

'It's me, Hester.'

'What are you doing in them clothes?'

'Never mind about that. Where are the other women, Ellen? Is everyone else being fed?'

'Must be. They said they'd bring me something a bit later, but I ain't bothered. I feel sick.'

'Not a fever?'

'Oh, no. I'm just not up to eating. They gave me some broth when I'd given birth.'

Hester jumped when she heard a tread on the stair, but whoever it was had a change of heart and turned tail.

'What did you have, a girl or a boy?'

'A boy. A bit scrawny, but healthy enough.' She looked pleased, fit to burst with pride.

'Where is he now?'

'With the other children, miss. It's him you can hear crying.'

She heard it now. The thin, reedy sound from undeveloped lungs. It sounded like a cat mewing, but Ellen knew the cry of her own child.

'You don't keep him with you?'

'Oh no, miss. Mrs Kirkham would never allow that. They bring the baby to me to be fed and that's it.'

Hester sat on the bed, her plans hitting a block. She'd intended to hide in the dormitory near Ellen, but her heart told her she needed to keep close to the child.

'Where do the children sleep?'

Ellen reached out to grasp Hester's shawl.

'You'll watch over my baby for me?'

'I'm going to do my best, but I need to be careful. I can't help you on my own. I need to watch, see with my own eyes who your enemy is, and then go for help. It'll be good if I can take the baby away from here.'

'You?'

'You trust me, don't you?'

She saw the girl shake her head.

'Listen, Ellen, am I the pale lady?'

'Of course not.'

'Then you have nothing to fear from me.'

Hester felt her head swim and her ribs ache with the older wound.

*Mercy, appear before me, please*, she pleaded. *Give me strength when I most need it.*

The room remained still as the grave. Another tread on the stairs brought her to her senses.

'Listen, Ellen. Is there somewhere to hide in the children's wing?'

'I don't know. My baby's always brought to me. I told you.'

Hester could hear the footsteps get closer.

'I need somewhere I can watch over the child. When you've seen the pale lady in the past, which way does she come up to this floor?'

'Up the master's staircase, but we see her from our beds. She stands in the doorway as if taunting us that she's going to take away our child.'

'She taunts the women in the undeserving wing?'

'It's our bairns who are most at risk.'

'What do you mean?'

She was interrupted by a wail of a child but saw that Ellen wasn't interested.

'That's not your baby's cry?'

'Another who has been born.'

'What? Here?'

'Three nights ago.'

'And it's still here?'

'Of course. It's safe.'

'Why is it safe?'

'It was born in wedlock, wasn't it? The pale lady never comes for legitimate offspring. It's the baseborn children she wants.'

Hester, her head reeling, kneeled beside Ellen.

'They want the illegitimate children? But why? Those poor mothers are entitled to their children, aren't they?'

But even as she spoke, Hester was aware of the naivety of her words. Single women didn't go about their lives with children in tow. They were given to relatives, left behind in orphanages, passed to other couples.

Ellen moaned, putting her hands to her face.

'They started taking our money and then it was the babies, money or not. We have no hope.'

'Ellen.' She grasped hold of the woman's hand. 'I will save your baby.'

# Chapter Forty-Seven

The children's room smelled of whitewash and excrement. Rooms, it seemed, were continually whitewashed as a means of fumigating the building. In the general dormitories, Hester supposed it gave the rooms a fresh atmosphere, but in the children's room, it made for a sickly smell. Not all of the children were asleep – two terrified pairs of eyes peeped from under the blankets. She put a finger to her lips.

'I'm not the pale lady. Go back to sleep.'

The children slid under the covers and pulled their blankets over their heads. Hester counted at least eight bodies crammed into the double bed with about the same number squeezed into the one opposite. There were two cots with babies, one with a chubby stomach gurgling contentedly, the other containing what must be Ellen's child. It lay there with its eyes closed, the most beautiful thing she'd ever seen. The need to reach out and stroke its face was overwhelming.

'Will the pale lady come tonight?' asked a small voice.

She turned and saw a fair-haired child trying to get up from under the thin blanket.

'If she does, let her take the baby. I'll be nearby.' She looked and saw a cupboard in the corner. 'Do you think I could fit in there?'

The child shook her head.

Hester opened the door and saw it was useless for her task. It was fitted with shelves that were stuffed with an assortment of linen. Hester looked at the beds. It had been her plan to hide under one of the women's cots, but in the children's dormitory, the beds were pushed together and were lower to the ground.

'Go to sleep,' she whispered to the child. 'I'll be nearby, I promise.'

She returned to the passageway and pushed open a door. It opened on to a cream room, no whitewash here, with a double bed in the centre and a couch to one side. This must be the Kirkhams' bedroom. Joan had been wrong, though. Although undoubtedly smarter than the dormitories, it didn't give off an air of affluence.

Hester saw that hiding in here would be useless. It gave her no view of the children's room once the door was shut. Back in the passageway were two doors set to one side. The first was the privy, but the other opened on to a store cupboard smelling of washed blankets. She slipped in, keeping the door ajar, so a sliver of light could be seen. It gave her a view of the children's room and the top of the stairs.

For the first hour of her vigil, Hester was happy enough to listen to the sounds of the workhouse. The children settled in their beds, snuffling as they dropped off to sleep. The women followed not long after, their voices muted as they undressed. Hester remained still, praying that no one would open the door. Eventually, at the sound of footsteps, she peered out of the gap. It was the Kirkhams, who entered the bedroom together and shut the door behind them.

The workhouse creaked and groaned in the night. A bitter wind entered the cracks in the windows, cooling the air, and Hester pulled one of the blankets around her to ward off the cold. A child cried out in its sleep and the babies bawled. Hester waited for someone to go to them, but the doors remained shut. Deserving or undeserving poor, babies didn't receive comfort at night.

She dozed, her aching ribs and pounding head urging her towards sleep. She wondered if Matthew had noticed her absence and if Joan had come up with a suitable excuse. What she didn't need was him intruding on her before she saw who the pale lady was.

Her doze was interrupted by a noise so soft that she thought she'd imagined it. She held her breath and it came once more. Hester put her eye to the gap. She saw nothing but heard the creak of a door opening. Footsteps passed the cupboard and made their way down the stairs. Unlike the weary but firm treads of a person coming to bed, this was the soft sound of someone trying to avoid detection.

She considered leaving her hiding place and following the footsteps, but caution stayed her. She tried to imagine how either the master or his wife might treat her if they caught her in the building. There were no excuses she could make. If she were discovered, she'd lose the chance of finally revealing the identity of the pale lady and another child would be gone. She'd follow her original plan and stay with the baby. She stood, shaking her deadened leg. There was the sound of a bolt undoing and another footstep entering the building.

Eventually, there was the tread of two footsteps up the stairs. Mrs Kirkham came into view, holding a lamp to light the way.

'Are you sure the baby's healthy? That it would live if I didn't take it?'

Hester took a breath and thought her lungs might burst. Edward. She stayed absolutely still. Even after everything Matthew had told her, his presence was a shock.

'Them babies are always healthy when I give them to you. I'm not so sure afterwards.' Mrs Kirkham sniffed.

She heard him chuckle softly.

Hester exhaled, all of her illusions dissipating. Matthew's suspicions were right. Edward was a participant in the taking of these children.

The two disappeared into the children's ward and Hester heard one of the children cry out in fear.

'Get back to sleep,' she heard Mrs Kirkham snap. 'Or you'll go without breakfast tomorrow.'

Mrs Kirkham emerged carrying the baby while Edward held the lamp. It cast a sickly amber glow on the woman, her grey attire casting a shadow on the wall. Was she the pale lady? Hester could hardly believe it. The women would be able to recognise the form of the matron who ruled their lives from daybreak to nightfall. She might inspire fear and submission, but she wasn't a supernatural figure.

Hester watched as they crept down the stairs, the baby still snuffling. Now that the child had been removed, she was spurred into action. She opened the door at the same time as a figure emerged from the adjacent room. Her heart nearly stopped – was she finally about to see the pale lady? But it was Ellen panicking at her baby's cries.

'Where are they taking my child?'

Hester put her finger to the girl's lips.

'Ellen, we're in danger but, most of all, your baby is in mortal peril. I thought I'd be able to take the baby from the pale lady, but I see I have to contend with both Doctor Holland and Mrs Kirkham. How well do you feel?'

'I'm still bleeding, but I'm well enough.'

'Will you run to the inn? Tell Matthew Alban, the keeper, that I'm in danger and that Joan will know why. Get him to come as quickly as he can. I'll try to stop the coach leaving with your child. I'll have more standing than you. Trust me. Your baby will not be taken from you, if you do as I say.'

Hester could see the girl hesitating. Eventually, her belief in doing whatever other people told her to do won out and she nodded.

'Go out through the back courtyard. You won't be spotted there.'

The two descended the stairs together and parted company at the bottom. There was no sign of a coach in the courtyard, which would have made too much noise. It must be in the stables out beyond the high wall.

'Hurry,' she whispered to Ellen.

She felt a grip on her arm and a voice in her ear.

'She's not going.'

# Chapter Forty-Eight

Confound all women, thought Matthew, seized by a desire to grab his cousin and friend by the throat. He knew how women conspired together, but they didn't have a brain in their heads. Whoever had come up with the plan, and he was pretty sure it wasn't Joan, had been heedless of the danger that their actions brought about.

Kirkham had a temper on him and so had his wife. He remembered opening the door that one time to the boy, his back raw with shreds of flesh hanging down after the beating meted out to him. Matthew wasn't sure what had shocked him more. The extent of the boy's injuries or his insistence that it had been Mrs Kirkham who had wielded the belt.

Matthew heard that they split the sexes in the workhouse. Women looked after by the mistress. Men, split up from their wives and forced to bow down to Mr Kirkham. Why that young lad, surely too old for the children's ward, had been given to Mrs Kirkham for attention, he didn't know. Perhaps he'd cheeked her or had come to the aid of a female relative. Either way, he'd fled the workhouse for whatever freedom that cold winter's night.

Matthew had intended to offer him a job as a stable lad. He'd been soothed by the horse and slept in the barn. There was always work in the stables. But by morning, the lad had gone, too frightened to spend another hour in Southwell.

Matthew hadn't expected Joan to show any remorse and she didn't.

'The girl's entitled to do what she thinks is right. God only knows what goes on inside that building. Her sister died and the bairn is missing. It's only right that she wants to find out what happened to them.'

'At the risk of her life? What use is she to anyone lying dead alongside her sister?'

Joan chewed her inner lip. 'They wouldn't kill her. What has she done?'

'Oh, it's not the Kirkhams I fear the most. It's the people who line their pockets.'

'What do you mean?'

'The servant is not greater than his master.'

Joan stared at him. 'Quoting the Bible now? That girl's got under your skin.'

'What I'm saying is on a wage of £30 per annum, how can the Kirkhams have bought a farm near Oxton?'

'What?'

'They're nearing retirement and looking for somewhere to rest their bones. That's what they told old Pitt when they bought the farm off him.'

'So, how *did* they afford it?'

Matthew kept a lid on his boiling temper.

'Because they've been supporting a trade in babies and they're not likely to give up their secrets without a fight.'

## Chapter Forty-Nine

Hester's heart nearly failed at the female voice. Was she at last about to see the pale lady? But when she looked down, it was Little Pinch – not in her nightclothes but dressed in her work-house garb.

'I'll go. Ellen's too sick. Shall I fetch the parish constable?'

'Explanations will take too long. Go to Matthew Alban at The Black Griffin. He knows some of it. Not all, but enough. Do you know the place?'

The girl nodded. 'I'll go. I can run faster even on short legs. What if the coach has already left before we return?'

'It'll be still here. I'll see to that.'

'What about me?' asked Ellen. 'And my baby?'

Hester considered. It was too much of a risk for Ellen to return to the dormitory. If she were spotted, the angelmaker might stay in the shadows and Hester would be no nearer to uncovering her identity.

'Go and find the coach. It's most likely in the stable. They'll need to keep it hidden. Wait in the trees nearby. I'll try to make sure the baby doesn't make it to the carriage but, if it does, then you'll need to use your wits. Can you do that?'

The girl regained some of her previous confidence.

'Ain't no one taking my baby,' she said.

The two hurried into the dark, leaving Hester bereft. Both women out in the cold night to save this child. She realised what a fool she'd been to come here alone. She'd thought it would be her pitting her wits against a woman on a quest to steal babies for her own ends. But she hadn't acted alone. Edward was as complicit as Mrs Kirkham and both could easily overpower her. She must wait for Matthew and together, they'd act.

The minutes ticked by as she kept vigil. The temperature dropped to near freezing and her dingy charcoal shawl gave little comfort. She swallowed to keep at bay the nausea caused by her headache. She could hear the taken child crying – not the bawls of earlier but plaintive little gulps coming from a room along the passage. It must be the kitchen. It was the only place where the vestiges of heat would remain.

She crept further along the passage and tried to listen. A woman was speaking – not Mrs Kirkham's reedy intonations but a refined, cultured voice. Who was it? Hester strained to hear, thinking she recognised the rise and fall of the words.

'Why can't we leave now?' she heard the woman say.

'The horse is lame.' Edward's voice was patient. 'We've got a boy changing a shoe, which might be the problem, but we can't go until it's done.'

'I can't be found here.'

Hester leaned in close.

'I shall have a job explaining my presence.'

Hester felt her heart beating fast in her chest. It was Dorothea Francombe, she was sure. No wonder she'd wanted Hester away from her home. It was she who was at the heart of the plot to remove children from the mothers – Ruth's own childhood friend. She heard footsteps approach.

'Sir, I've changed the shoe. It still limps but it's better. He just needs a ride out.'

'Then we'll go,' said Edward. 'Perhaps the pale lady would like to take the baby.'

At the sound of his mocking tones, knowing its heartbroken mother was standing outside in the cold, a flash of fury rose in Hester's chest. She pushed open the door and looked at the baby in a simple wicker basket on the table.

'What are you going to do with that child?'

Mrs Francombe turned and Hester saw with a jolt that she'd got it terribly, fatally wrong. For the woman wasn't Dorothea but Caroline. The girl looked different in the firelight. Gone was the refined and vain expression Hester was used to seeing, replaced by a rigid determination.

'So,' Caroline said, looking across at Edward. 'Who do we have here? Hester, who I've heard has been hiding out at The Black Griffin in the bed of the innkeeper. Now what would the Bristol Friends think of that?'

Hester swallowed, trying hard to keep the terror out of her face. She thought she'd been frightened of her father, but his words were nothing to the danger this woman posed.

'I don't understand . . .'

The girl swept her eyes over Hester's outfit, taking in, Hester thought, her feeble attempts to pass as one of the poor.

'Of course you don't understand.'

It took all of Hester's strength not to take to her heels and run. Only the sight of the newborn in the crib gave her the courage to speak.

'Why, Caroline? Those innocent souls. Not for the money, surely.'

Caroline kept her eyes on Hester, her expression mocking.

'Of course I don't do it for the money. Although I was rather impressed by the profitable scheme that Edward and the Kirkhams had going here.'

'You weren't involved at the beginning?' asked Hester, wondering if Little Pinch had made it to The Black Griffin yet. 'How did it all start?'

Caroline took a seat after shooting Edward a look of contempt.

'As you guessed, Hester, with money. Women came to South-well Union expecting and, naturally, not all mothers would want to keep their babies. So Mr and Mrs Kirkham, along with Edward here, came up with a plan. An arrangement was made – for a fee, of course – to take the babies and place them with foster families. It wasn't difficult to organise. Edward was already providing the service to the wealthy of the county. He just expanded it into Southwell Union. For women not yet showing, they were introduced to a woman who would remove the child from the womb.'

'For God's sake!' shouted Edward. 'Do you want to get us hanged?'

'So, who's Quare?' asked Hester. 'The man who promised that these babies would be humanely taken care of.'

Caroline's eyes slid to Edward.

'You?' said Hester, aghast. 'You're Quare?'

Caroline was amused by Hester's reaction.

'They were all Quare. Edward, the Kirkhams, Reverend Flint, the midwife he uses for abortions. Doctor Quare is a figment of their imagination.'

'Does Rope Walk even exist?' asked Hester.

'It's an address near the asylum.' Caroline sounded bored at having to give explanations. 'If you get that far, the landlord at the inn on the corner knows to direct women to Edward.'

Hester felt sick thinking of the fine woman and gentleman in the carriage.

'But you say the object was money. The women in the work-house are paupers. There's no money to be made on them.'

'Even paupers can spare a few coins,' said Caroline.

'But that goes to the child's new mother, surely.' She thought of Amos's blood money sent from Bristol.

'Not every child,' said Caroline, her voice dropping to a whisper, 'reached its destination. I heard you found the pit. If you think it was my doing, think again. It had been opened long before I was involved, for a few of that old sop of a midwife's mishaps during surgery.'

Hester winced.

Caroline carried on, her voice still full of ennui.

'They'd realised, of course, that there wasn't much money to be skimmed off from fostering workhouse brats, so newborns began to be put in the pit. It doesn't take a young one long to expire from exposure. That way, they got to keep all the money.'

The explanation was one that Hester had expected, but to hear of it so casually told made her nauseous.

'And you?' she asked.

'I saw the card with Doctor Quare's name slip out of Edward's pocket. When I guessed what was going on, I told him I wanted in.'

And Edward couldn't resist Caroline, thought Hester.

'But why? You must be the pale lady who steals these women's babies. They don't hand over their babies by choice.'

'You have to understand, Hester, that for Edward and the Kirkhams, it's purely a financial arrangement. For me, however, it's a matter of morality. If a baby is born to loving parents, then the child stays in the workhouse. The women have nothing to fear.'

'You decide if a child lives based on the marital status of the parents?'

Caroline inclined her head.

'And what gives you the right to choose?'

'God,' she said, her eyes boring into Hester's. 'God gives me the right to choose.'

Hester saw it all. The small vanities and emphasis on fripperies had been a ruse. The girl was as unrelentingly pious as Amos had been, but more deadly, as she wore a mask so effectively.

Hester turned to Edward.

'And what motivates you?'

Caroline laughed. 'Don't feel so sore-hearted about Edward. An addict makes a poor husband. He never was for you.'

'So,' said Hester, 'children die at the altar of your piety and Edward's addictions. What a pair you make.'

Edward stepped forwards, his hands outstretched as if to placate her.

'Hester, no one wants these children. The mothers are anxious to rid themselves of the child whether they seek Quare out or not. I'm sure of it.'

Hester remembered the desperation of Elisabet, so sure that her baby would be taken even though it had been conceived in wedlock, and the act she'd committed to remove herself from living in fear. And there was Ellen, waiting in the cold for news of the child who lay in the crib in this room. These women hadn't wanted to rid themselves of their children.

'And those poor souls are dead and buried in the potter's field.'

'It's a common enough place to bury paupers,' said Caroline, shaking her head. 'I don't know what your issue with it is.'

'Paupers aren't usually murdered first,' said Hester. 'Is that where my niece is? In the field?'

'Ah. Is that what this is all about? You want to know where your kin is.'

'It's about all those dead children and their inconsolable mothers who would never have given up their children. Like Lizzie, who haunts the streets looking for her child. She's never got over the loss.'

Caroline raised her eyes to the sky, but Edward put a hand on her arm. She halted and looked pityingly at Hester.

'Surely you, Hester, a Friend, know that having an illegitimate child is an offence. It's the law of the Church.'

Hester became aware of the enormity of the gap between Caroline's madness, her focus on the poor children of women like Mercy and the sober but strict teachings of their faith. This was her father writ large, but worse, in Devil's clothing.

'I'm going straight to the constable,' said Hester, turning. 'You can answer to him.'

A figure blocked the doorway. Mrs Kirkham, her arms now empty.

'What does she know?' she asked, nodding at Hester.

'Everything, it seems.'

Edward's refined voice, which had once seemed so attractive to Hester, now repelled her.

'Then she can't leave here. She's not putting my retirement in jeopardy.'

Hester spun round, looking for another exit, but there was only the mean glass window. Mrs Kirkham grabbed her arms and Hester lashed out with her feet, desperate to flee. Edward was too quick for her and had her in his grasp.

'Take her to the coach.'

Desperately, Hester twisted and turned, but the pair of them were too strong for her. Caroline followed them out into the night. An owl hooted as Hester was bundled through the courtyard, past the high walls towards the outbuilding. Hester writhed until Edward slapped her face so hard that her ears rang.

'We'll take her to the potter's field. She'll know the grave well. It's the second time she'll have lain in it.'

Edward might have been talking about laying a dog to rest, such was his disinterest.

'Perhaps it better she's killed now,' said Caroline.

'My dear, it goes to show how little you know of the human

anatomy. Dead bodies are harder to carry than live ones. We'll kill her once we get there. She won't be missed. As far as everyone's concerned, she's left Southwell.'

'She'll be missed by me.'

In her swoon, Hester heard the voice of Matthew, his rough tones as welcome as any she'd ever heard.

'And the pair of you will rot in hell for this.'

'Get her in the coach,' said Edward. 'I'll deal with Mr Alban.'

'You think I'm scared of a fop like you? I can beat you to a pulp.'

'I think,' said Edward, reaching into his jacket, 'you might struggle against this.'

# Chapter Fifty

The flintlock held by Edward Holland was as elegant as the physician, its polished rosewood barrel reflecting the flames from the lantern. Matthew had no doubt that it was already loaded with gunpowder and shot. Edward would use it if cornered. The only thing stopping him from shooting now was the sound that the gun would make. Mrs Kirkham had Hester in her control, but where was her husband? He must be in a deep slumber to sleep through the comings and goings of the baby farmers, but would he miss the shot of a gun? And the other residents must surely hear the noise, too.

'You won't shoot,' Matthew said to Edward, hoping his voice didn't betray his fear by quaking. 'It's all over for you and you know it.'

Edward lifted the gun in response. 'On the contrary, it's all over for you, you'll find.'

Matthew charged at his foe, roaring like the bullock his father had once owned. There was a loud bang followed by the smell of gunpowder. Matthew saw that the shot had been deflected into the air, but he was blinded by the flash. He stumbled, rubbing his eyes.

'Hester, where are you?' he shouted.

'Matthew!' he heard her cry. 'I'm here.'

He stumbled towards the voice, still unable to see. Suddenly, he felt a small hand in his, guiding him away from Hester's cries.

'No.' He tried to shake off the touch, but, powerless, he surrendered to the spirit. He felt his hand being guided to the water pump. He grasped the lever and felt water gush onto his boots. He put his head under the tap and, as his sight cleared, he turned to thank whoever had led him there. There was no one.

'Matthew!' screamed Hester, and he ran towards the barn, picking up one of the hammers lying against the wall for the stone breakers when they resumed work the following morning.

In the barn, he saw Hester already in the coach, along with the vain Quaker woman. Mrs Kirkham was hurrying off with the baby.

'Give her to me!'

It must be the child's mother, thought Matthew. He saw her pick up a pitchfork and jab it at Mrs Kirkham's head. As the matron clutched her scalp, the mother grabbed her wailing baby.

Matthew charged through the coach house doors, hearing Edward's steps behind him. He turned to see the physician lift the reloaded gun. Matthew threw himself at the doctor and Edward reached out to steady himself, his arm knocking the oil lamp. As they rolled to the ground, Matthew's last vision was of the carpet of fire spreading out along the hay.

# Chapter Fifty-One

Fire. It was the smoke that first alerted Hester that something was amiss. The hay and wood of the barn's construction went up like tinder. There was a barrel of some foul-smelling liquid in one corner that also caught alight, creating a stinking black smoke. Hester banged against the window of the carriage.

'We have to get out of here!'

Caroline lowered the window, allowing smoke to fill the carriage.

'Move on,' she shouted to the boy, but they remained still.

Their driver had fled.

Hester saw the two men tumbling around in the straw as the fire raged around them. Matthew was the larger of the two, but she saw he was wounded, a dark stain on the left side of his waist. Edward climbed on top of him and hit him with a blow to the face.

'No. Matthew!'

She turned to Caroline and launched herself at her captor, momentarily stunning the girl, which was enough time for Hester to open the carriage door. Coughing, she put her arm over her forehead, straining to find a way to Matthew. Edward surely couldn't reload a pistol for the third time in these flames.

'Matthew!'

Her voice competed with the cracking of flames and the falling of timbers. She saw Edward kick Matthew and pass around the back of the fire towards the coach.

'I'll drive. Get back in the coach, Caroline.'

'We've lost Hester.'

'Never mind her. We need to leave!'

Edward whipped the horse, but it was terrified by the fire, its shying causing the carriage to rock perilously. Hester saw Matthew trying to sit up and crawled across to him, the heat rising and the smoke thickening

'Matthew. Can you get up?'

There was no way she'd be able to move him.

He lifted his head.

'Get out of here, Hester. Save yourself. I've been shot. I can crawl but that's about it.'

'Then crawl.'

She saw the flames had crept around to the barn's side door. They'd be alight if they tried to get through that way. The opening of the double doors was blocked by the bucking horse, it's jerking movements increasingly panicked.

'I can't. We're trapped. I'm sorry, Hester. I tried to warn you.'

Hester opened her mouth to reply and found her eyes stung by liquid so sharp she thought she was going blind. She felt arms gripping her and she looked up to see Little Pinch pulling her away from the flames, across the singed ground where the fire had been extinguished by ice-cold water from the well next to the barn.

'Matthew is in there, too. You need to get him out.'

'I don't have the strength. Leave him to Heggs.'

Hester turned on her side and saw Heggs the porter pulling Matthew, screaming, across the ground. But Matthew's screams were nothing compared to the cries of Edward and Caroline, so anguished that it was as if the souls from the pit had risen up.

Hester turned and finally saw the shape that had followed her from her first visit to the workhouse. A wraith, not desperate any longer, but vengeful, standing in front of the terrified horse. The beast reared and twisted away from its straps, rocking the carriage until it tipped on its side. With a shriek, the horse bolted through the fire, away from the burning barn, its hooves receding into the distance.

'Don't look.'

Little Pinch put her hands over Hester's eyes, but she'd already seen Edward flung from the carriage into the flames and Caroline lying crushed beneath the weight of the trap.

Hester felt a searing pain and began to scream as her arm caught alight.

'She's on fire,' Matthew shouted at Little Pinch, and Hester found herself back on the floor again, and water being thrown, drenching her until she could bear the pain no longer.

# Chapter Fifty-Two

For three days, Hester was plunged into a fever. She pitched in her bed, the searing pain soothed only by a succession of cold poultices placed on her arms. As her fever raged, Hester had few visitors, but the ones who came were the best kind, comforting and silent.

On the fourth day, Hester opened her eyes, aware that the pain, although present, was in a distant place. She frowned, suspecting the relief was laudanum-induced – she'd heard of patients tell of the altered state resulting from the tincture. She focused her gaze on a spot on the whitewashed ceiling where the plaster had peeled away from the surface.

'Hester, are you awake?'

At her bedside, she saw a figure out of the corner of her eye. She turned her head in alarm, wincing from the flash of pain.

'Susanna.'

'It's me, all right. Come halfway across the country to look after you.'

Hester struggled upright but felt a pair of cool hands pushing her down onto the pillow.

'Don't move. You've been ill. I thought I'd be burying you in the same plot as Mercy.'

She groaned. 'Where am I?'

'In the house of Joan Alban. Go back to sleep.'

'Matthew?'

'He lives. Now's not the time for explanations.'

Hester closed her eyes and submitted to the pull of the dark. When she opened them again, night had fallen. Susanna was still in the chair, looking out of the window.

'You're awake. How do you feel?'

'Terrible. What's that smell?'

'One of Joan's home-made unguents. A right tartar she is, but she knows her healing, I'll give her that. Your arms have been covered in pig fat, which has saved your skin. I'll be putting it on my arms myself when I next catch them on the range.'

Hester tried to laugh, but it caused darts of pain in her head.

'Oh, Susanna. You don't know how pleased I am to see you.' A thought struck her. 'Ruth . . .'

'She's well. She would have come herself, but there are problems at the house. One of your father's creditors has turned up. Ruth says she'll sort it, but she needs to be at the house to make sure the bailiffs don't come while she's away.'

'Bailiffs?' Hester's head pounded with an insistent thud. Her throat was parched and she had trouble forming her words. 'That sounds bad.'

'Your mother says it's a misunderstanding, and Ruth has never been one to lie to me. The house is to be sold and she has her eye on a smaller place outside the city.'

Hester, bitter with recriminations, turned her head away.

'It sounds like she has everything sorted. Shame she didn't apply herself in the same way to Mercy.'

Susanna was having none of it.

'You're not to be blaming Ruth for your father's acts. Women don't always get a voice in family affairs.'

'But that's the whole point, isn't it? All the acts of goodness we did outside the home came to nothing once the front door of our house was closed. Women have a voice. We were educated and sent out into the world but put back in our allotted roles once home.'

'Your father wasn't all bad.'

A note in Susanna's voice made Hester pause. A wistfulness she hadn't seen before. Their eyes met and a thought, so fleeting that she couldn't catch it, made Hester wonder about the true nature of the relationship between her father and Susanna. That their bond might have been one of lovers rather than master and servant. It went to show how far she'd been changed by events. It would never have crossed her mind two months earlier.

'What happened to Edward and Caroline? The last I remember was screaming and flames.'

'They died.' Susanna's voice was flat. 'And good riddance.'

Hester bent her head so Susanna wouldn't see her tears.

'There's no point crying. I've heard that you liked Doctor Holland to begin with, but the man was no good. He was a devil with two faces from what Joan tells me, and he'll be in the right place now.'

'Susanna,' she hissed, shocked. 'I don't believe in hell. You know this.'

'After what he did to Mercy's child? You'd have joined her in that churchyard, too, if he'd had his way. Don't ask me to feel sorry for him.'

'And Caroline?'

'Crushed. And her mother in disgrace. She's making plans to move to Scotland. Perhaps she'll find the cold more conducive to her sensibilities.'

'But Dorothea wasn't like that. She was . . . kind.'

Susanna sniffed. 'But her daughter was tainted by evil.'

Hester shook her head. She'd never, until the end of her days, understand the acts of Caroline – a girl she'd thought of as vain and shallow. To have interfered in those women's lives in the name of a God whom Hester no longer believed in was incomprehensible. Those poor women with their missing and dead children. If anyone was the devil with two faces, it was Caroline, for she'd deceived everyone.

Hester swallowed. Susanna noticed her distress and passed her a glass of water.

'Why pretend to take the children to a baby farm? If they wanted to take the children, they could have just snatched them. The women were helpless.'

'It's a dubious but legitimate business, placing unwanted children elsewhere for money. Mercy knew it and she made arrangements to give up her child. When she died in childbirth, they had both her money and the baby. That was one way to obtain the babies.'

'And the other?'

'If there was no money, then the baby was just taken from the children's room. It's where the story of the pale lady came from. A spectre picking up babies.'

'The women will rest easier now that the spectre *has* disappeared,' said Susanna.

'I hope so. And Ellen's child?'

'It lives. She's been here to see you. I shooed her away as I was afraid the baby's bawling would wake you. Also another inmate. About as small as a child. If you ask me, she's showing, too.'

'Little Pinch? Does she have news of the workhouse?'

'The master and matron have been removed, that's all I know.'

Hester sighed, placing the glass on the table with shaking hands. 'And Matthew? The man who saved me.'

Susanna gave her a keen glance.

'He was shot but he'll live. He escaped without burns, unlike yourself. He hasn't spent much time in bed, although he was supposed to. He said he had an inn to run. It'll take more than a wound to stop a man like that.'

'You've met him?'

'When I arrived there was a man, his back as broad as an ox, hanging around your chamber. He's been here every afternoon for the last three days. I wasn't sure if he should be allowed. You weren't in any fit state to give your permission. But anyway, he's not a man you want to say no to.'

Hester smiled, although it felt like her scalp would split in two.

'Of all the people I met in Southwell, he was the one who never liked Edward.'

'Well, he wouldn't, would he?'

'Different class, you mean?'

Susanna sighed and picked up the square of embroidery in her lap.

'Sometimes, Hester, you can be incredibly obtuse.'

# Chapter Fifty-Three

Hester was asleep when her visitor arrived, dropping quietly into the chair. How long her caller had waited, she couldn't tell, but when she woke, she looked straight into the eyes of Dorothea Francombe. Hester's throat constricted in alarm and she began to choke, bringing Susanna hurrying in with a beaker of water in her hand. As the cool liquid trickled down her throat, Hester regained some of her composure, pulling herself up the pillows.

'Please don't distress yourself. I'm leaving on the afternoon coach. I had to see you first. I am so very sorry. I shall never forgive myself for putting you in danger.'

Hester asked the question that had been plaguing her since Caroline had been revealed as her nemesis.

'Why did she ask for me to return to Southwell? She knew I was upset at Mercy's treatment, but there was little I could do from Bristol. It was the invitation to return that was the catalyst for everything that happened.'

'Caroline . . .' Dorothea's voice trailed off, forced to accept the truth of her child. 'Caroline liked to play games. I think it was all one big joke for her.'

Hester shook her head, remembering the look of determination as they'd carried her to the coach.

'She would have allowed me to die. It was no game.'

'Hester, I strongly believe she was under a terrible influence in her partnership with Edward Holland. I should have listened to his mother when she and her son first became estranged.'

'She tried to warn you?'

'Money and some items of value went missing. Servants were dismissed, but the trend continued until a pawnbroker was caught with stolen candlesticks and identified Edward as the culprit.'

'But you never said. You and Caroline treated him as if he were a respectable member of society. You were even trying to arrange an attachment to me.'

'He was young at the time of the thefts. He ran up debts training to be a physician, his heart was so set on it. We both forgave him and I had high hopes that he'd reunite with his family.'

'He hired men to kill me, Dorothea.'

'I'll never forgive myself. I believe he was motivated by the fact that you were about to expose him. The apothecary of the town says he was known as being generous with his prescriptions of opium. Not all reached the patients.'

So that had been his addiction. Another physician enticed by the lure of the heady potions prescribed to the unwell.

Dorothea stared at Hester, stricken. 'We're all victims of him. You, me, his parents, those women and children, and yes, Caroline.'

Hester swung her legs out of bed, desperate to get away from the woman. She'd hear no more.

'It wasn't a man who terrified the undeserving women in Southwell Union. It was a woman. Your daughter, Caroline.' Her throat swelled again and she reached for the beaker.

'Did she threaten you herself? I cannot believe my daughter wished you harm.'

'One of them wrote the note I received. I only had Caroline's word that it was delivered by hand.'

'But surely it was intended to save you from harm. So that you'd leave Southwell.'

'It was intended to threaten me. Those men had already been commissioned to assault me. I was attacked in the market that very afternoon.'

'But the note didn't sound like Caroline. Surely that's another mark to lay at Edward's door.'

'She stood by and allowed others to harm me, and that makes her equally guilty. What's more, it was she who shaped the work of the baby farming. Edward might have been the one to initiate it, but the taking of babies from their mothers, when they were desperate to keep hold of them, was her.'

'Mrs Kirkham—'

'She was involved for the money, like Edward. It's she who played the hand of God who is the most evil in my eyes. Had you no idea?'

But Dorothea was a mother grieving for her daughter. She shook her head.

'Caroline was always a law unto herself.'

'What's she doing here?'

They both turned to see Matthew standing in the doorway. He'd crept up the stairs without either of them noticing. Susanna stood in the background giving Hester a helpless look.

Dorothea stood. 'I think I should go. I had to see you, Hester. I hope both you and Ruth will one day be able to forgive me. I shall write to your mother from Scotland.'

She brushed past Matthew without looking at him.

'Is that how rich folk give their apologies? By saying they'll write?'

Hester was aware of her nightdress, which smelled fusty like a warm feather bed. She caught Susanna's eye, and she approached with a blanket.

'Don't keep her long.'

Matthew dropped into a chair at the side of the bed. Hester saw him wince as he sat.

'Were you badly hurt?'

'The shot nicked the side of me. Those flintlocks can do a lot of damage. I was lucky. I told you it was a bloody stupid idea to go to the workhouse. Only you and Joan could have come up with such a miserable plan.'

'I wouldn't have survived without you. I shall be forever in your debt.'

He grunted, refusing to meet her eyes.

'Your maid has asked me to book you on the coach home to-morrow. Do you think you're up to it?'

Hester shrugged. 'Susanna will make me as comfortable as she's able. I'll have to bear it until I get to Bristol.'

'You won't go without saying goodbye?'

'Of course not.' She looked down at her arm, wrapped in its stinking poultice. How foul she must smell. 'I haven't seen Joan since I woke.'

'She's been staying at the inn. You're in her bed.'

'Oh, no.'

'Oh, don't worry. She's been back and forth like a clucky hen. She'll miss you when you go.'

What about you, though? she wondered, but saw his thoughts had moved on.

'The night of the fire. The horse shied.'

'I remember.'

'There was a figure, a girl holding a child. Not Lizzie, another.'

'I know.'

'Your phantom?'

'I prefer to call them my sightings. She's gone now. I'm quite alone.'

'Your sister?'

'Gone too.'

'And that's the end of it?'

She shrank from the note of hope.

'They've all gone, but there will be others. There always are.'

# Chapter Fifty-Four

Hester left Joan's house leaning on Susanna's arm, her limbs stiff and ungainly after days of lying in bed. Despite Susanna's best efforts with soap and a flannel, she could still smell the fire on her, the stench of burning flesh permeating her hair and grains of soot still in her nostrils.

She'd allowed Susanna to give her a draught of laudanum before leaving the room. The concoction made her nauseous, although it did dull the agony of her raw, burned skin as it rubbed against the bandages. Between them, Joan and Susanna had done a good job with their poultices and unguents, but Hester would carry the scars of the fire for the rest of her life.

The town was busy as they passed down the main street. Hester had dressed in the severe navy given to her by Dorothea. Susanna had made a face, but there was little point in letting a decent gown go to waste. Hester accepted that it was impossible to shrug off your upbringing completely. The dress would be reused until it was no longer wearable, despite all its associations with the previous owner.

At the far end of the street, standing on the corner, she saw a familiar figure and, for the first time, it didn't make her breath catch with fear.

'I need to speak to that woman.'

'Where?' Susanna put her arms around Hester's shoulders, taking care to avoid her arm. 'We need to get to The Black

Griffin to catch our coach south. I don't want you out in the air longer than necessary. Is this the reason you refused a trap to the inn?'

'There's a farewell I need to say.'

They were close to the girl, who turned at their approach. Her baby had grown since Hester last saw the child and, for once, it wasn't crying.

'How's your baby?'

The girl gripped the child to her and, sure enough, it began to wail.

'They's planting trees over in potter's field. My baby is to have a mark for its grave.'

'A headstone?'

'A tree, I said. Elm – and it will grow as high as a house.'

Hester smiled, although Susanna was restless to move on.

'An elm tree sounds like a perfect grave marker. Your baby isn't forgotten.'

The girl nodded.

'I never found out the name of your babies.'

The girl looked down at the crying child. 'This one's Tom. The other is nothing to do with you.' She turned away, staring once more at the street as it went about its business.

'Poor soul,' commented Susanna. 'Is she one of the girls?'

'Yes, I'm sure of it,' said Hester. 'It gives me some comfort to know that Mercy's child will be marked by a tree, too.' She stopped. 'I organised a headstone for Mercy's grave . . .'

'It's in hand. The mason is carving it as we speak. Give the man a chance to do the job.'

'I need to pay him.'

'We can send the money from Bristol. Can we please get moving, Hester?'

The three of them set off down the street – three as Mercy was once more walking by their side. The Mercy she remembered, calm and at peace.

'There's a coach at eleven o'clock and we'll need to hurry to catch it. I should have insisted on that trap.'

The coach, thought Hester, had been such a source of excitement several weeks ago and now it was to speed her home to Bristol. The problem was that she didn't want to leave. Her father was gone, it was true, with all his rigidity and deceit. He'd been appealed to, had been asked to adhere to tenets of Quaker beliefs – compassion and charity – and had been found wanting on both counts. He lay in the peaceful earth next to Hermit's Cave, and it was up to Ruth and Hester to pick up the pieces.

Bristol might be far from this Nottinghamshire town, but it would give her no peace, she was sure. She'd be haunted not by future sightings, but by memories of the horror of that last evening at the workhouse, which would stay with her as long as the scars on her arm. She thought she knew the difference between a friend and an enemy, but she was, as Matthew had said, naïve. She'd liked Edward, and Caroline she'd dismissed as harmless and vain. She'd never again trust her own instincts.

'I don't wish to catch the coach at eleven. My goodbyes cannot be rushed.'

'But the mistress said . . .'

'I've a pretty good idea what Ruth said, but here I am telling you I'm not rushing my farewells. Can we take a later coach please, Susanna?'

Susanna dropped her arm from Hester's shoulder.

'I saw how Matthew Alban looked at you while you were feverish in bed. There's no doubt about his feelings. You're playing with fire. Remember what happened to Mercy. Is that what you want for yourself?'

Hester tottered without Susanna's support.

'I'm going to say a proper goodbye to him. I owe him at least that. He saved my life.'

'He says the same about you. You saved each other, so what? You can be forever grateful to him from Bristol.'

'Susanna, please.'

'As long as it's goodbye.'

Hester remained silent, concentrating her effort on not swooning on the Southwell street.

'Hester,' said Susanna. 'He's a publican. Who knows what kind of people frequent such places.'

'His inn is perfectly respectable. It's where I stayed, remember. When no one else in Southwell would listen to my concerns, he and Joan helped me.'

'And we know why, don't we?' hissed Susanna. 'Did he try anything while you were staying there?'

'Of course not.' Hester shook away the image of Matthew in her bedroom that first night after he'd despatched Edward's paid thug.

Joan was washing the cobbles of the inner courtyard as they entered. When she saw Hester, she threw down the brush, tripping over the tin bucket, causing sudsy water to spread over the cobbles.

'I told you to be careful, you foolish girl,' Joan muttered into Hester's hair. 'I've been worried sick. I got into so much trouble with his lordship. I don't think he'll ever forgive me.'

'I could never have left without saying a proper goodbye. Where's Matthew?'

As she spoke, Hester felt his presence behind her and she turned to see him standing in the doorway as he had at their first meeting. This time there were no insults and he came out of the shadow into the light of the morning sun.

'I've made all the arrangements. Your trunk is already here.'

Matthew approached Hester, his eyes on her arm. 'How are your injuries?'

'They're painful, I can't lie. Joan did a good job with the dressings, though. I'm sure my arm will recover.'

She was lying. There was a network of honeycombed tracks, red weals that pained her as she spoke. She saw Susanna exchange a glance with Joan.

'Now, what about this famous cup of tea I've heard about here.' said Susanna.

Joan looked delighted and steered Susanna into the inn, neither of them looking behind at Matthew and Hester.

'Is it busy?' Hester asked him, at a loss where to begin.

'Not yet. The morning is fair, though, so perhaps I'll get a decent crowd. Although maybe those days are long gone.'

'What do you mean?'

'The railway's coming to Nottingham – steam is the new thing. Who will be wanting to travel by coach and horses in the future?'

Susanna looked around the courtyard, where the stable lad was whistling while leaning against a wall, and the ostler brushing down a horse ready for the next carriage.

'I can't imagine this way of life disappearing.'

Matthew smiled and looked towards the door through which Susanna and Joan had disappeared.

'We've missed you here. I keep listening out for you saying your prayers.'

'Saying my pray . . .' Hester laughed when she saw his expression. 'You're jesting with me.'

She wanted to touch him, give him comfort, but didn't dare. Soon, she'd be racing away from this city and it would all be a memory.

'Perhaps . . .' she hesitated. 'Perhaps you'll keep a room for me. I'd like to return.'

He folded his arms, regarding her.

'Your maid told me a little about your family situation. Money is difficult, I hear.'

'My mother's buying a small place outside Bristol. I'll live with her there.'

'There's always another option – that you don't go.'

Hester looked round the inn that had been her refuge in the dark days of the last weeks.

'I've never felt more looked after, but I can't see this as my home.'

'That's just as well, as I can't quite see you as an innkeeper's wife, either. I have an offer as a manager on my uncle's farm. He made it that day I took you to Newstead. He's a decent sort, unlike my father. He's made the offer before and he always said I'd take it up when I wanted to settle down. Perhaps now's the time.'

'A farm? Is that what you want?'

Matthew shrugged. 'The hours will be the same – early starts, late finishes. The prospects are better, though. As I said, it's the end of days for coaching inns. The question is, Hester, what do you want?'

What did she want? She looked up at this tall, imposing man, someone she'd once thought uncouth but who had proved himself twice the worth of Edward Holland or, for that matter, her father.

She made her decision.

'Is there money for a servant?'

He smiled. 'Joan's settled in Southwell. There will be other work for her.'

Hester shook her head. 'Little Pinch helped to save our lives. She deserves a home and she's an excellent worker.'

'The midget?'

'Don't let her hear you say that.'

He frowned. 'I hear she's with child.'

'I think, given everything that's happened, we ought to help one mother and baby, don't you?'

He looked grim. 'Do-gooding. I was right first time. I suppose I could afford a small wage. I thought you were talking about Susanna. I'm not sure she and I could live under the same roof.'

'Susanna isn't much enamoured of the country. She'll be glad to get home to Ruth.'

'Will she visit, your mother? I'd hate to start a marriage with you estranged.'

Hester thought of Ruth and the decisions she'd made – and the ones imposed on her.

'I think it's possible my mother might understand the choice I'm making.'

'Then,' he said, smiling, 'that's settled.'

# Acknowledgements

Thanks to my editor, Rachel Neely at Trapeze, who has an excellent feel for what works in a novel, and, as ever, to my agent, Kirsty McLachlan at Morgan Green Creatives. Also, heartfelt thanks to my first reader and eagle-eyed proofer, Tony Butler, for his continued support.

Thanks to bookish friends for writing encouragement including Charlotte Baker, Judith Butler, Tana Collins, Alex Davis, Kathy Durkin, Gill Hart, Karen Meek, Dea Parkin, Chris Saccali, Ricki Thomas, Ettie Williams and Joanne Williams. Also to Vicky Dawson at Buxton International Festival, Nick Quantrill at Hull Noir, Sian Hoyle at Derby Book Festival and Sara Gilmore at Newark. And to the readers who chat on my Saturday morning Facebook posts. We have a lovely community talking about books, if you want to join in at: https://www.facebook.com/SarahWardCrime

This book was written during the COVID-19 pandemic when I was also being treated for breast cancer. Thanks to all of the NHS staff I met during the course of my treatment including my GP, Doctor Pauline Love, the staff at the Breast Unit at Chesterfield Royal Hospital, the nurses at Barlborough Hospital, and my oncologist and the radiographers at Weston Park in Sheffield. Eternal thanks to Vicky Dawson, to Mog and Pauline at Warwick Books and to Heledd Davies for being particularly heroic in their support.

Finally, thanks as always to my family in this strange year. Dad, who sends my books to friends and relatives around the world, Adrian and Amelie, Ed, Katie, Jacob and Luke. And, as ever, to Andy who, along with Sonny and the much-missed Tubbs, was my rock during the writing of this novel.

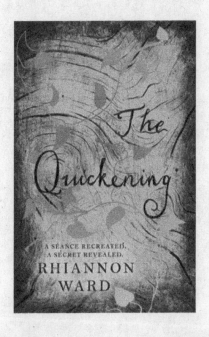